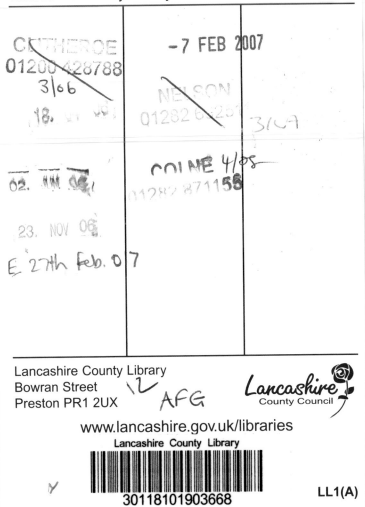

SHANGHAI NIGHTS

ALSO BY

Juan Marsé

Fiction

Lizard Tails

Juan Marsé

Shanghai Nights

TRANSLATED
FROM THE SPANISH
BY

Nick Caistor

Harvill *Secker*
LONDON

First published with the title *El embrujo de Shanghai* by Plaza y Janés S.A., 1993

1 3 5 7 9 8 6 4 2

This edition has been translated with the financial assistance of the
Spanish Dirección General del Libro y Bibliotecas, Ministerio de Cultura

First published in Great Britain in 2006 by
HARVILL SECKER
Random House, 20 Vauxhall Bridge Road,
London SW1V 2SA

Random House Australia (Pty) Limited
20 Alfred Street, Milsons Point, Sydney,
New South Wales 2061, Australia

Random House New Zealand Limited
18 Poland Road, Glenfield,
Auckland 10, New Zealand

Random House South Africa (Pty) Limited
Isle of Houghton, Corner of Boundary Road & Carse O'Gowrie,
Houghton 2198, South Africa

The Random House Group Limited Reg. No. 954009
www.randomhouse.co.uk

A CIP catalogue record for this book is available from the British Library

ISBN 1843431505

Designed and typeset in Fournier MT
Typeset by Palimpsest Book Production Limited, Polmont, Stirlingshire
Printed and bound in Great Britain by
Mackays of Chatham plc, Chatham, Kent

To the memory of Rosa of Calafell
and of Berta de L'Arboç.
For Carmen of Santa Fe.
For Joaquina of Herguijuela.

The truest, deepest nostalgia is not
directed towards the past but the future.
I often feel nostalgia for the future: I
mean nostalgia for those days of
celebration when everything was on
the move before me, and the future
was still in its proper place.

LUIS GARCÍA MONTERO
Moon in the South

CHAPTER ONE

I

'The dreams of youth rot in adult mouths,' said Captain Blay as he strode out intrepidly in front of me, looking more than ever like a frail Invisible Man: head swathed in bandages, and dressed in a raincoat, black leather gloves and dark glasses, with those abrupt, inexplicable gestures that so intrigued me. He was on his way to the kiosk to buy some matches when all of a sudden he came to a halt on the pavement. He sniffed anxiously at the air through the gauze that covered his wraith-like nose and mouth.

'And that rotten garbage is in the street, you can smell it. But there's something else as well . . . I've no wish to offend, but there's a stink of rotten eggs here. Can't you smell it?' the old man went on, getting a whiff of his favourite obsession, his head darting nervously back and forth. I stopped to sniff the air. The Captain had such a way of seizing my imagination with his gravelly voice that all at once I felt an emptiness in the pit of my stomach and my head began to spin.

This is how my story begins. I would have liked there to be room in it for my father, to have him with me to give advice in order not to feel so helpless confronted with Captain Blay's ravings and my own daydreams, but by this time my father had been confirmed as missing, and he never came home. In my mind's eye I once again saw his body tossed into a ditch, the snowflakes drifting down and covering him, but then my mind flitted back to the old crackpot's enigmatic pronouncement as I followed at his heels in the direction of the kiosk in the Plaza Rovira. Just as we were passing by the doorway to number eight, between the grocery store and the chemist's, the Captain came to a halt again as his indomitable nose, normally so useless beneath the bandages, picked up the rotten smell.

'Don't you recognise that stench, boy?' he said. 'Has that precious little nose of yours been so led astray by the incense of Las Animas and the stale sweat of those priests' cassocks, that it can't make it out any more?' He broke off, craning his neck and snorting like a nervous horse. 'Is it rotten eggs, or cat shit? It's neither . . . over there, in that doorway. I know what it is! Gas! That's all we need!'

There certainly was a permanent stink inside the doorway, because several tramps slept there at night, but the Captain could immediately distinguish one smell from another, and insisted this one did not come from the doorway but from the crumbling pavement beneath our feet, from the cracks where straggly weeds poked through.

He took it on himself to warn everyone living in the vicinity. He mentioned it at the kiosk, in the chemist's and at the tram-stop, and although everyone knew about his fits of senile dementia, from that day on, whenever any of them had to walk across the top end of the square and breathed in, they were startled to realise it was true. Some of the women took fright and called the Gas Company.

'There must be a broken pipe that's letting all that shit out,' the Captain never tired of telling them in the bar on the square. 'It's very dangerous, you mark my words. We'd be well advised to avoid walking past there: in fact, the best thing would be for all of us to stay at home . . . and be careful when you light a cigarette by the kiosk, any of you.'

'And above all,' his friend Señor Sucre told the regulars listening with a mixture of suspicion and disbelief, 'be careful with those flashing looks of yours, and the incendiary or perverse ideas some of you still harbour deep down. Take care! And that old woman selling chestnuts outside the cinema is a danger too, with her brazier and her forked tongue. It'd only take one spark, or a curse from her and boom! we'd all be in hell.'

'You two are the ones who ought to be careful, dammit, the way you burn newspapers behind the kiosk,' a tram driver drinking a glass of cheap brandy retorted. 'One day you'll send the lot of us flying through the air, the tram terminus, the fountain and . . .'

'And what were we brought into this world for if not to fly through the air in bits, eh, you you silly old fool in your khaki corduroys!' the Captain roared, whirling his long arms around like the sails of a windmill and shuffling his feet on the sawdust and olive pits strewn on the floor. His bandages had come loose, and strips of yellowed cotton hung down by his ears. 'Fly off in a thousand pieces, go on, you'll feel a lot better for it!'

'I might just do that, you'll see,' the tram driver said. Then turning to me, he added: 'Take him away, kid. He's off his rocker.'

A fortnight went by, and the smell still persisted. In spite of repeated complaints by the residents to the Catalan Gas Company and the City Council, nobody came to check the reports. Day after day, from the door of the bar, it was obvious that nothing had happened; passersby who were in the know stepped down into the street to avoid walking past the doorway, and the people living in the building (three storeys with balconies overflowing with geraniums) scuttled in and out like terrified rats. But the Chacón brothers and myself would deliberately use the pavement, our minds racing with the sense of danger, the feeling of imminent catastrophe.

At that time I found myself in a very special, unusual situation, which in turn left me extremely bored or in a kind of daydream: I had left school but had no work. Or rather, I had a job, but in the future. I had always shown some talent for drawing, and so on the advice of Señor Oliart, a jeweller friend of my mother's, she had arranged for me to be taken on as an apprentice and errand boy in a jewellery workshop not far from us. But they told her they would not require a new apprentice for another ten months at least, after the next summer holidays. Despite this, she decided the jeweller's

3

trade was right up my street, so she promised to send me to the workshop on the agreed date. My supposed ability to draw and my love of reading were the deciding factors: guided first and foremost by her common sense – she could not afford to pay for my studies, and we needed another weekly wage at home – but probably even more by her intuition, my mother wanted to channel a destiny she saw as linked to some kind of artistic sensibility, however vaguely and prosaically interpreted. For myself, in those days I could see no connection between the jeweller's art and my real concerns. Apart from reading and drawing, all I liked to do was to wander round our neighbourhood and the Parque Güell.

I used to meet up at the bar on the corner of the square and Providencia with two boys of the same age as me. They were the Chacón brothers, whose insolence and freedom of movement I secretly envied. Their means of support were scarce and irregular, as were their appearances in our neighbourhood. They had left school much sooner than me, and had worked off and on as delivery boys and general assistants in stores and bars, but now they roamed the streets all day long. I never knew exactly where they lived: I think it was in a shack on Calle Francisco Alegre, up in El Carmelo. On Sundays they sold second-hand comics and battered paperbacks at knockdown prices.

It was November; the grey, enclosed square was filling up with yellow leaves from the plane trees. The chill in the air promised a long, hard winter. Everyone except for Señor Sucre scurried along hunched against the cold. He always looked as though he were sleepwalking, talking to himself and behaving as though he doubted his own existence or was afraid he might turn into a ghost at any moment. Whenever it was stormy or windy, he would announce he had to go out to try to find the self he had lost somewhere. We would see him searching for himself in the streets of Gracia, hands behind his back and head down, entering bars, chemists and drug stores, or hidden, dusty bookshops and modest art galleries, interrogating everyone he met until someone could tell him his name and address. And to the Chacón brothers and me he would confide that it was so hard for him to discover the person he had once been, and he got so little help, that sometimes he felt like abandoning everything and just accepting the idea that he was nobody, and sitting quietly in the sun on a bench in the Plaza Rovira. Usually though we would see him searching anxiously and angrily for himself in the most unlikely places. Once he was said to have turned up at the Civil Guard barracks in Travesera and asked the sentry for his name and address – his own, not the sentry's – which scared the soldier so much he shouted for the duty sergeant, and there was an incredible fuss.

'Look here, boys, could you do me the favour of telling me my name and where I live?' Señor Sucre was standing in the bar entrance, and succeeded momentarily in diverting our attention from the number 8 doorway. 'Please.'

'You are Don Josep María de Sucre, and you live in the Calle San Salvador,' I replied automatically.

He nodded thoughtfully. He seemed pleased with the information, but before he entirely accepted who he was, he suddenly became suspicious again:

'And does it seem to you possible or likely that I was born in Catalonia and am an artist, with little or no reputation, but an old friend of Dalí's, and that I don't have a penny?' he asked us, a mocking glint in his eye.

'Yes, sir. That's what they say.'

' Ah well, what can I do about it?' he sighed, ruffling my hair and Finito Chacón's. 'You boys are very kind and polite to this silly lost old goose . . . Thank you.'

In order to completely reassure him, and not make fun of him as many people might have thought, Finito Chacón supplied him with further details:

'And you come every day to have a chat with the tram drivers at their terminus, then you buy a newspaper in the kiosk and set fire to it with a match sitting on a bench, sometimes with the Captain. Then you come to the bar.'

'OK. Understood. And now could you kindly tell me what I've come to the bar for?'

'You've come,' Juan Chacón added patiently, 'to have your aniseed and coffee drink, and to see if that Forcat fellow finally decides to show his face in the street.'

'You must be right,' Señor Sucre admitted, shuffling resignedly over to the counter and muttering: 'That must be how it is, what can I do about it?'

On the reddish facade of the Rovira cinema over at the far side of the square, all week Jesse James had been toppling from his living-room chair, gunned down in the back by a coward. On the other garish poster The Madonna of Seven Moons peered above the tops of leafless trees wielding a dagger and glowering at all the trams negotiating their way round the bend of the Torrente de las Flores. But that afternoon it was not the cinema that concentrated the attention of the locals gathered in the door of the Comulada bar, nor the famous gas leak. It was not even the exciting possibility of an explosion which made it impossible for us to take our eyes off the house: what we were all curious to see was if a man was going to come out. At first, we boys were interested only because the grown-ups were so keen to catch a glimpse of him. We had never seen him before and knew nothing about him; later on, we learnt his name was Nandu Forcat, that he was a refugee who had come back after living almost ten years in France, and that he was a friend of Kim, Susana's father. He had only been in the house a few days, with his aged mother and an unmarried sister, and everyone said the police must know about him and have taken him down to Headquarters for interrogation, but for some reason no one could explain, must have let him go.

At that moment the three of us could not have suspected how unlikely a figure he was, like Kim himself: pure invention, someone who only came to life in the mouths of the adults when they talked in hushed tones of what some called his misdeeds, others his exploits. We were sure he would never become a legend like Kim, even though Forcat had fought or perhaps was still fighting in his group. Opinion about him was divided. Some said he was a cultured, educated man who had fought for his ideals, an honourable anarchist born into a fisherman's family and brought up in Barceloneta, someone who had worked as a waiter to pay his way through teacher-training college. Others thought he was nothing more than a criminal, a bank robber who had probably betrayed his former colleagues and who, now he was back in the city, would have to face several people who had scores to settle with him. Which was why he was so chary about leaving the house. When we tried to imagine him, the Chacón boys and I preferred to see him as a man of action, risking his life revolver in hand, always side-by-side with Kim, protecting each other . . .

For four days, Nandu did not come out into the street. He did not even appear on the balcony. The smell of gas still hung in the doorway day and night, so that now as we passed by we felt a double thrill, as though the gas and the gunman had formed a dangerous alliance. At nightfall on the fifth day, Captain Blay bought a copy of *Solidaridad Nacional* and set fire to it behind the kiosk, quite close to the doorway of number eight. Two women passers-by panicked and ran off shrieking, but there was no explosion.

The next day, at about four o'clock on an afternoon that threatened rain, something unexpected happened. A Gas Company gang of two workmen and a foreman showed up. They used their picks and shovels to demolish the pavement and dig a trench outside number eight. Everyone in the square got tremendously excited. The men uncovered a tangled mess of pipes that looked like rusty guts. They put up a barrier, and laid planks to make a bridge from the doorway to the edge of the pavement for the tenants to cross. That was all they did. It did not look as though they had made a thorough job of it: they dug up six or seven metres of pavement, but the trench was no more than a couple of metres long, and it was not very deep. And they stopped at that. One of the men came to the bar with an empty pop bottle and asked for it to be filled with red wine. He paid, then went back to his colleagues, and the three of them sat on the pile of pavement tiles, spending the rest of the afternoon drinking and sleepily watching the comings and goings at the tram terminus and round the kiosk. From time to time their foreman spat into the blackish mound of earth they had heaped on the pavement, and stared coldly down into the trench. When night fell, they put up a small canvas tent and stored their tools in it. Then they left.

On the sixth day after Forcat's return, the road gang was even more conspicuously inactive. Not one of them so much as lifted a pick or shovel. They came to the bar in turns, to use the toilet or fill their bottle with wine, but did not talk to anyone. On another occasion, the youngest of them, a rough-looking, sturdy fellow with a beret pulled down over his eyes, strolled over to the cinema to examine the photographs on the board outside. He frowned as he did so, as if he did not understand what he saw. We also noticed him, hands in pockets, next to the brightly-painted side of the kiosk, laboriously trying to decipher the comic covers hanging from pegs.

In the bar they said they must be waiting for the engineer from the Gas Company, but Finito Chacón and I had a very different idea. Saturday and Sunday went by, then first thing on Monday morning the workmen reappeared. Two more days passed, with no change: the open trench, the three men sitting with arms folded keeping watch over it, waiting for nobody knew what. In the bar somebody said dammit, it's very odd, there's something fishy going on, and another regular replied there was nothing strange about it: the workmen weren't from the Gas Company, they were from the Council, and hadn't he ever seen how lazy those people could be; the odd thing would be if they ever did a stroke of work, he laughed.

We boys though knew there was only one possible explanation to the mystery: those were not workmen from the Gas Company or the Council, they had not come to repair any leak and were not waiting for an engineer or anyone of the sort. They know the refugee is back, they know he's inside the building and that some day he will have to come out of that doorway. The trench and all the rest are a blind, a pretext for them to guard the place without arousing suspicion. The trench could well turn out to be Forcat's grave.

2

On Thursday morning a fine rain fell and the earth from the trench became spongy, turned a darker colour and formed huge clumps. At midday we were prowling round the kiosk to get a good look at the three men sitting on the edge of the pavement silently passing the bottle of cheap wine round. Granny Sorribes who lived at number eight and was just returning from a shopping expedition was stepping carefully across the muddy planks when she slipped and almost fell. A mandarin toppled out of her bulging bag and rolled to the bottom of the trench. The old woman was furious.

'How long is this nonsense going on? I'm talking to you lot, you lazy good-for-nothings! Are you never going to fill in that blasted hole?'

'We'll do that when we're told to, granny,' the foreman growled. 'But we'll probably have to dig deeper first.'

'What are you waiting for then? You're lazy louts, every one of you!' Still grumbling at the slippery planks, she went inside. 'It's filthy! You've made a real mess!'

'Hey lady, all this crap was here before we arrived!' the youngest of the three protested. 'Give it a rest!'

When it was lunch-time, the men got out their boxes, knives and napkins. I was supposed to take Captain Blay home, but that day he refused to go with me. He said his wife would come and fetch him, so I left him in the bar with Señor Sucre. I went off with the Chacón brothers, and as we passed by the workmen, the tallest, the one with a shaven head, called out to us.

'Hey there, kids.' We could see his lunchbox was full of a sticky mass of rice. 'Do me a favour, one of you go to the bar and ask them for a pinch of salt. I don't know what the old woman was thinking of today, but this is inedible . . . Go on, yes, you.'

Juan ran towards the bar. His brother and I stayed rooted to the spot, watching the other workman and the foreman eat; the latter had bean and cod soup; the workman lentils with bacon. They chewed their food quickly and seemed bored. The foreman only glanced at us once, and even then it was as though he had not seen us; his eyes were watery, with puffy lids. He stretched out a limp hand to take the bottle of wine his companion was offering him. We could smell a stink of cat shit from the trench behind them. Juan came running back with a twist of salt in a piece of paper, and the shaven-headed workman said thanks. Then, as if he had just been waiting for this moment, Finito plucked up courage to ask him why they didn't finish digging the trench and why they weren't doing anything about the gas leak.

'Who said there's a gas leak?' the man grunted, sprinkling salt on his rice.

'Everyone knows there is,' said Finito.

'Oh, they do, do they? You're all very smart here in the square then. All we've found up to now is a skull.'

'A skull?'

'That's what I said.' The shaven-headed workman glanced at his colleagues and went on: 'A skull and a few bones. That's why we've stopped digging for the moment. Someone has to come and take a look at it, some professor . . . Underneath this square is a cemetery full of dead people. Hundreds, thousands of corpses. They're very precious old bones, very important ones, get it? Ask my mates here if you don't believe me.'

'It's true enough,' the youngest one said.

'Where's the skull?' asked Finito. 'Can we see it?'

'Of course not. It's being examined.'

That didn't fool us. They might have been pulling our legs, and we were expecting them to guffaw at any moment, but instead they simply kept on eating, scraping the bottom of their boxes with their forks and downing the wine.

'That's why,' the bald-headed one went on, 'you think you can smell gas. There is no gas leak. The stench comes from the bones of the dead when they're all heaped up together. They also give off a green glow like phosphorus, I've seen it myself at night in cemeteries . . . the smell is very similar to gas, in fact it is a gas really, the gas of the deceased. On my mother's grave it is.'

None of us said a word. This nonsense only confirmed our suspicions; they were there for some other reason, the trench was just an excuse. I looked anxiously at it and at the doorway, then I noticed the foreman's watery eyes staring at me.

'What are you worried about, kid?' he asked in a hoarse voice.

'Me? Nothing.'

He stared silently at me for a moment with his sad, weary eyes, and eventually he said:

'Are you scared?'

'Me? What of?'

He fell silent again, as if he had given up trying to make himself understood, not only by me but by himself. I could tell as much from the way he said:

'Go off home with you. Your mother will be expecting you to eat. You other two as well. Be off with you.'

It was not the words that wounded me so much as his lifeless eyes. He stopped staring at us, sat there lost in thought and shook his head slightly, as if feeling sorry for himself and at the same time powerless. Almost inaudibly, he muttered 'holy shit' without giving any indication of who this was aimed at, or what past or future injustice he might be referring to. A black cat climbed onto the pile by the trench to sniff the dark clods of earth, and a tram turned the corner by the cinema, screeching in its tracks and in my head. I can still remember that man's eyes and the desolate feeling of abandonment and confusion that filled me, exactly the same as when someone whose name and affection for me I have completely forgotten greets me enthusiastically.

The three of us went home. We were agreed that however harmless the workmen seemed at close quarters, they must be concealing their real intentions, whatever those might be. We also said we would meet one another again in the square after our meal to spy on them some more.

By mid-afternoon, a squally, wet wind had risen, which heaped the yellow leaves up alongside of the kiosk and blew them into the trench. I stood in the bar thinking of the silent, shrivelled men standing alongside me at the window, as well as in other bars in our neighbourhood and throughout the city; obscure, withdrawn men who drank standing up peering out of the window or at the counter, or crowded round the wine barrels as though that was where life had washed them up, on this spit and sawdust floor. A short while later Finito and Juan arrived. We were watching a pigeon preening itself in the fountain in the middle of the square, as though it was dangling from an invisible string, when all of a sudden Nandu Forcat appeared in the doorway of number eight, just by the trench. A grey trench-coat was slung over his shoulder, he had a pair of dark glasses on, and an unlit cigarette dangled from his mouth. He was wearing a bright orange and purple tie, and looked tall, with muscular shoulders and a strong chin. For a few seconds, he stared at the kiosk and the tram stop, and then without moving lit his cigarette with a lighter. At that moment it did not occur to me he might blow up the whole square: I was too busy watching the three workmen sitting on a bench and passing the bottle of wine round yet again. The foreman saw him straightaway, but did not move a muscle or alert his companions.

Before he set out across the planks, Forcat looked down into the trench. He must have seen the twisted mass of rusty pipes and electric cables, the dead leaves and the rotting mandarin; he looked up to peer round the sooty, peaceful square, without so much as sparing a glance for the three men on the bench. Behind his dark glasses, his eyes seemed fixed on some distant point in space, perhaps on his defeated life, on something that had more to do with his sad heart than anything he could see by the kiosk or the tram terminus beneath the leaden sky, as people came and went in the clear early evening light like furtive shadows, and children wrapped in thick scarves, their knees purple with cold, rushed from the stand selling *churros* to the fountain.

However hard we stared at him, standing there gaunt and immobile, however long we watched his long, dark hands and his taut mouth, we could not see any sign that he was about to meet his death, no gesture that betrayed his cornered, condemned state of mind. He did appear to be on edge and wary, but this impression came from the cat-like tension in his strong shoulders. Ready at last to cross the threshold of who knew what drama, he took a couple of deep draws on his cigarette, but then, against all expectation, he flicked it into the trench and turned on his heel. We looked on in disbelief as he disappeared back inside the doorway.

Two days later, the workmen shovelled the earth back into the hole, covered it with the same worn slabs, loaded their tools and the barrier into a van, and left, never to return. It was then we realised something that had completely escaped our attention: all the time the pavement had been lifted, laying bare its rusty pipes and fraying cables, we had noticed no particularly noxious smell, apart from the faint suggestion of cat shit that always emanates from freshly dug earth. But as soon as the trench and its rotten innards had been covered up again, the smell of gas filled the air once more, and not only outside number eight. The fetid atmosphere seemed to go on spreading, to the extent that – perhaps because it stuck to your clothing and skin – you could detect the smell in streets well away from the square, and even in distant neighbourhoods of the city.

3

After spending several more days with his sick mother, Forcat too left the flat. We were not to see him again until the following Spring, in even more remarkable circumstances. His departure was as discreet and unexpected as his arrival. People said there was nothing to keep him there, apart from burying his aged mother when the time came.

A short while afterwards, someone said they had seen him wiping glasses behind the counter of a bar in Barceloneta that belonged to his other married sister, but it seemed unlikely because according to the postman, letters were again arriving for his mother from him in France, which suggested he had gone back to Toulouse.

Some time later, at the start of a new year, the Chacón brothers stopped coming to the square. Occasionally they could be seen with

their second-hand comics and books laid out on the pavement opposite the Colegio del Divino Maestro, on the corner of Calle Escorial.
One Saturday three months later I caught sight of them outside a
take-away greengrocer's in Calle Providencia. The two boys stood
hands in pockets staring at the barrels of fragrant olives outside on
the pavement. They were even dirtier and more ragged than before.
They seemed to have shot up, and were all eyes and dirt; their bodies
quivered like animals stalking their prey. Inside the shop, half a
dozen women were queueing to buy cooked chick peas and lentils.
Hoping to surprise them, I crept up behind the brothers, but when
I tapped Finito on the shoulder he turned slowly to face me with
rolled-up eyes, then started to shake uncontrollably and fell moaning
to the ground. He began to kick his legs and a green froth started
to pour from his mouth. His brother Juan knelt quickly to grab his
head and shout for help. A few passers-by halted, the women came
out of the shop, and a circle of locals soon collected. No one had
the faintest idea what to do. Desperate groans of a kind I had only
ever heard in the cinema came from Finito's throat, and the ghastly
green foam was still bubbling out of his mouth. The women said
how sorry they felt for him. They bemoaned the way some children
were neglected these days, the hunger and misery the poor immigrant children from the south suffered in their shacks . . . For a
moment, I was paralysed by shock and fear; then an overwhelming
feeling of sadness overcame me as I saw my friend writhing around
as if possessed by the devil. I threw myself down beside him,
desperate for him to clamber out of the dark well he was drowning
in: 'Finito, Finito, what's wrong!' I shouted, and was trying to grab
his flailing legs when, still howling and foaming at the mouth, the
little rogue winked at me . . .

I scrambled to my feet and waited to see how this tawdry melo-
drama would end, although I already had a good idea. With Juan
holding on to his head so it would not explode, Finito gradually
calmed down. He dragged himself across the pavement until, painfully
and laboriously, he succeeded in propping himself against a wall.
One of the women who lived nearby wiped his mouth clean with a

handkerchief, and told anyone who would listen that attacks like these were due to debilitation and empty stomachs. 'We haven't eaten for five days, señora,' Juan said. A granny living opposite came out with a tin of condensed milk and gave it to these poor starving immigrant children. As Finito was struggling to his feet, the woman selling cooked dishes came out of her shop with a bag full of at least two kilos of steaming chick peas. She handed it to Juan, and told him: off you go and eat them at home. Juan asked me to help, and between the two of us we supported Finito as we walked away, the women's pitying comments still echoing in our ears.

No sooner had we turned the corner than Finito straightened up, smiled, and cuffed me round the ear: 'You're a real dummy,' he said. At that moment I both hated and envied him: in the three months since I had last seen them, he had learned tricks to stave off hunger like buying and selling second-hand comics and foaming green at the mouth: all I had learned was to play billiards. Sitting on a bench in the Plaza del Norte, they ate their fill of hot chick peas, which I refused, then used a penknife blade to make two holes in the tin of milk. While they were sucking at it, they explained their trick: before he fell to the ground, Finito chewed on a green water-colour tablet, and put a handful of sherbet in his mouth. The rest was simply a matter of playacting, and his precocious talent as a fraud. I felt cheated and foolish, angry I had been taken in by such a simple hoax thought up by two illiterate, flea-ridden outcasts like them. When I saw how they were laughing at me, their mouths still full of chick peas and condensed milk, I walked off without so much as a goodbye.

I was unaware then what other pantomimes and frauds – far more destructive and unappetising – lay in store for me that Spring. They were played out not far from there, in the Calle de las Camelias, with Captain Blay as my faithful companion.

4

My mother worked in the kitchens at the Sant Pau Hospital and did not eat at home. She went out before I got up, leaving me my lunch already prepared – almost always boiled rice or beans with a piece of cod, sometimes leftovers she brought from the hospital. She was so exhausted by the time she came in that she went straight to bed. We lived in a tiny third floor flat up at the top end of Calle Cerdeña, close to the Plaza Sanllehy. Whenever I had been playing billiards in the Juventud bar, and got back later than her, I used to open her bedroom door a little way and look in. It was too dark for me to see anything, but I stood by the door waiting to hear something: the sound of her breathing, her body stirring between the sheets, a creak of the bed-frame or a cough, something to reassure me that my mother was at home and asleep.

Only a few days prior to Nandu Forcat's arrival and all the excitement over the trench, I had been given the delicate task of looking after the obstinate, eccentric Captain Blay. His wife, our neighbour Doña Conxa, suggested to my mother that as long as I had nothing better to do, I could usefully employ my mornings by accompanying the old lunatic on his wanderings round the neighbourhood.

'You're to go with him and make sure nothing happens to him,' my mother instructed me. 'Keep an eye out for trams and cars, and steer him away from that gang of louts who make fun of him in the street. Don't let him go very far, and don't go further into town than the Travesera de Gracia. And for God's sake stop him burning those newspapers: what kind of nonsense is that!'

Señora Conxa gave the Captain a few coins for a glass of wine here and there, but she warned me only to let him go in bars where he was already known, and not to let him get into arguments or drunken shouting matches. Above all, she said, he wasn't to talk politics to anyone he was unacquainted with: God forbid he came out with one of his provocative comments, then we'd have to go and rescue him from the police station. I told both her and my mother

I'd do what I could, but I thought to myself: who on earth can shut that old crackpot up, or force him to go anywhere he doesn't want to?

During the first few days, I was very worried. For almost three years, the Captain had not walked more than a hundred yards out in the street. In fact, he had not even left his house. He sometimes still shut himself up in a tiny disused bathroom he reached through a backless wardrobe shifted in front of the bathroom door. By the time he finally decided to go out into the world again, he had lost thirty kilos in weight, a war and two sons, his own wife's respect, and, to all intents and purposes, what little common sense he had ever had. At first, none of the locals could identify him, because he was so terrified he only went out heavily disguised as a 'pedestrian run over by a tram,' as he liked to present himself in bars: an anonymous patient convalescing in the nearby Hospital de Colonias Extranjeras in Calle de las Camelias, out for a while to stretch his legs and have a glass of wine, with the doctor and nurse's permission of course. And he showed the surly early morning drinkers listening open-mouthed to him the striped pyjamas under his baggy raincoat, his felt slippers, his proud, feverish head completely swathed in gauze like a giant egg, with the bandages and strands of cottonwool surmounted by tufts of wild grey hair. Soon, when he became well-known in the area and had me to accompany him, he left his dark glasses at home. The Captain confided to me that during his lengthy seclusion, he had imagined that when he emerged he would find the city in ruins beneath a cloud of ashes, and jumbled piles of furniture, goods and coffins being bought and sold: the final humiliation of defeat, while a storm raged all around: thunder and lightning, doors and windows being flung open, the hurricane spattering the wallpaper of bedrooms visible from the street through the shell-holes in the housefronts with trails of blood ... The first day we went up to the top of Guinardó and stood in the doorway of a wine-cellar, as he stared out blindly down at Barcelona, he told me had the feeling he was returning to an empty city, somewhere abandoned to the plague or air-raids, his memory washed away in the deluge.

Being not only shy, but timid and apprehensive as well, at first I went along with the Captain's ravings, his manias and extravagances, but bit by bit I learned how to combat his erratic nature. By now, in exchange for my services as guide and guard, or perhaps simply because Doña Conxa felt sorry for my mother when she saw how exhausted she was, I ate at the Captain's flat three days a week. Doña Conxa was a plump, cheerful woman, with full lips and long eyelashes always smothered in mascara. She was a lot younger than the Captain, and was extremely good-natured. The Chacón brothers called her 'Bettibu'. She lived on the fourth floor just above our flat with the old lunatic, although for a long while I thought she was on her own, and only knew of Captain Blay by name. To all appearances, 'Bettibu' was a widow with no other means of support than the cleaning jobs she did in a few houses, and her exquisite bobbin lace, much sought after by the women always praying at Las Animas and by the rich ladies of the neighbourhood. She also darned socks and did sewing. Because of their long friendship and the fact that they were some sort of distant relative, my mother was very fond of her, and whenever she came back from a visit to our grandparents in Penedès with potatoes, oil and other provisions, she always made up a little basket for Doña Conxa, which I had to take up to her: aubergines, tomatoes and peppers, artichokes and walnuts, and occasionally a homemade sausage. One day as I was trying to sneak a walnut out of the basket I was taking upstairs, I came across two cheroots wrapped in a scrap of newspaper. I said to my mother, does 'Bettibu' smoke cheroots in secret then? Or are those stinking weeds for one of the fancy men everyone says she has: the watchman, the dustman . . . ? My mother frowned at me and chose her words carefully: what's in that basket is no business of yours, Señora Conxa is a good woman who feels very much alone since she lost the Captain and her two sons . . . she deserves our respect and help, and yes, the cheroots are for her . . . we all have our little vices.

My mother was lying, and it was not long before I found out why. I had been in 'Bettibu's' flat several times, but I had never got any further than the hall, and did not yet know that Captain Blay and the Invisible Man, the ragged phantom we always saw in the neigh-bourhood surrounded by a swarm of kids shouting at him: 'Take your clothes off, Invisible Man, no one will be able to see you!' — were one and the same person. I discovered this when my mother sent me to collect some socks Doña Conxa had been darning for her. On this occasion, instead of asking me to wait in the hall as she usually did, she told me to follow her into the dining-room and had me sit down while she finished the socks. In the centre of the oilskin tablecloth was half a water-melon with a knife stuck in its crimson flesh. 'Bettibu' asked if I'd like a slice, but I said no — I had already eaten the other half of the melon at home. It was then I noticed the huge, ancient black wardrobe pushed to a corner of the room. It looked like one of the ugly confessionals in the parish church. I wondered what a wardrobe was doing in the dining-room, although I was accustomed to furniture appearing in strange places and being put to strange uses, because for a while my mother and I had rented a room stuffed full of the oddest objects. Despite this, I had never seen such an enormous piece of furniture in such an inappropriate place. I was thinking that perhaps it covered up a patch of damp or a crack in the wall, when all of a sudden its doors creaked open, and a pair of filthy, scrawny hands pushed back the moth-eaten dead man's suits hanging inside. With a giant stride, arched over like a wary cat, half an extinguished cheroot dangling from his mouth, dressed in his striped pyjamas and his long brown coat, but without the bandages round his head, Captain Blay stood before me. He looked like a messenger from a devastated, long-lost world, the world of his two dead sons and his shattered ideals, the world of defeat and madness.

'Cunt,' he declared without a hint of spite, as though he had just remembered something.

Pursued by images and voices whose origin and meaning I gradually learned to decipher, the Captain crouched for a moment in front of the wardrobe, his eyes alert, his body tense as a spring, his mind yet again hearing the echo of a shot resounding on the far side of the River Ebro, yet again seeing his son Oriol fall between his horse's hooves, his pack and rifle strapped across his back, his field glasses still slung around his neck . . .

He stared straight through me. His wife, her attention concentrated on the socks she was mending, did not heed him at all. Weighed down by his heavy soldier's cape, the Captain straightened up laboriously in the mists rising from the river. The insides of the wardrobe doors were plastered with cards that had prayers and pious verses written on them.

'I'm going out, Conxa,' he announced, speaking so softly it was as though he had given up all hope of ever being heard. Then, as he rummaged around in one of the drawers for bandages and bits of cottonwool, he added, even more quietly but with no hint of bitterness: 'Where do you think he was buried?'

His wife did not reply or even look at him.

'They could at least give us back his field glasses,' the Captain went on. 'They were a very good pair.'

'*Vols parlar com Deu mana, brètol?*' said 'Bettibu'.

'God doesn't give the orders any more, Conxa. They're the ones who give the orders now.'

He looked at me as if this was the first time he had seen me. 'Who are you, boy?' he asked, and then began to bandage his head, spinning round like a top. At the same time, in his mind's eye he could see himself furiously tying up another long, dirty bandage round his bleeding forehead: he must have banged his head against the canvas of the ghostly tent pitched on the river bank, and as he stooped, for the thousandth time he saw the bullet knocking Oriol from his horse. And as always, he could see a body sobbing on a stretcher behind him – his other seventeen-year-old son who was back from the Ebro and was dying of typhus. The Captain cursed and told him to be quiet.

'*Prou, nen! Calla!*'

The soldier moaned that he wanted to die in his own bed, but in the end did fall silent. The Captain glanced at him pityingly out of the corner of his eye:

'That's right,' he said. 'Die quietly like a little bird. Here or at home, what's the difference, son; just die like a little bird. Don't make a fuss.'

'*Què dius?*' she grumbled.

'I'm not talking to you,' he said, his raging head bumping into another tent rope as he staggered out into the mist. 'Last month two stray bullets whistled across the river. The first had Oriol's name on it, the second hit me in the head. The bitch reached my brain, but when it burrowed inside I wasn't thinking of anything in particular. So now I'm going out for a walk.'

Doña Conxa shook her round china-doll face and her black shiny curls. She pursed her jaunty lips, redder than the water-melon's heart. Even now she did not deign to look at him, and she may not have heard what he said because she was quite deaf, but she knew he was there, up to some more mischief. She always used his surname when talking to him:

'*Blay, ets un cap de cony,*' she said in her stony, vindictive Catalan. '*Estàs boig.*'

'I'm going out, my love,' the Captain repeated. 'And I reckon that if I pass by Las Animas church on the way back, I might just gobble up a priest.' He scrutinised her face to see the effect of his words, and added: 'If it's true I'm such a bloodthirsty bolshevik and degenerate mason, I have to behave like one. Don't you agree, sweetheart?'

Doña Conxa continued shouting at him in Catalan, the language they had always spoken together. Later, my mother told me that one day years earlier when the Captain had been talking to his wife, in Catalan as usual, he had suffered a stroke and collapsed onto the floor. When, a long time later, he came to, he was seeing double and also started speaking in Spanish, without being able to explain why and apparently unable to prevent it, however hard he tried. He had spoken in that language ever since, even though Doña Conxa, whether she was listening or not, always answered him in Catalan.

'*Ja n'ets prou de ruc, ja.*'

'I said I was going out, and that's what I'm doing,' the Captain said in a voice his wife could now hear perfectly well. 'I'm a lot thinner, more of a tramp and uglier than ever, so nobody will recognize me. I've become a creature in the service of Moscow, I know, but I'll dress like a pedestrian knocked down by a tram, so I'll go unnoticed.'

'*A mi em parles en català!* Blabbermouth! *Capsigrany!*'

The Captain quietly buttoned up his raincoat.

''Bye, my love. I'll be back soon.'

'*On vas ara, desgraciat?! Ruc, més que ruc!*'

I do not know if the Captain did in fact go out that day, because I escaped beforehand. Doña Conxa had finished darning the socks. Her plump fingers turned them inside out in a flash, then she rolled them up and gave them to me. I ran out of the flat.

6

In mid-March, the next year, the Chacón brothers moved their pile of dog-eared comics and tattered Westerns to a corner on Calle de las Camelias, by the garden fence of the house where Susana Franch had been in bed for a year and a half, suffering from tuberculosis. Susana was fifteen years old, and was Kim's daughter. We did not really know her, apart from the fact that for a while she went frequently to Las Animas and made friends with the girls in the orphanage, but when we heard she had been spitting blood and was consumptive, we could scarcely believe it: how could that happen to someone like her, who seemed so healthy and full of life, and who lived in that lovely villa with a garden, and with all the money they said her father had. But according to Doña Conxa, when the mother was left on her own with the girl, she could not cope. She had to sell her jewels and had been forced to go out to work. Now in the afternoons she was a box office attendant at the Mundial cinema on Calle Salmerón, and supplemented her meagre income making bobbin lace whenever the Captain's wife asked her to. Even so, she must have found it hard to make ends meet, especially now her daughter had TB; word had it that her husband did not send her any money from France any more, and that she did not protest if any of her men friends offered her a bit of help. These rumours about her love life incensed 'Bettibu', who had never managed to free herself from similar gossip – she always claimed they were spread by three or four bigoted women from church.

Susana spent the day in a bed set up in a covered semi-circular verandah which was the brightest and sunniest room in the house, and gave onto the garden. From the street we could see her lying back on a mound of pillows, enveloped in aromatic vapours that kept the atmosphere humid and misted up the windows. She usually wore a mauve or pink nightdress, her black hair loose around her shoulders, and spent the time painting her fingernails mother-of-pearl or cherry red or reading magazines, listening to the radio or cutting film adverts out of newspapers. A pot full of water and eucalyptus leaves simmered constantly on an attractive iron stove in one corner of the room. Its outlet pipe twisted like a sinister black hook up to the ceiling, then snaked out of the room through a round hole cut neatly in the windowpane.

When I took the Chacón brothers to task for having chosen the street corner on Camelias so they could spy on Susana in bed, Finito said: who do you take me for, it's nothing like that, and anyway don't you know the poor girl's going to die soon? And he said he and his brother hadn't chosen that spot either because they hoped to see her father, Kim, turn up some day, but for a less exciting but much more practical reason: simply to be close to the market on the opposite pavement by the wall of the Europa football club, a bit higher up than Susana's villa. The two of them also took turns to hang around the fruit and vegetable stalls to see if there was any work to do, hauling crates, sweeping up the rubbish or carrying bags. And if there was nothing doing, Finito would fling himself to the ground in one of his spectacular epileptic fits. He was so convincing that despite knowing it was a trick, the sight of him writhing, shaking and having a spasm, his eyes like a drowned man's and all that green foam coming from his mouth, still scared the life out of me. There was a shop that sold *churros* on the corner of Cerdeña, and some charitable soul from there who felt sorry for this poor immigrant kid almost always brought him a bag of doughnuts, while one or other of the market stall women gave him a couple of apples or bananas.

Thanks to their pitch by her railings, Juan and Finito had established a silent but affectionate relationship with the sick girl, a cheerful code of signs and suggestions. They frequently lent her comics and paperbacks and brought eucalyptus leaves for the stove. Susana's mother would come out into the garden and send one or other of them to the market to buy fruit, or to the coal merchant's or the baker's. When she had to go to the cinema in the afternoon, she asked them to keep an eye out to make sure no one got into the house. I would occasionally stop to thumb through some of the brothers' novels, and would see Susana get up from bed and wave with a sad smile to her protectors from the far side of the window.

One bitterly cold evening when I was in Calle de las Camelias after the brothers had gone, probably driven away by the damp and mist that had crept up the street and blurred the outlines of the garden and house, I thought I saw a pink blotch turning like a spinning top behind the windows: it was the consumptive girl dancing with her pillow. The vision only lasted a moment, and then she fell back on the bed. A short while later she sat up again, and I clearly made out her hand wiping the condensation from the glass and then saw her pale, distant face pressed up against it, staring out at me as though she were floating inside a bubble. I do not think she spotted me, because I waved my hand and she did not respond; soon the warm, moist atmosphere in the room had steamed up the window once more, and her face vanished.

CHAPTER TWO

I

One day sometime before he went completely off his head, Captain Blay asked me to draw Susana in her consumptive's bed with my coloured pencils. He needed a portrait of the sick child for something extremely important. He said he had already spoken to her mother, Señora Anita, and she had agreed.

'Could you do it without going to her house? Draw her from memory?' the Captain asked me.

'I don't know how to draw from memory.'

'I only meant if you're frightened you might catch the disease . . .'

'Of course not! I'm not scared!'

'Then you'd better go as soon as possible. I don't think she's long for this world.'

The Captain strode along stiffly, his head bandaged and his open coat revealing his pyjamas beneath. He took me to a stationer's in Calle Providencia, bought me six sheets of drawing paper and explained why he needed the portrait. He had decided to dedicate himself to collecting signatures in the neighbourhood for a petititon he was drawing up to present to the Council, protesting at the criminal gas leak in Plaza Rovira which threatened to poison us all, and which was definitely killing off those with weak chests, like poor Susana . . . But that wasn't all, he said: in addition to the toxic fumes, which all the docile, short-sighted locals seemed to have got used to, there was another equally insidious threat: the chimney at the plastics factory on the corner of Calle Cerdeña. According to him, the red-brick chimney was below the legal minimum height, and spewed out a black noxious smoke day and night that did not rise in the sky, but smeared the entire neighbourhood with soot. He had grown tired of sending letters to the director of Dolç Ltd., the factory owners, asking them to add to the height of the chimney. He had never received a reply, so now he was determined to go onto the attack: he would collect signatures from everybody protesting not only about the smell of gas, but the chimney as well. He said it had to be a devastating, incriminating letter signed by at least 500 people. He had already got Susana and her mother to sign. The girl's signature was of the utmost importance as a vital piece of evidence, the Captain insisted, because the poor thing's lungs are ruined and she needs pure air, not that choking smoke that's making her even worse.

I knew the chimney and the back yard at the Dolç factory very well, because with Finito and his brother we had often jumped over the warehouse wall to filch bits of plastic belts that looked like coloured snakes, celuloid fish and little ducks, or defective ping-pong balls. But that had been three or four years earlier.

'As well as the petition,' the Captain went on, 'I want to present something else to those idiots on the Council, and that's where you come in. Your mother tells me you draw very well . . . As you know, the chimney is behind the garden where that poor sick girl is, and every morning when she wakes up she's greeted by a plume of that black poison. I was thinking that to make the protest more effective, a good drawing of Susanita coughing her lungs up in bed with the chimney nearby spewing out that deadly smoke would be worth more than all the signatures put together . . .'

'Hang on, Captain! Who exactly is coughing their lungs up?'

'Let's get things straight, my painter friend. We have to be clever. You've got to paint the consumptive girl looking very pallid and emaciated, very sad, with that porcelain face of hers, prostrate in her bed with eyes closed, one hand on her chest, gasping for breath, like this, look . . .'

'Have you been to see her?'

'I visited her yesterday with my wife.'

'Is she still coughing blood?'

'Not while I was there.'

'Doña Conxa says she's curing her by rubbing elderflower on her chest and back.'

'That's nonsense. Boiled elderflower is only good for the sort of piles that bishops and homosexuals get, everyone knows that. Anyway, don't interrupt me, what I'm asking you to do is very important,' the Captain growled, as we stepped out across Calle Martí. 'Just remember: it has to be a very moving drawing, one that makes you want to cry. And it has to show the choking smoke hovering above the sick girl on her death bed, like a deadly black cloud, with the brick-red chimney looming like a curse over us . . .'

'Will Susana let me draw her?'

'Her mother told me she had almost convinced her.' The Captain took a crumpled cheroot from his coat pocket. 'Tomorrow morning, go to the house and say I've sent you. You can start at once. If you need more paper, just tell me. I suppose you've got some coloured pencils, haven't you?'

'You want it coloured?'

'Of course. How long will it take?'

'Hmm, I don't know. I'm very slow, I find it hard.'

'Just so long as it's a good likeness . . . Go on, kid, you'll enjoy it! Show them what you can do! Between us we're going to stuff those nobs with their poisonous smoke and killer gas!'

When we reached the square he sat for a moment on a stone bench and cut the cheroot in two with his penknife. He kept one half and lit the other with a match, protecting the flame with his scaly hands, making sure he had his back to the pavement with the gas leak. 'Just in case,' he muttered. His bandages with their red-coloured ticking were filthy; he had not changed them in a fortnight, and perhaps even slept in them. By contrast, his tobacco-brown gloves with their white stitching, which he had thrust into the belt of his raincoat, were impeccable. All of a sudden the Captain leapt up from the bench as though he was completely deranged.

'Let's go home and sharpen the pencils,' he said. 'Quickly!'

'Didn't you want to go to the bar?'

'And another thing: when you go to the house tomorrow, take some of your other drawings to show Susana you're an artist. Come on, we've a lot to do!'

That night I could not sleep for thinking of the consumptive girl. All sorts of fears and apprehensions kept me awake. I could hear her racking cough full of microbes, see her furtively spitting into her pretty lace handkerchief, then immediately tucking it under her pillow. And half asleep in the early hours, with an intensity and precision I had never experienced in my erotic dreams until that moment, I imagined her snow-white breasts between the starched sheets, her pale, feverish thighs covered with a fine film of sweat as she stirred restlessly in her sleep.

2

The next morning I set off for Calle de las Camelias, my folder of drawings under my arm. Just thinking of the consumptive girl left me exhausted and feverish, gasping for breath as if I had no air, as if I had already caught the disease. Above and beyond Susana's villa, the smoke from the chimney that Captain Blay loathed so much was not going straight up into the sky, but spread horizontally like black froth, hanging round its mouth repulsively for some time before drifting down in sooty streaks over the surrounding roofs and gardens.

I met the Chacón brothers spreading out their tattered wares on the pavement outside Susana's garden railings, and spent a pleasant few minutes leafing through Edgar Wallace paperbacks in the Mystery Collection. There were three other kids rummaging about in the pile of dog-eared comics. The street market was less than fifty yards away, and some of the women who came shopping with their kids left them to amuse themselves looking through the brothers' wares. On the far side of the garden I could see Susana behind the verandah windows. She was lying in bed, a blue shawl round her shoulders. Her eyes were shut and her head was tilted back, but she did not seem to be sleeping or in pain, because she was waving her right arm as if following the beat of a tune, which must have been on the radio.

When I told Finito and Juan the Captain had asked me to do a portrait of Susana, at first they did not believe me, then they were upset and almost offended. I realised how far the two brothers considered themselves her exclusive guardians, and felt responsible for everything that happened in the garden and house.

'OK, but be very careful,' Finito warned me. 'If you see she's getting tired, or looks sad and out of it, her mind straying heaven knows where, you have to leave at once,' he said, taking half a dozen hairslides out of his pocket. 'Give her these from me. And this Rip Kirby annual that looks brand new.'

'Have you seen her close up, have you been in the room with her?' I asked.

'Sometimes. When she's on her own.'

Finito explained that every afternoon, including Sundays and holidays, Susana's mother left the house at half past three to go to work, and did not get back until after eight. She always asked them to take the message if anyone came to the house, because she wanted her daughter disturbed as little as possible. The first time Susana had opened the verandah door to them was because she needed something: the stove had gone out, and she wanted them to bring some coal from the shed, which they did. Sometimes they went in when she wanted a book to read, or eucalyptus leaves to put in the pot boiling on the stove, or because the flowers in a vase in the room were giving her a headache, or simply because she was bored with being alone.

'Make sure you behave with Susana, or you're for it,' Finito concluded, pushing the gate open for me. 'You can go in, little angel.'

As I walked across the small, neglected garden, where oleander bushes drooped in the shade of a willow-tree and lily beds were drooping from a lack of sun, I wondered how those two ragged kids had managed to gain such authority when they spoke of her. It occurred to me yet again that although barely four months had passed since the time we were all threatened by the gas leak and used to meet up in the Comulada bar and at the Juventud billiard tables, it seemed as though years had gone by.

3

Señora Anita greeted me in a frilly pink dressing-gown that had lost all its silky lustre. She had a towel over one shoulder, and a glass in her hand. She was from a village in Almería whose name I had heard for the first time on Captain Blay's lips: Cuevas de Almanzora. Standing in the doorway, she looked at me absently with eyes that seemed veiled by sadness. She was thirty-eight years old, had curly, unkempt blonde hair, a slender but lively body, and the bluest eyes I had ever seen. Her weary face, with its puffy lids and pale mouth, gave the impression of vulnerable, injured sweetness.

'Captain Blay sent me,' I said. 'For the drawing . . .'

She stared at me for a moment uncomprehendingly. Then she smiled:

'Oh, yes. Come in. But I don't think Susana's made her mind up yet. That daughter of mine's a bit whimsical, you know.'

'I can come back another day if you like.'

'No, no, come in.' She pulled me by the arm and closed the door. 'Don't tell poor old Blay this, but I think his idea is a load of nonsense . . . But anyway, it'll keep the child occupied, it'll mean she has company in the afternoon when I'm not here. What's your name, sweetie?'

'Daniel.'

'Daniel. What a nice name. That's what I planned to call my Susana if she'd been a boy . . . Daniel in the lion's den! I always liked that story. So, go down this corridor to the dining-room, then the verandah is on the left.' She raised her voice so her daughter could hear: 'Sweetheart, it's the boy to do the drawing!'

There was no reply, and I did not move. The music on the radio stopped.

'Don't worry, come with me,' Señora Anita said, linking arms. 'And don't pay any attention if she scowls. She's been expecting you.'

She led me along to the doorway of a bedroom – hers, I guessed – then smiled to encourage me to carry on to the verandah. From within, the villa was not as big as it looked from outside. But on this first visit I was confused by the darkened corridor: it seemed endless, so long that as I walked down it I felt the strange sensation that I was going beyond the villa and entering into another space. I passed beneath a mouldy stucco ceiling; on the walls were old paintings in artistic frames, speckled art nouveau mirrors and lots of marble and porcelain figures on pedestals, some of them chipped and accumulating dust; I caught the smell of pieces of musty furniture and remembered that Susana's parents had once been rich. The heavy mahogany furniture looked cumbersome and somehow baleful, as if they had been silent witnesses to a drama that had happened here years before, from which neither Susana nor her mother had recovered. As I drew nearer to the verandah, I also noticed the scent of eucalyptus and the hot, moist atmosphere: the air was heavy and smelt in a way I had never come across anywhere else. I felt excited and apprehensive. I decided to keep a safe distance from the sick girl's bed. As I crossed the dining-room, I spotted an open wine flask on the table, and when I poked my head round into the verandah, I heard her say:

'Come in. Hurry up, will you, before my mother pushes her way in!'

The pot was bubbling on the stove. A pale sun filtered into the verandah like an aquarium, lighting up the small bed with its metal frame against one wall, and the bedside table with an already antique radio set on it. At the other end of the room were a round table, two chairs and a white rocking chair. One of the chairs was pushed back against the wall, and on it lay some unfinished bobbin lace.

I was surprised to find the consumptive girl sitting upright on the edge of the bed, legs crossed and nightshirt raised to her knees. She was barefoot, sat with her arms akimbo, and was wearing an artificial daisy in her hair, with the shawl draped round her shoulders. It took her a lot of effort to sustain this pose, and there was a mixture of trust and defiance in her gaze, as though she were demanding my approval. There was no way I could have guessed that this studied position and haughty charm were the result of hours of thought and rehearsals in front of the mirror: she was sitting this way because that was how she had decided I should draw her, and the nervousness she transmitted, coupled with her desperate desire to please, the animal energy quivering in her pale, dry lips and slender nostrils, was so intense and direct she was the most beautiful girl I had ever seen. A mass of black curls framed her waxy forehead pearled with sweat; her cheeks glowed pink where she had pinched them. Her top lip was plump and well-defined, and tilted slightly upwards, making it seem broader and fleshier than the lower one. This made it look as though she were continually pouting in a childish, disturbing way. She did not have dark circles round her eyes, sunken cheeks or a collapsed chest; she was not extremely pale or struggling to breathe through an open mouth or anything of the sort. In fact, she was nothing like the consumptive patient I had imagined, who might infect me with her poisonous exhalations and tortured visions of death no sooner than I breathed the same air as she did. On the bed beside her were photos she had cut out of magazines and newspapers, a pair of scissors, a bottle of cologne, a pack of cards and a black felt cat with green glass eyes which she clasped to her.

'I know you,' she said. 'You're Daniel.'

'Yes.'

'You're the boy who discovered a big gas leak in the Plaza Rovira.'

'It was Captain Blay who discovered it.'

'And you live in Calle Cerdeña.'

'Yes.'

'And you don't have a father.' She lowered her voice and whispered: 'Is that true?'

Her voice had a sleepy quality that somehow caught on the phlegm of her vocal chords. I imagined she must have a high fever, and that her voice was in some way transmitting the illness and the infected phlegm.

'Is it true you don't have one?'

'I don't know.'

'You don't know if you have a father or not? You're a fine one! Are you stupid or something?'

I stared at the cherry red polish on her manicured nails.

'He never came back from the war,' I explained. 'But we don't know whether he was killed or not. Nobody knows. He might be alive somewhere, and have lost his memory or been badly wounded – I mean, so that he doesn't remember his family or anything, or how to reach home . . . So I can't really say I don't have a father.'

Susana looked at me quizzically, then said:

'But it's as if you didn't. The same as me.' She took a handkerchief from under her pillow, soaked it in cologne from the bottle beside her, and dabbed it on her temples and neck. She threw me a wary glance, and added:

'You are a bit odd, aren't you?'

I shrugged: 'Me? Why?'

Her eyes still on my face, she seemed to think this over. Then she said with a scowl:

'Haven't they told you I'm very sick and that you shouldn't come too close to me?'

'Yes.'

'And do you know what's wrong with me?'

I took my time answering:

'You have sick lungs.'

'No, sir. Not lungs. Lung. Only one of them. Do you know which?'

'No.'

'The left one.'

She fell silent for a moment, still staring me in the face. Her expression was a combination of sly mischief and controlled tension. So great was the effort she made to create this impression despite the torments of her fever and her exhausted blood, that often over the coming months it was this determination that frightened me much more than the idea of catching her illness. All at once she looked very tired. She closed her eyes and took a slow, deep breath, as though she were afraid of hurting herself. I said:

'Finito gave me these for you,' and I handed over the hairslides and the Rip Kirby annual. She did not even glance at the book, but chose two slides and while she was lifting her hair from the back of her neck to push them in, I noticed a silver-framed photograph of her father on the bedside table: Kim in a light-coloured coat with the collar turned up, looking to one side with his hat brim pulled down over one eye, and a lop-sided smile. There was a disturbing glint in his eyes, the spark of adventure.

'And is it true you can draw?' said Susana.

'A bit.'

I opened my folder and showed her the drawings I had chosen: one of an almond tree in bloom, a pink cloud I had copied from life in the Baix Penedès, and two of the Parque Güell I liked a lot because of their bright colours: one of the ceramic dragon on the steps, the other of the twisting bench in the square with the outline of Barcelona in the background. She was not impressed, so I showed her one more I had kept in reserve: Gene Tierney in a tight green dress sitting on a stool at a casino bar looking seductive and dishevelled, with cigarette smoke curling up around her face. I had copied it from a film handbill, and the technique was nothing special. It did not even look like her, but this was the one Susana admired.

'This one's very good. She's beautiful.' She passed back the folder, took out the hairslides and shook her hair loose. She uncrossed her legs then crossed them again, and said in a whisper: 'Is Mum still in the bathroom?'

'I don't know.'

'We'll have to hurry. If she sees me out of bed, she'll have a fit.'

She ran her tongue round her lips to moisten them, bit them, then pinched her cheeks again. 'Now look: what do you think?'

I didn't know what to say. She looked like a paper doll. She insisted:

'Am I all right like this?'

'I don't understand.'

'Like this, sitting on the bed. I want you to draw me like this, as if I was better and just about to go out, with colour in my cheeks, wearing shoes and a green dress I can't put on yet but which I'll show you some day. But I don't want the nightdress or the woollen shawl – none of that. I ought to have something in my hand . . . a mirror, or a very pretty bag my Dad gave me. What do you think, can you draw me like that?'

I told her that wasn't what I had agreed with Captain Blay, and that I was supposed to draw her slumped in bed with a waxen face as she breathed in the toxic smoke from the factory chimney.

'And with dark lines round my eyes, pinched cheeks and looking like a scarecrow, I bet!' she cut in, furious again. 'A poor consumptive about to kick it! No chance!'

'It's not that, ' I said to try to persuade her. 'Anyone can see you're almost better. You look wonderful. But the Captain wants the drawing to give a different impression . . .'

'I know exactly what that old lunatic wants!'

She was very angry, and dropped her pose. Then she thought she heard her mother's footsteps in the corridor, so she raced into bed, leaning back on the pillows and pulling the sheets and blue bedcover up to her chest. But her mother did not appear.

'Well that's not how I want you to draw me,' she said without looking in my direction. 'Stuck in bed, coughing like a poor idiot, no.'

'We could have you lying on the bed as though you were resting . . . and I won't draw you too pale, just enough. And you can wear a flower in your hair if you like. If the drawing was for you, I'd do it exactly how you want.'

Susana turned her head slowly and looked at me curiously.

'I don't want a drawing for me,' she said. She thought for a few

35

moments, then added more brightly: 'OK, here's what we'll do. I'll let you draw me like that for the Captain, as if I'm wasting away surrounded by medicines, but on one condition: you have to do another drawing of me in a pose I choose, dressed and with my hair the way I want, with lots of colour and everything very nice. The portrait of a happier and prettier girl, a portrait of me how I'll be quite soon, in a few months' time . . .'

'The Captain's drawing will be nice too, you'll see.'

'I don't care about that.' She picked up the toy cat and held it to her chest. 'You can draw me ugly and scrawny, with my face the colour of wax and my eyes bloodshot with fever, you can even draw me spitting blood, I don't care. But I do care about the other drawing, because I want to send it to my father, and I don't want him to see me sick and horrible-looking. Got it?'

'Yes.'

'It'll be a surprise gift for him, get it?'

'Yes, I said yes.'

'You'll do it then?'

'I hope I can get it right . . .'

'Of course you can! It'll be lovely!'

'And shall we put the chimney with the smoke poisoning you in the background, like in the drawing for Captain Blay?'

Susana shrugged.

'I don't care. That dreadful smoke and the gas leak and everything else going on out there has got nothing to do with me . . . nothing at all.'

'Why do you say that?'

Her burning eyes were still staring in my direction, but she did not seem to see me.

'Because some day soon I'm going far away from here,' she said with a wicked smile. 'That's why.'

4

The next Monday afternoon, I embarked on the drawing that was supposed to be so controversial and moving it would miraculously save not merely the consumptive girl but the entire neighbourhood from a slow but certain death. I was full of optimism, but nothing went right. Even though I tried and tried a thousand times, not a single line was as it should have been. I stared as hard as I could through screwed-up eyes to size up and capture the tenuous harmony of her delicate body, as she pretended to be prostrate on the cushions, shrouded in eucalyptus vapours – although Susana made fun of my efforts by writhing about and exaggerating in pure *dame aux camélias* style, dying in agony with one leg dangling from the bed – but my pencil would just not respond. In order not to waste good drawing paper, I made laboured sketches in a school notebook. Then for a while I gave up on her figure and tried to compose the windows of the verandah, the stove and the fateful chimney (even though I could not actually see it from where I was), but with the same result. I found it impossible to resolve the perspective.

'I told you it wouldn't work if you drew me like a stupid sick child wasting away, with collapsed chest and bulging fish eyes,' Susana said, picking up the cards from the table. 'Why not make a start on the other one?'

'No, this one first. The Captain asked me before you did.'

'Go on, leave it for now.' She spread the cards like a fan in front of her face, her shining eyes peeping over the top. 'Shall we play rummy?'

'OK.'

I did not get far the second day either. Midway through the afternoon it came on to rain, and we saw the Chacón brothers gather up their books and comics and run for shelter under the willow-tree in the garden. Susana called to them and they came in through a small door at the far end of the verandah. Finito's pockets were stuffed with eucalyptus leaves. He threw them into the pot with his filthy hands, then got out a piece of comb and drew it several times through his greasy mop of jet-black hair. Susana sent him and his brother to wash their hands in the bathroom, and when they got back suggested a game of parcheesi. The three of us sat on the bed; my back was to the table with Kim's portrait on it, and I could feel his eyes boring into the nape of my neck. I shook the dice as hard as I could for luck, and moved my yellow counters with all the skill I could muster, but I could not prevent the Chacón brothers eating them every game, nor could I stop myself thinking the whole afternoon about the legendary gunman and the dark gleam of his eyes focussed on the back of my head.

5

When Nandu Forcat's mother died, everyone said he would come to the funeral and we were all hoping to see him, but he did not appear. The unmarried daughter who had looked after the old woman went to live in Barceloneta with her married sister and sold the flat in Plaza Rovira, so it seemed unlikely Kim's friend would ever be seen again in the neighbourhood.

My mornings were still taken up with accompanying Captain Blay in his tireless trek through the streets of Gracia, Perla, Bruniquer, Montmany, Joan Blanques and Escorial. In his quest for signatures, he climbed stairs and rang bells everywhere. We sometimes ended up in gloomy taverns with pungent-smelling counters and solitary drinkers, while I pestered him with questions about Susana's father: Were they already after Kim for being a red when he got together with Señora Anita, Captain? Is it true they're not married by the Church? Is it right what they say about Señora Anita, that she worked in a dance-hall called the 'Shanghai' and that was where Kim met her? And is it also true that before that she had been a poor house-maid, and then a dancer in a burlesque show on the Paralelo, and that she danced naked?

The Captain said yes, damn and blast it, but it wasn't as simple as that and certainly wasn't something to be blabbing about to a fourteen-year-old still wet behind the ears, but that the most important thing to remember was that blue-eyed women lied as easily as they drew breath, everyone knew that; and the only really true thing about Kim's life was that he had been a rich young man, someone with a lot of class and a first-rate education, the eldest of an extremely rich family of textile manufacturers from Sabadell.

'A libertarian is what he was and is, if he still is what he used to be, or wanted to be – although Conxa and I can never agree about that either.' The Captain came to a halt in front of some kids playing football in Calle Legalidad. 'Hey, you lot, don't come too close to this drain here, there's a build-up of gases! I'm serious, you idiots! The leak has reached this rat's nest, and if you breathe it in, your bones won't grow! And whatever you do, don't throw a firecracker in there . . .'

'Go on, Invisible Man, take your clothes off!' one of the boys shouted, and then they all clustered round the Captain and chanted: 'Pull them down, pull them down!'

'Fine, as far as I'm concerned you can all choke to death!' The Captain forced his way between them, lashing out to right and left. A few yards further on he shook his head sorrowfully: 'Too bad, they've got the shit inside them already, they'll never grow.'

I returned to the attack with my questions about Susana's father. For some reason, the Captain could not stand Kim, even though he did not doubt his courage or the legend that had grown up around him, his strange role as a clandestine hero. He told me that a long time before he was known as Kim, when everyone here and in Sabadell still called him Joaquim Franch i Casablancas, he was already a man of action and progressive ideas, someone with an indomitable spirit determined to forge his own destiny. He had almost finished his studies as a textile engineer when he fell hopelessly in love with Anita, the family maid, and ran off with her to Barcelona. It was then that his father disinherited him, or rather he disinherited himself: he never saw his family again. Anita, Susana's mother, was twenty-one at the time. She had come from a village in Almería to serve in a rich family, following in the footsteps of one of her cousins, who eventually became a chorus girl at the Paralelo. Remember, this was at the start of the thirties, kid, so Kim found work wherever he could: he did many things, although none of them were in his own line: he sold coffee-grinders and razors, managed a gym, became an agent for variety artistes, then a secret policeman for the Generalitat, and finally the representative for a German firm of cinema projectors, which enabled him to travel all over Spain and make a lot of money.

'But it all vanished like the morning dew,' the Captain added, as we were climbing Calle Cerdeña, close to home. 'Because no sooner had he set himself up in the villa with his wife and daughter, who must have been around three years old at that time, than all hell broke loose, and it was pa-pa-pam on the trumpet, to arms everyone . . . !'

And from then on what can I say, kid, he concluded, slowly climbing the dark, narrow staircase with its sticky handrail, with me behind him hanging on every word he grunted and groaned rather than said outright: that was when he met up again with Nandu Forcat and his bunch of utopian dreamers, first at the Ebro front and then here in Barcelona, and their friendship rapidly led him to the anarchist paradise, that libertarian ideal which turned the world upside down, and changed forever not only his own life but that of his beloved Anita and that poor consumptive child of theirs.

'Bettibu' opened the door, and the heartwarming smell of lentils and bacon wafted out into the corridor.

'Time to eat,' said the Captain, rubbing his hands. With his wife looking on as patiently as ever, he unwound the bandages, took off his coat and went to wash. He came back and sat at the table and for once revealed his bare, ghostly features. His face was haggard and devilish-looking, and with his white-flecked beard and bushy eyebrows, his startled lizard's eyes, his trembling hand groping for the spoon on the tablecloth, he looked to me like some decrepit, domesticated Buffalo Bill who had lost his shiny silver locks, his Winchester and his marksmanship, but was still ready and willing to do battle.

6

'Do you like films?' Susana asked me while she was sorting out her cuttings. She did not wait for me to reply, but went on: 'I haven't been to the pictures in ages. Sometimes I see films in my dreams. Once in a nightmare I saw the light from a projector shining in the darkness, and I woke up with a start when I realised it was one of my father's. Did you know it was he who installed the Erneman projectors in all the Barcelona cinemas and lots of other cities too?'

'In all the cinemas? I doubt it.'

'Well, in almost all of them anyway.' She thought about it for a moment, then insisted: 'Yes, yes, in all the cinemas in Spain. Why not? His projectors were very good, the most up-to-date and everything.'

Susana was naturally disposed to this kind of daydreaming, where everything she wanted, or thought was pretty and appropriate, came true. She did the same with the collection of film adverts and handbills her mother brought back each week from the Mundial cinema. Sometimes she would cut out faces and figures, then stick them together on films they had nothing to do with, just because that was how she would have liked it to be, or because it amused her to see them like that: she had joined the beautiful Sheherezade and Quasimodo in *Wuthering Heights*, had placed the shadowy Heathcliff at a poolside with Esther Williams in her bathing suit, Sabu flying on his magic carpet over Baghdad together with Charlie Chaplin and the house-keeper from *Rebecca*, Tarzan clinging to the top of one of the towers of Notre Dame with the gypsy Esmeralda and Chita the monkey. She also distorted reality, transposing images and memories to produce bright hopes or sad forebodings. And among this jumble of memories was that of her father the last time he crossed the border clandestinely to visit her, almost two years earlier, when she had fallen ill.

'He arrived in the early morning. He came in here without switching the light on, and bent down over me. He had been talking to Mum, and was almost in tears . . . He had no idea I was so ill. When he saw how weak I was, he gave me a big kiss on my forehead and told me he couldn't take me with him yet. Well, he didn't exactly say that, but that was what he meant . . .' Susana hesitated as though she could not remember exactly how it was, then went on: 'His icy lips were pressed against my burning brow, Danny, some nights I can still feel them there when I'm turning things over and over in my mind and can't sleep . . . I'll come for you in Spring, he whispered in my ear. His leather jacket smelt of rain, and I think he was wearing a beret, though I couldn't see it properly. All of a sudden there was a sound in the garden, and he ducked down even lower beside me. He turned and his hand felt for something at his waist; it was then that I saw his tormented face, but couldn't make out his features clearly, though I know he's handsome from the photos and from what Mum has told me . . . When he stood up I couldn't see any pistol in his hand, and there wasn't one tucked in his waistband. The noise wasn't anything or anyone: perhaps it was just a cat in the garden or a pot of geraniums blown over by the wind. Then he kissed me again, took my hand and stayed next to me until I pretended I had fallen asleep because I felt sorry for him.' She sighed and fell silent. She was frowning, and licked her upper lip, which looked dry and puffy. 'Then he left, but not before he wrote me something – I know it off by heart, it was: "sweet sleeping dove, never be afraid of night, because night is my friend, and I'll come with her for you . . ." That's what it said, he wrote it on a piece of paper for me.'

She told me she'd show it me some day, together with other letters he had written her, but she never did. She was also fond of remembering how, when she was very small, her father used to lift her with one hand until she almost touched the glittering dining-room light, an antique chandelier that years later suddenly crashed to the floor one day, though no one had touched it, and smashed to smithereens. She could picture the scene vividly: she was very aware of her father's strong arm, his tender grasp, the secure feeling she had so high in the air, the blinding light from the crystal chandelier, then the dizzying descent and her mother's laughter. Still now, she said, especially some nights when she felt so ill and weak, with stabbing pains in her chest, all at once the memory of her father would come flooding back in that explosion of light in her blood and the loving impulse lifting her high above fever and loneliness, above the terror of spitting blood, the fear of dying.

CHAPTER THREE

I

I crossed Calle de las Camelias carrying my drawing folder and box of Faber pencils under my arm. As usual, I stopped to talk to the Chacón brothers outside the railings, but just as I was about to go into the garden, I heard a squeal of brakes that made me turn my head. It was a Wednesday, the only day of the week Señora Anita did not work, and that afternoon I could see she was out in the garden beyond the willow tree, singing to herself as she hung out the washing, with two clothes-pegs between her teeth.

The Balilla had come to a sudden halt just beyond the corner of Alegre de Dalt, and it seemed as though the driver had realised he had overshot the turning and was now reversing back along the street. The car was only there a couple of seconds, and we did not see anyone get out or hear its door slam, but after the Balilla had shot off round the corner, there he was, as if he had suddenly materialised out of the tarmac. He was carrying an old cardboard suitcase held together with a piece of string, and he kept the other hand in his trouser pocket. He was middle-aged and looked rather rough but still good-looking, with a strong chin and a wary look to his eyes beneath the brim of his grey hat. He slowly scanned both sides of the street, then the garden and the house, before dropping his chin and staring down at his own feet. He gave no sign of being lost or confused as he stood there in the middle of the road; it was as if he simply wanted to confirm the disastrous state of his tan and white shoes. There was a nervous energy to his broad shoulders that seemed familiar to me.

It flashed through my mind that this might be Susana's father, but then I realised who he was: Nandu Forcat. He had changed. He was not wearing sunglasses, and he looked thinner and more vulnerable than he had when we saw him for the first time five months earlier in the doorway of his mother's place, by the danger-filled trench. As he had done that day, he was standing motionless, lost in thought. He gave the impression not so much of just arriving from some unknown and distant place, but that he was about to step off again over the edge of yet another trench, leaning forward slightly as if nervous about the outcome. I exchanged glances with Finito and his brother, who had also recognised him, and stood with the gate half open as he walked towards me. He came closer slowly, carrying the suitcase and with his hat pulled down over his eyes. When he raised his head to talk to us, his cross-eyed look confused me so much I could not tell which of us he was addressing:

'Is this where Señora Anita Franch lives?'

'Yes, sir,' we all replied together.

I am sure he had already seen her and was only asking to avoid seeming like an intruder. I pushed the gate open and we watched him stride purposefully into the garden. Susana's mother did not notice him. I do not know why, but I was sure the two already knew each other, either casually or intimately, although at that time I had no evidence. Later on, the Captain told me that many years before, when Anita had been the maid in Kim's family home and had not yet fallen in love with him, she might have met Forcat in the bars of the Paralelo and flirted with him. Be that as it may, that afternoon Forcat saw her hanging out the washing and walked across the garden towards her, slowly but determinedly, with steps he seemed to have already rehearsed in his mind.

I followed his footsteps into the garden. But I was headed for the verandah, and when I reached the door I turned and watched him deposit the suitcase on the ground, take his hat off, and hold his hand out to Señora Anita. She looked surprised but very pleased to see him. Her hands went to her face, and he brought a letter out of his pocket. I could not hear how he greeted her, but I could clearly make out his warm, mellow voice as he said:

'I've come from Toulouse with news from Kim.'

Struggling with her feelings, unsure whether to be pleased or annoyed, it took her some time to react:

'Good God! Can it be true? That madcap really sent you?'

'Yes, really.'

'Why . . . why didn't he come himself?'

'You know very well why not.'

'How is he? What's he doing? Does he still remember his family?'

'Of course. He gave me this for you.'

Forcat handed her the letter in an unstamped envelope. She recognised the handwriting and, after reading a few paragraphs, gave a little squeal of delight and flung her arms around him. She let go almost immediately, ashamed perhaps to be so excited when, as she would soon discover, there was no justification for it. In the letter, the first thing her husband asked was if she could please receive his friend Forcat on his behalf, and put him up in the villa as discreetly as possible while he sorted out an extremely important matter in Barcelona. I learnt all this some weeks later, and although naturally Señora Anita could not be aware of it at the time, the favour her husband was asking for his friend turned out to be the start of the only decent, satisfying thing to happen to her in years. At the end of the letter Kim repeated his often expressed desire to take the girl with him some day, when she could travel without risking her health, but failed to say whether he was hoping to start a new life outside Spain with his wife as well.

They stood talking in the garden for a few minutes while she finished hanging out the washing. A short time later, when I was struggling yet again at the round table struggling yet again with my drawing, and Susana was shifting nervously in her bed because I had already told her the visitor was bringing news of her father, Señora Anita came into the room smiling, and presented the man on her arm:

'Sweetheart, this is Señor Forcat. Your father loves him like a brother,' she said, then quickly added, looking straight at Susana with those sparkling blue eyes of hers: 'And so do I. He'll be staying with us for a few days . . . and this serious, polite young man . . .' – she turned towards me – 'is a good friend of Susana's who comes every day to keep her company. His name's Daniel.'

Stiff and rather formal, Forcat shook hands first with Susana and then with me. He asked her how she felt, and she kneeled up on the bed, clutching the felt cat to her.

'Fine,' she said. 'Absolutely fine. Better every day.'

'Really?' said Forcat. 'Your father will be pleased to hear it . . .'

'Did he send you?'

'Yes.'

'When did you last see him? Is he all right?'

Her mother was stoking the coals in the stove. She tried to coax Susana back under the sheets.

'I'll go and see what state the room upstairs is in,' she said, smiling at her guest. 'You can bring the case up later on. Give me your coat though, you must be sweltering in here.'

He passed it to her and she left the room. Susana was so impatient she was bouncing up and down on the bedcover, still hugging her cat. She repeated her question:

'When did you see him?'

'Less than a month ago,' said Forcat, folding his arms and smiling slightly as he sat at the foot of the bed, apparently happy to satisfy Susana's curiosity: 'What else would you like to know?'

'I've no idea . . . what did he tell you?'

'Well, he told me lots of things. He had just come back from a long trip and was already preparing to set off again, on a special mission, you might say.'

'Where did you see him? In Toulouse?'

'Yes, but he's not there now.'

'Where is he then?'

'Well . . . much further away. You know your father, he's always got itchy feet. But now I think you should get some rest, we'll leave

all that for some other time. I'm a bit tired from my journey as well
... and you heard what your mother said, you should get into bed
properly.'

I was studying his face: his bushy, raised eyebrows and the one
lifeless squinting eye, which we never saw looking directly at any of
us, neither at Susana, her mother, me nor anyone else; a cold,
unmoving metallic eye with its slightly hooded lid which seemed to
repel light and detect a different reality, to answer another call beyond
his immediate surroundings, most probably located somewhere in his
past. He had an elongated face which conveyed a sense of knowing
wonder, a kind of clown-like sadness. But when he spoke it was not
this expression nor even his strange eyes that captured one's attention. It was his ample mouth that became the focus, his thin, taut lips
and perfect teeth, so regular and straight it seemed they must be false.
He spoke with a forced correctness, the sort of precise, polite way
of speaking of those who have had to fight to improve themselves
in a hostile environment.

Forcat had got up from the bed in order, I think, to try to avoid
any more questions from Susana. He glanced over at my wretched
drawing, which was little more than a sketch of the verandah windows
and the murderous chimney looming in the background over the tops
of the garden trees – I had not managed a single acceptable line of
the bed or the stove, let alone Susana. He patted me on the back, but
made no comment. Señora Anita came back and made Susana get
into bed. She tucked her in, then plumped the pillows and straightened the sheets and blankets. Forcat helped her without being asked,
smoothing out the eiderdown carefully with both hands. These were
criss-crossed with prominent blue veins, but what was more disturbing
still were the stains on the skin. There were yellowish patches like
iodine, others with intense silky pink outlines that gave the impression they had been damaged by fire or acid, or as if a strange illness
had partially eaten them away. I could also detect a smell like boiled
cauliflower, a stale odour reminiscent of kitchens and households,
one I would never have linked to a gunman like him.

Señora Anita took Forcat upstairs to show him his room on the first floor, and I carried on with my scrawl. Susana lay back lost in thought for a while, then opened a small bottle of varnish and began to paint her nails. A short while later we could hear their voices from the dining-room. 'Are the police after you?' Señora Anita whispered. He replied: 'I don't know . . . perhaps not any more. I wasn't an important member of the group. But you never know, and anyway, I have nowhere else to go.' We heard her offer him a seat and a glass of wine, and then she must have started reading the letter, because we caught him saying to her in a sad tone: 'Don't read it again, woman, it'll only torture you. And above all, don't give up hope.' 'It's too late,' she said, 'I can't forgive him. I could have accepted anything else, going off with another woman, for example . . .' 'I can vouch for the fact that there is no other woman in his life,' said Forcat. 'There's something worse,' Señora Anita murmured in that throaty voice of hers in which the overwhelming sadness of her everyday existence was more evident than any amount of wine: 'You know what I mean.' 'Yes,' he said, then both of them fell silent until all at once she cleared her throat and seemed to return to a topic they must have been talking about earlier: 'So that was all he said to you.' 'No, there was lots more. He also told me he could never forget you. I mean . . .' 'I know exactly what you mean,' she said, interrupting him, and we heard the familiar clink of a wine glass against the top of the flask as it was refilled. Then Forcat insisted: 'Don't let it upset you so much. It's all been over for a good while now.' Señora Anita asked: 'Did he say that, that it's all over? Did he tell you that? How can he be so sure?' Her voice tailed off until it was almost inaudible: 'Well, at least he can count on his daughter . . . what does it matter if I go under? If you think about it, we're always in the shit.'

I looked at Susana: I wished she had not been there, nor me either. She was sitting head down, putting all her attention into painting her nails. Maybe this was not the first time she had heard her mother complain of being alone and unloved, something she had apparently accepted. But then, after a much longer silence from the other room, we heard a chair being pushed back and its legs scraping on the floor tiles, followed by a faint sigh, then silence once more . . . I pictured

Señora Anita burying her face in her hands to prevent herself bursting into tears, or perhaps stifling her sobs on his chest, allowing him to fold her in his arms. Susana lifted her head and stared at me, as if trying to tell from my expression what was going on next door. Then she bent over and returned to her task once more, her black curls cascading down either side of her neck.

I sometimes think I never felt as close to her as I did at that moment, when I suddenly saw hovering about her defenceless head the same sense of being a lost orphan that I secretly endured at my mother's side. She must have felt it even more keenly because of her illness and because her blonde, vibrant mother liked to have fun, hated being alone, and enjoyed the challenge of men. Susana must have deduced what I did from the sudden scraping sound of the chair, the stifled cry and the ensuing silence: a sudden, irrepressible outburst of her mother's which she felt ashamed of. All at once she grabbed a bit of cotton-wool and started furiously rubbing off all the nail polish. She screwed the top back on the bottle, then threw it onto the bed. She slid down inside the sheets, with her knees up and legs spread. She switched the radio on and off again, stared at me, and then resorted to some of the tricks she used to poke fun at me to try to put me off the drawing she hated, the one I was doing for the Captain. She stuck her tongue out, coughed like a dog, beat her chest, kicked off the sheets, wafted her hand in front of her face as though to clear the foul air, pinched her nose as if she could not stand the stink of gas and the choking black smoke which, according to Captain Blay's eccentric, lugubrious predictions, would dry out her lungs. On this occasion though her nervous reaction was a reflection of something that affected her far more deeply. So that when with barely concealed impatience she suggested a game of parcheesi, I put down my pencils and sketches to keep her happy. We heard nothing more from along the corridor.

When it was evening and time for me to go home, Forcat came into the verandah. He was wearing an odd pair of wooden-soled sandals, and was wrapped in a long black dressing-gown decorated with flowers and a Chinese character. He was hiding something behind his back and smiled at Susana. For a moment he leaned on the table where I was busy picking up my sheets of paper, and once again I caught the vegetable odour of his hands, this time even more strongly: they smelt of strained cauliflower, or perhaps artichoke.

'Your father gave me this silk kimono,' he said, walking slowly over to the bed. 'Now for your surprise. He gave me this for you.'

He handed her a postcard of Shanghai and a green silk fan. The photograph on the card, he explained to her, was the River Huang-p'u and its thronged and picturesque docks by the Bund, the most famous avenue in the entire Far East, with its proud skyscrapers and the old Customs building. The other side of the card, which Forcat explained had no stamp because Kim had handed it him personally, was filled with a tiny, forceful handwriting that Susana immediately recognised as her father's. It read:

My beloved Susana, I'm sending you this postcard with a messenger I respect and trust completely. Treat him as you would me, and offer him hospitality and your affection, he's always been at my side and helped me in everything (and he's a very good cook!) but now he has problems (as I've explained to your mother in my letter to her). He brings with him an authentic Chinese fan – green, because I know that's your favourite colour, and lots of kisses and thoughts from me, this globetrotter who never forgets you. Be good and eat a lot, do everything your mother and the doctor tell you to, and above all get well soon. Your father who loves you, Kim.

Susana sat staring into space for a few seconds, then turned the postcard over to look at the bustling River Huang-p'u again.

'I don't understand,' she said. 'Why did he do that? Why did he go so far away . . . ?'

'It's a long story. I'd say . . .' Forcat fell silent, plunged his hands into the wide sleeves of the kimono and sat on the edge of the bed, his eyes still on Susana. 'I'd say he's gone in search of something he lost here . . . But enough of that for the moment. We've got lots of time to tell each other stories.'

2

Each day, by one o'clock in the afternoon all I could think of was to deposit the Captain back at his flat, eat as quickly as I could, then run on aching feet to Susana's villa. One day I suggested to Captain Blay that he come with me.

'Nonsense,' he said.

'But wasn't Señor Forcat a friend of yours, Captain?'

'That's right, he was,' the old lunatic replied, coming to a halt at the top of Calle Villafranca and looking down at his list of signatures. 'There's not many, dammit. We have to get more.'

'Well then,' I insisted, 'don't you want to see him?'

'What for?' he grunted. 'We're in another war now.'

After a rambling explanation of the different kinds of friendship and anger that a war can create, the Captain began to tell me how fifteen years earlier Forcat worked in the La Tranquilidad bar in the Paralelo, a haunt of Proudhon anarchists and utopian dreamers. While he was serving his clients chasers and seafood, he tried to sell them books by Bakunin and revolutionary pamphlets he printed himself.

'He was a *somiatruites*,' said the Captain. 'A simple soul who preached paradise. It's true his chasers were out of this world too: they were so generous, and had so much aniseed in them . . . but that's enough chit-chat, we've got a lot of work and not much time.' He studied the narrow pavements and closed doors along both sides of the street, and added: 'Do you think anybody in this place will sign? I could swear the gas got up here too.'

Captain Blay might have been pig-headed and crazy, but he was not stupid or blind, and he quickly realised how little enthusiasm there was in the neighbourhood for his fight against the chimney and the gas, how much of a joke he was, and how hard it would be for him even to get the first dozen signatures. As a result, he no longer tried to hurry me up with the drawing of Susana prostrate and suffering in her bed, which was a relief to me as I was in no hurry either. On the contrary, I liked having to go to the villa every day, and wanted this situation to carry on at least until the autumn, when I started work.

Many afternoons I never even picked up a pencil, preferring to play draughts or rummy with Susana and above all, if the Chacón brothers were there, games of parcheesi. Sometimes when she felt tired, Susana would reproach me for not even having started her drawing, the one she wanted to send to her father with a dedication. But she also stopped harassing me when Forcat developed the habit of coming to the verandah at about five o'clock in his long black silk kimono, his hair shiny and smart, wearing his clattering wooden sandals. Refreshed after a lengthy siesta, he would sit on the sick girl's bed, and slowly and lovingly evoke some of the adventures he had lived through with her father: how they met and became friends in a poverty-stricken Barcelona that was full of hopes and welcomed the whole world – a city they had loved and lost together; how after that defeat they both had to escape to France, and all the troubles, dangers and misfortunes they had faced there, the many hardships but also the joys they had shared . . .

I cannot recall exactly when it was – I think it began on the day Susana demanded an answer to her oft-repeated question: what was so important that it took her father to such a remote and mysterious city as Shanghai, a question he had always evaded before – but I do remember that Forcat's tales started to bewitch us from the moment he began to explain why a man like Kim, so attached to his family and his home city but whose moral convictions meant he often had to respond to unforeseeable international calls, and more especially when he embarked on a description of the shady business that took him to the far ends of the earth: although I'm not sure I should be telling you this, he said, staring at us with that squint of his, the eye that seemed perpetually fixed on a point somewhere behind us beyond normal sight, but Susana insisted, and so in the end he relented. Well, he said, it's a long story which begins in France two years ago, in a rented room Kim and I had shared in Toulouse since the early, most difficult days, so perhaps that's where I'd better start, then we'll take it step by step . . .

3

One of the first people Captain Blay asked to sign his petition was Señor Sucre, whom he ran into on Calle Tres Señoras one drizzly morning.

'Dammit Blay,' he said with a smile, 'how can you ask me to sign when you know I've lost my name, my home address, my sex and my affiliation . . . ? What are you trying to do?'

'Oh come on, that's enough of that old wives' tale,' protested the Captain. 'I bet the gas has got to you as well. It's not something to joke about . . .'

'All right, give me your famous manifesto.' Señor Sucre cut him short, took his pen and signed and initialled it. 'Here you are . . . Do you know something, Blay? I really appreciate you, you slyboots. One day I'll paint your portrait. But this crusade of yours is ridiculous. Can't you see the extent of the emptiness all around us?' Then as if responding to some exhausted memory, a sensory throwback to ways of behaviour long since dead and gone, his limp, cindery artist's hand swept round in an elegant gesture to show us the nauseous swamp he insisted surrounded us: 'You know what I mean. A void of dreams drowning in nothing, as the man said . . .'

'See how you know perfectly well who you are, you old rogue?' said the Captain with a knowing smile. 'Thanks anyway, your signature is very valuable.'

'Blay, you may not believe this, but there are days when I'm not the least bit interested – not the least bit – in knowing who on earth I am. It doesn't matter a jot. Our identity is a sham, and it's so fleeting . . . We are nothing more than cosmic waste, my friend. The only thing that worries me now is to remember as clearly as I can what I did tomorrow and to forget forever what I will do yesterday. Farewell.'

By way of taking his leave, Señor Sucre slapped the Captain on the back, winked at me, and set off bent but lightheaded through the fine rain towards Torrente de las Flores. We went on our way, the Captain smiling because his old friend trusted him enough to make fun of him as he always had. Above us in the grey, overcast sky, in the centre of a jumble of black, ominous clouds that seemed to be devouring themselves, the yellow scrawl of a lightning flash hung motionless.

4

Kim always says that, whatever the danger he might find himself facing whenever he takes up a gun and risks death, he is doing it not in the name of freedom, justice or any of the great ideals that lead men to dream – and to kill each other – but for a pretty young girl who is so ill and poor that she cannot escape from the house or city she is stuck in. That girl is you, and you are imprinted on his dreams like an indelible tattoo. Not a day goes by when he doesn't imagine you lying in this bed like a wounded dove, a prisoner in a glass cage threatened by that grim black smoke. Tell her there must be no room in her heart for despair or sadness – those were the exact words he used, I'm repeating him word for word; that's how he sees and feels about you, that's how he remembers and loves you, above and beyond his own misfortunes, because he has survived all the defeat and disillusionment he's suffered since the end of the war – the loneliness of exile, missing your mother, the deportation and death of his comrades and the Germans' sadistic cruelty – and he says that was nothing compared to the despair he felt at not being able to help his sick daughter, to cheer her up and give her the will to live . . .

Now I'm going to tell you how Kim's latest adventure began, and how it took him so unexpectedly from Toulouse to Shanghai on the trail of a Nazi spy, a former Gestapo officer he had never seen before. But so that you'll understand why Kim decided to embark on such a perilous mission, first of all I have to tell you of an earlier unfortunate incident on what was his last trip to Spain, originally planned to raise funds for the cause...

The first thing I remember is the click of a Browning magazine being unclipped, that metallic sound I could never stand. We are in Toulouse, a little over two years ago, in a small room with a balcony overlooking the Rue de Belfort, not far from the railway station. Kim is checking the fake identity papers I've just handed him. He smiles and puts them in his pocket: 'You've done a good job,' he says to me as I am putting the finishing touches to the other safe-conducts, and adds: 'You're a real artist.'

There's something I have to get straight from the start, kids: don't imagine me with a pistol or sub-machine-gun, holding up banks or wielding a gun like the others in the group. Don't for a minute picture poor Forcat doing that kind of thing, because as we'll see, that wasn't his mission . . . Now the person I can see is Luis Deniso Mascaró, known to everyone as 'Denis', Kim's right-hand man. He's stooped over the pistol to grease it, and his leg is in plaster. He was wounded in a skirmish with the Civil Guard close to the border, and now uses a silver-topped cane that adds a new elegance to his way of walking; he knows how to accentuate his limp for the women. 'Denis' the clown, always ready with a smile and a joke, young and good-looking and Kim's loyal companion, the spoilt child of all the refugees still fighting from Toulouse: someone who like so many of the others is deep down a pessimist hounded by despair and madness. He's a good marksman and very courageous, and there's nothing he likes more than to clean and grease Kim's weapons before he sets out on a mission. A clock is ticking on the wall, a train whistles as it sets off for the south or arrives at the station: early morning trains puffing as they come and go in Toulouse station and in our recurring nightmares, ghost trains that appear and disappear every night of our exile.

'Don't bother,' Kim tells him. 'This time I don't need to go armed.'

He has two reasons for going to Barcelona: first, to hand over money and fake safe-conducts to comrades who have to travel round the south of Spain, and also to deliver personally the message countermanding the mission of three men who had travelled to the Catalan capital two days earlier. Two of them, Nualart and Betancort, had travelled from Tarascón; the other one, Camps, from Béziers. They are to suspend a raid on an electrical factory in L'Hospitalet planned by Kim. He was meant to join them in Barcelona on the eve of the attack. But a few hours before he is due to leave, Kim receives instructions from the Central Committee to call off all actions, and since Nualart and the others are already in Barcelona waiting for him, he decides to meet up with them anyway to warn them off and bring them back. A quick return journey; a routine job without risk.

As I hand him the documents for the other comrades and wish him good luck, we stare into each other's eyes. His reflect the dying embers of what had once been a dream; in mine there are only ashes, and Kim knows it.

'You don't approve of this journey,' he says.

'Not this one or any others now,' I answer. 'This one least of all. I don't see the need for you to go: they'll get by without you.'

'Maybe. But what about the documents and the money?'

'I don't think any of it makes sense any more . . .'

'You don't?' he cuts me short. 'Well even so, I have my reasons for going.'

He intends to take advantage of the trip, he tells me, to pay a lightning visit to you and your mother one night, to give you a kiss and renew his promise to get you out of here some day. By now the pistol has been greased and re-assembled. 'Denis' offers it to his leader, but he refuses to take it. Kim has never crossed the frontier without a weapon before.

'What the devil's wrong with you?' asks 'Denis'.

'It's not worth taking so many precautions just for a few papers and an order.'

This isn't the only reason why 'Denis' is so upset. He'd dearly love to kiss Carmen and his son as well, and if it weren't for his leg in plaster, he'd willingly go with Kim. In all his clandestine trips to Barcelona, Kim spends the night in 'Denis's' parents' home, a small chalet in an out-of-the-way spot in Horta, where 'Denis's' partner and their seven-year-old son also live. She is very young: she was only sixteen when she got together with 'Denis', and it wasn't long before he marched off with the boy soldiers to the Ebro front, and then away into exile. On her own with a son of only a few months, Carmen was taken into his parents' house. When 'Denis' met her she had just arrived from Malaga; she was very beautiful, but always seemed frightened. She lived and slept in a hairdresser's salon run by an aunt of hers, who exploited her dreadfully. And just like your father, Susana, 'Denis' never gave up hope of bringing Carmen and his son to live with him in France. At first he was kept in a concentration camp, then during the occupation he worked in a mine for the Germans, but managed to escape and joined the Resistance. It was there he first met Kim, and worked with him in the *maquis* when the war was over. But 'Denis' is a different story . . .

A train whistle blows in Matabiau station. The last of the evening sun bathes the *ville rose* in its glow, and there's a flash of impatience in Kim's eyes as he looks at my white smock streaked with paint. He smiles and says: 'Poor old dauber,' he says, 'you should go back to your mother.' The thing was, here in Barcelona I had been an illustrator as well as a waiter, but in Toulouse I could only find work as a house-painter, like 'Denis'. I wasn't complaining, it wasn't a bad job.

'See you when I get back. Behave yourselves,' says Kim, tucking the papers inside his shirt. 'I swear that one of these days I'm going to throw all caution to the winds and bring Susanita back with me.'

'Are you crazy?' 'Denis' objects. 'How are you going to cross the Pyrenees with a sick child? What you could do, if you get the chance, is see about bringing Carmen and my son. If you think there's a possibility this time, I'll give you money for the expenses, and some more for my parents.'

Kim thinks about it while he's putting on his fleeced leather jacket.

'If I see there's no danger for her or the boy, I'll bring them. You can count on me.'

'Denis' hands him a letter and 5,000 pesetas, half for his parents, the other half for Carmen. The two friends embrace in the centre of our tiny rented room, enveloped in that rosy pink glow that always floods in from the balcony at this time of day. And that's how I'll always picture them: clasping each other in a halo of light that makes them look as though they are floating in the air, both of them aware deep down that in spite of all the precautions and good intentions, they might never see one another again. In the end, Kim accepts the freshly-cleaned pistol his companion is still offering him. I've forgotten all the list of things 'Denis' mentioned: how delicate Carmen's feet were, and how easily she caught colds, and how he was to be sure not to let her sleep on the ground during the mountain crossing, but I'll never forget Kim's determined gaze as he tells him:

'Trust me, my boy. I'll bring her to you safe and sound.'

He heads for the door and at that moment a black cat, which I'm not sure I really saw, which perhaps only purrs and stalks across the room in my imagination – I mean I don't remember it having been in that room, so perhaps it doesn't really exist – at that moment a black cat crosses in front of him, goes out onto the balcony and jumps down into the street. I only just stopped myself crying out.

'What's the matter, Forcat?' Kim asks.

'Nothing. The kitten.'

'What blasted kitten are you talking about?' he says, peering round and seeing nothing.

'Don't listen to me,' I say. 'Go on, good luck to you.'

We watch from the balcony as he heads off down the Rue de Belfort towards the station, in his leather jacket and wearing a dark-brown hat. He strolls along thoughtfully, cigarette between his lips and hands in pockets, for all the world as if he is out for one of his regular walks along the banks of the Garonne.

5

'Hello there! You're a godsend, my boy. Let me lean on your arm, my shoe's come off,' Señora Anita said.

She had run into me on the street corner, and stood there unsteadily on one foot, shoe in hand. She grabbed my arm, causing my folder and box of pencils to fall to the ground. I could smell her wine breath all over me. When she smiled, there were streaks of lipstick on her teeth. I had just left the villa, it was gone eight o'clock, and I could feel the cold pricking my fingers despite my woollen gloves. She was coming back from the Mundial cinema in Calle Salmerón, and had probably stopped off in several bars on the way. Still clinging to me, she tried and failed to put her shoe back on, and fell onto the pavement, scraping her knee. I struggled to help her sit up in a doorway, where she almost banged her head. She lifted her knee to her face and shook her head. The stocking had a hole in it as big as an egg.

'Would you like me to go home with you, Señora Anita?'

'That's very kind of you, but there's no need. It's this shoe, I don't know what's wrong with it.' She held it up to her face without knowing what to do. She examined it top and bottom, but it looked perfectly all right. 'It's worn-out, that's the trouble . . . and the heel must have twisted. Cinderella's slipper, look . . . !' I smiled back at her, half-heartedly I am sure. 'Have you come from the villa? You haven't left Susana on her own, have you?'

'Señor Forcat is with her.'

'Ah yes, of course. My daughter has such good company these days, doesn't she? She spends every afternoon with you, and sometimes those boys from Carmelo are there too, they're so funny, and then there's Señor Forcat, who knows so well how to keep her amused . . . We've been lucky, haven't we Daniel?'

'Yes, señora.'

'We're fine now, aren't we?'

'Yes, señora.'

'And what a good time we all have. We all have a great time, don't we?'

'Yes, señora, a very good time.'

'I'm very happy, do you know that?' she said with a sigh. 'It means my daughter does not have to be alone. But just look at these poor stockings! There's no way of darning them any more. And it's so cold today . . .' She fell silent and I had the impression she was trying to waste a bit more time by massaging her bruised knee. Then she saw my grey woollen gloves, grabbed my right hand and gently pressed it against the torn stocking and her grazed skin. 'May I? It's so warm and nice, it's so soothing . . . ! And they're such nice gloves. Did your mother make them for you?'

'No. Señora Conxa.'

'Did you know there are hands that can warm you just by looking at them?' She bent her knee a couple of times, closing her eyes. When she opened them again, there was a bright sparkle in her blue irises. 'If you think about it, all you need in this life is a bit of warmth at the right moment, just a tiny bit, that's all . . . but I bet what you're thinking right now is: Señora Anita is sozzled.' She finally succeeded in replacing her shoe, and stood up. 'But do you know something else? Nothing lasts forever, however bad it is . . . Ow, my knee!'

'Let me help you home.'

'No. I'm almost there . . .'

She was limping badly though, and finally agreed I should accompany her. She hung on my arm, and then before she opened the garden gate stopped and tried to get her breath back. She looked at herself in a small hand mirror, tidied her blonde curls and while she was putting fresh lipstick on, made me promise I would not tell Señor Forcat I had seen her in such a state. As she went in, she turned to me with a smile:

'Remember, if ever you go to the Mundial and I'm not there, just tell the usher you're a friend of mine and he'll let you in for free.'

'Thank you, Señora Anita.'

6

I was just part of the group, and not one of the bravest, not one of those who risked their life with a gun. All I did was use my nibs and inks; I scraped and changed numbers and names thanks to a few razor blades and a surprising range of implements. I made counterfeit documents and invented signatures, gave them new names and identities. It was me who made them dangerous, but I wasn't. I dreamed their dangers.

One rainy night at the end of April Kim arrives incognito in Barcelona. He hides out in 'Denis's' parents' house, and hands them the letter and half the money he was given in Toulouse; the other half is for Carmen, who receives it with little enthusiasm. She is a twenty-four-year-old woman ground down by work and loneliness. She is tired of waiting, and looks at Kim with something approaching hatred: his visits always mean fresh scares and sadness, there is always bad news – this time 'Denis's' scrape with the Civil Guard. How long will this uncertainty go on? Are all the sacrifices, all the people who have died, worth it? When will the nightmare end? Kim understands and confesses to her – and this isn't the first time, he's already said as much to me as we left a bad-tempered meeting in Paris – that he too is growing tired of fighting for nothing.

He tries to cheer her up by telling her of 'Denis's' great wish: since things are going slightly better for everyone in France, perhaps it's time for her and the boy to get out of Barcelona at last and join him. I can take you with me when I get back in three days' time, he says: crossing the frontier is tough, but we'll have a good guide. To his surprise, Carmen doesn't seem too keen on the idea, as if it were already too late, as if 'Denis' were already dead to her. She hugs her boy and thinks it over . . . can't you just see the three of them huddled round the fire that rainy night, after their supper when the old folk have already gone to bed, the boy refusing to go to sleep and sitting on his mother's lap: his eyes staring wide open just like yours are now, a mixture of fascination and disbelief, can't you picture him gazing and listening to Kim, his father's intrepid friend who has travelled from the far side of night and fear, from a place where his mother's weary bitterness could finally come to an end? She too must be listening as closely and silently as him, that beautiful young woman who can barely read or write, who ended up here from Malaga during the war . . . I don't know the details, but Kim finally succeeds in convincing her by telling her of his experience of ferrying children across the mountains into France. Years earlier, when he was organising the first armed group of the Confederation and used to cross the border frequently, he would sometimes take an exile's child back with him. The last time, he took two boys aged eight and twelve, whose father had been a Republican commander who died in Mauthausen concentration camp. Why haven't you got your wife and daughter out then? Carmen asks. He replies: How was he supposed to look after them in the years when he was always travelling to and fro as a member of the Resistance? And now when it might be possible, my daughter is ill . . .

Much later that same night, almost at first light, Kim decides to come and see you and your mother. It is raining heavily, so he walks quickly across the waste ground of Horta and Guinardó until he can hail a taxi.

He says you were asleep and he didn't want to wake you, so he didn't even switch the light on. He told me how fragrant the smell of eucalyptus was here on the verandah, how startled he was when his lips brushed your burning forehead. He left a green plastic handbag on the bed for you, because that is your favourite colour. He left some money for your mother too. He was here less than five minutes, but that short time spent beside you made up for all his disappointments . . .

The next day is Sunday, and it's a bright sunny day with a fresh breeze and such a clear blue sky that it stirs memories he has tried hard to suppress – perhaps of a similar light in this very garden in happier times – as he crosses the city by tram. Through the window he can see the fresh shoots of the plane trees, yellowing Easter palm fronds on balconies, people out for a stroll holding their children's hand. And he feels again a sudden stab in his heart: to be a stranger in your own city, a foreigner in your own country, the feeling you get when you've been blinded by hatred and gunsmoke as he has been for so long. Far from you and your mother, he has imagined Barcelona as a hell of repression and misery, an endless calvary he has cursed time and again, but now all of a sudden this peaceful spring day makes all that evaporate, as passers-by in their Sunday best enjoy themselves with no thought for the past . . . We cannot be on the tram with Kim as he travels through the city from north to south, but we can guess what he is feeling yet again, and tries hard to dismiss: not only how ridiculous the freshly greased Browning is in its shoulder holster, close to his heart, but the futility of the ideals that heart still cherishes. Each time he crosses the frontier, each time he re-encounters this spring light of Barcelona, he is close to despair.

But this feeling of being an outsider has its advantages: it makes the instinct warning you of danger sharper, and keeps you alert. Kim has hidden the false papers in an old briefcase, and remembers the orders: all money-raising armed raids are suspended, including the attack next day. That's what the Central Committee has decided, and it's Josep Nualart who has to hear the instructions. The two men are to make contact at eleven o'clock on the terrace of a café close to Sants station. Kim gets off the tram and pauses to look at the papers in a kiosk. He spots Nualart waiting on his own with a vermouth at a table near the far end of the terrace. Everything seems normal. The terrace is crowded with people who are being served by a busy blonde waitress wearing a white cap and pleated skirt. Nualart is engrossed in his newspaper, whose pages rustle in the wind. He has not yet seen Kim. He is a strong-looking thirty-five year old, with a crewcut and metal-framed glasses. I've already mentioned Kim's sixth sense for danger, but what saves him this time is that he thinks of you, Susana.

There is a squeal of brakes, and Nualart lifts his head sharply from his newspaper, but sees nothing unusual. Two boys are scampering in among the tables; the wind is getting up and becoming a nuisance. Nualart seems to sense that Kim is nearby, and turns his head in the direction of the kiosk, but at that precise instant a gust of wind lifts the waitress' skirt as she goes by with a tray of drinks, and this attracts not only his amused glance but that of other customers in the café. Flustered, the young woman tries to smoothe down her skirt, and as she does so almost tips the contents of her tray over Nualart's head. Some of the men laugh, and it's the young girl's legs, that unexpected sight for sore eyes – as Nualart himself might have put it, laughing – which prevents him noticing that Kim has arrived and is perhaps signalling to him. It's this, together with the fact that your father lingers at the kiosk a few seconds longer because he's looking at the illustrations in an adolescent novel called *The Dangers of Susana*, which he thinks might amuse you, that saves Kim.

He is about to buy the book, but suddenly there's no time for anything. The wind snatches a black mantilla from a woman's head; it flies like a crow across the terrace until it is caught in a low tree branch. This is a sign, the ill omen that Nualart does not spot. Kim is asking how much the novel is; as he turns to look, he sees Nualart on his feet but almost falling over as he fights the gust of wind and his surprise: two men in trenchcoats are either side of him, Nualart is trying to bend down to pick something up, a beret, but they grab him and one checks his papers while the other snaps on a pair of handcuffs. Nualart offers no resistance as they push him roughly through a gaggle of curious bystanders to a waiting black car, but he still has the time and spirit to give a last look over his shoulder at the waitress' legs, perhaps in the hope that the wind will play a trick with her neat little skirt once more. That's Nualart for you, always so irrepressible, so in love with life and with women . . .

Kim remains by the kiosk until the car disappears, then leaves. He surmises that the police did not know Nualart was going to meet him, otherwise they would have waited for him to reach the café and nabbed him too. But the cops must have been acting on a tip-off, because at that same moment Kim's other men, Betancort and Camps, as well as our contact for distributing propaganda, a car mechanic in Gracia, are rounded up in a Poblenou apartment.

Kim hears about this a few hours later, after spending the day on the run, and decides it's best to get away. He doesn't think it is wise to go back to the chalet in Horta, so he telephones Carmen and arranges to meet her at the railway station. She arrives with her son and one small suitcase, and that same afternoon the three of them embark on the first stage of a journey that is to take them across the frontier during the night.

The mission has failed, but Kim is determined to keep the promise he made to 'Denis' to bring his partner and their son back safe and sound to Toulouse.

CHAPTER FOUR

I

Ever since I had turned into Captain Blay's morning shadow, caught up in the spider's web of extravagant nonsense the old lunatic spun ever wider with his words and gestures, I found myself immersed in a completely unreal atmosphere: the dreary, petrified world of La Salud and its fearful dreams seemed to me a world away from the exciting emotions awaiting me every afternoon in the villa. My only desire was to be with Susana and Forcat once more.

At first, as we roamed about collecting signatures, I felt very ashamed, and hid behind the Captain whenever a door opened, pretending I was not there. Gradually though I got used to it. I had to carry a folder with the protest petition and a sheet of paper where the Captain made me write down the name and address of everyone who signed, as well as all those who refused. There were far more of the latter. The Captain went into bars and shops, markets and schools, in an ever wider radius around the loathsome chimney, until he had covered almost the entire neighbourhood, and part of Guinardó. He knocked at every apartment, where busy, suspicious housewives blocked the half-open door and greeted him reluctantly and incredulously. If they knew him, they signed just to get rid of him, but this happened only rarely. Most of the tenants – especially if it was the man of the house who opened the door – sent us on our way with a flea in our ears. You want me to sign a petition to add a few feet onto the height of a chimney, and to stop a gas leak? What damned chimney are you talking about, what blasted poison gas leak, what the devil do you mean? they would shout furiously, and slam the door in our faces.

'You're a fool and a dimwit, my good man,' Captain Blay would shout at them through the closed door. Once we were out in the street again, he would mutter: 'They're up to their necks in shit and they refuse to see it. I bet that last idiot is wallowing in the regime.'

'You mean following the regime, Captain.'

'I meant exactly what I said, smart aleck. There are followers, then there are those who are so scared and weak-minded they aren't even that, they just wallow in it. And they're all being gassed.'

Despite all this, he never lost heart. By the end of May, a month after Forcat had arrived at the villa, we had still not gathered even a dozen signatures. According to the Captain's calculations, we needed at least 500 if the Council was to pay any attention, so I could see myself going up and down staircases, knocking on door after door until the autumn, when the jewellery workshop would finally rescue me from this crazy rushing about.

More than one dismissive housewife near Calle Camelias and Alegre de Dalt took advantage of the visit by the eccentric signature collector, whom they thought must be in the know about everything going on in the villa thanks to his wife, to ask him straight out: is it true the man that trollop is giving bed and board to didn't come from France at all, but from Burgos jail? Why doesn't he ever leave the house, what's he doing all day long in there with a fifteen-year-old consumptive girl and this boy here . . . ? Is it true she walks around the house drunk and naked, in front of the jailbird, or is it all just gossip?

Captain Blay took the greatest pleasure in adding to this tangled skein of rumours, often in great detail. No, Señora Clotilde, you've got it wrong, in fact that man is a healer who's recently returned from China; he's treating the girl's TB by rubbing her with rose water boiled with glow-worms – it's a very ancient cure for the Koch bacillus. And in his youth, he was a steward on board ship. He travelled the world and was once madly in love with our cinema assistant, but

Joaquim Franch i Casablancas was more astute, and stole his sweetheart from him. He gradually got used to the idea and apparently forgot her, but who knows whether there's still something there: you can never trust adventurers like him, especially not one with that cross-eyed look and that scarred heart of his. Forcat is a transatlantic adventurer!

The Captain mixed truth and fantasy so naturally that a lot of people in the neighbourhood, even though they regarded him as mad and foul-mouthed, happily swallowed everything that fitted in with their own morbid expectations and who knows what intimate emotional fantasies, what wet dreams, especially among the menfolk, many of whom were obsessed by the blonde bombshell. And whatever nonsense the Captain came out with, as soon as he started talking about the villa and its inhabitants they were all agog. He himself pretended to have an interest and curiosity about everything going on in the villa that he did not really feel. He once told me he had discovered he was old the day he began to fake an interest in things which deep down bored him rigid. The truth is however that he rarely behaved like an old man, particularly with regard to anything related to his twin obsessions: the factory chimney and the menacing gas. This was the real driving force behind his odyssey around the neighbourhood and his exposure to all the malicious gossip and slander.

This was how I got to hear of all the rumours going round about concerning Señora Anita, some of which the Captain dismissed, and others he didn't, such as for example that this was not the first time she had taken a man into her house. Three years earlier, the projectionist from the Iberia cinema, where she was working at the time, had been eating and sleeping at the villa for almost a month; according to the Captain, the man was a distant relative of Anita's and was very ill. They had thrown him out of his rented room because he was coughing and spluttering the whole time – I've always thought it was he who had infected the girl, the Captain said – and though it was true he was a very good-looking and tidy sort of a man, Anita had told Doña Conxa he disgusted her, above all when she had to change his sheets.

One day, the Captain plunged into a florist's shop on Calle Cerdeña, near my house, claiming he felt an urgent need to smell carnations – even though as soon as he got inside he sniffed the air and exclaimed: 'The evil beast's rotten breath has penetrated even here!' Before deciding whether she would sign the petition, which the Captain forced me to read aloud yet again, the owner, a stiff, scrawny woman, told us she thought Susana's mother was an ignorant immigrant: 'all these years living here, and neither she nor her daughter have learnt Catalan,' she then went on to add that the worst thing about her wasn't so much her affairs, as her fondness for wine, her tight skirts and her way of walking – her bad taste, in other words, that air of a whore she could never get rid of, more's the pity. If her husband had been at home she'd have waggled her bottom a lot less, she said.

'Men do find that blonde woman soft and attractive, don't they?' the Captain said cheerily. 'Even though she's such a heavy smoker. But you see, Señora Pili, the older and more decrepit you get, the less you feel like judging anyone. Well, almost anyone. That's why I reckon that God, who must be much older and more decrepit than I am, will not judge me when I arrive up there. He'll simply say, come on in, Blay, and sit yourself down wherever you can. That's what he'll say to me . . . and anyway, Señora Pili, if you think about it, whatever that lively blonde may choose to do with her feelings or her pretty backside, the only thing that should really concern us is the harm the Koch bacillus is doing to her poor daughter, and the gas that's rotting your flowers already, and is threatening all of us . . . That's why I'm asking for your signature, to save the lungs of a poor innocent child who is condemned to die if we don't all get together to demand justice and make sure the authorities order that damned chimney to be pulled down, or have several more feet built onto it . . .'

'Fine, fine,' Señora Pili cut in indignantly, snatching the sheet of signatures from me. 'Give it here, boy. I'll sign. There's no talking to the old fool.'

She took the Captain to task for dramatising Susana's TB problem; she was convinced the girl wasn't about to die. She said TB was a very romantic disease, and that people shouldn't exaggerate . . . As the Captain paused in the doorway on his way out, he turned to warn Señora Pili she should be careful if one clear, still night she was led by her romantic soul to look up at the stars. The stars don't twinkle, he told her, that's all lies, what they do is give off a fine white powder that dries up the optic nerve and can leave you blind.

'That's enough nonsense, for Heaven's sake!' the florist exclaimed.

'The idea that they send us light is a hoax the Meteorological Service has invented,' the Captain assured her. 'They've been dead for millions of years now. They said so last night on *Radio Española Independiente*.'

The Captain was in his element as he roamed our neighbourhood. I asked him why he hadn't escaped from Barcelona like Kim, Forcat and many others had, and as my father would surely have done if he hadn't gone missing in action.

'I'll die in La Salud,' he growled. 'No one will move me from here, I'll bury my heart in La Salud . . . Ooohhh . . .'

He had fallen behind, and when I turned to look he was pissing calm as could be into the open drain on the lower side of Plaza Sanllehy. The jet of urine was thick, dark and silent.

'Not here, Captain, please,' I said, tugging at his coat. 'Please!'

'When the Invisible Man pisses, no one can see it,' he cackled.

'But you're not the Invisible Man, damn and blast it!' Powerless and scarlet with embarrassment, fearing someone would shout at us, I stamped my foot and in a horrid voice I was immediately ashamed of, I rebuked him: 'I knew we would end up doing something daft today!'

'What else do you expect?' he replied. 'Don't you know I'm an old loony?'

'Come on, Captain, it's getting late.'

A short while later he was talking to the owner of the dairy in the Calle San Salvador where Señora Anita bought milk for Susana. The Captain was asking him to sign to help a poor consumptive girl recover her breathing, but the milkman growled that this was nonsense and a waste of time. What on earth do you hope to achieve with three or four signatures, he said, gesturing to me to get this maniac who never stopped talking out of his establishment.

'What does one little signature cost you, eh?' the Captain said. 'I don't think you realise the danger you're in. You and all your family. Do you know what gas is?'

'Well now,' the milkman puffed, 'I have some idea . . .'

'I doubt it, my good man. Gas is an immaterial substance, like air, or the smell of cows, the lies blonde women tell, or the farts bishops let fly. It can be neither seen nor heard. And its chief property is that it can spread indefinitely, and nothing can stop it.'

'If you say so . . . Take him away will you, boy? Someone should tell him what's wrong with him.' He took the Captain by the arm and thought for a moment about what he was going to say, with such a pitiful look on his face that the Captain guffawed. 'Look Blay, you were shut up at home for a long, long time with a piece of shrapnel in your head, and you're still not properly cured, so they really shouldn't let you out to wander around like this . . .'

'Gas is a miasma, a fluid,' the Captain interrupted him. 'And it comes in many forms. There's firedamp for example, chlorine gas that is poisonous and chokes you. That gets into the trenches. There's cooking gas, which is silent and treacherous. There's the green gas of reservoirs and marshes, which puts you to sleep . . . Why do you think this regime is building so many marshes?'

'All right, all right, I get the message! Now be off with you, I've got a lot to do.'

'Yes, watering down the milk, that's what you've got to do! You're well and truly infected, in case you're interested! An ignoramus, that's what you are, an ignoramus! So, are you going to sign or not?'

With some effort I managed to push the Captain out into the street. That day I more than earned my afternoon's reward, my favourite seat in the warm verandah, apparently working hard at my drawing, but in fact impatiently waiting for Forcat to appear in his magnificent kimono with its wide sleeves in which he hid his hands. I would watch him sit down slowly and dreamily on the edge of Susana's bed, staring for some time with his unruly eye at the dying light in the garden, as he searched for the words to take up his story again. Then I would put down my pencil, get up quietly from the table and slip across to the bed to sit down next to Susana so I could listen from as close as possible and allow myself to be caught in the fine net of his voice, the open pincers of his gaze, those keen eyes delving into the past from their distant corners.

2

These days, the city and its bright spring days are bathed in calm, as if the hurricane of life were raging faraway and could not touch it, this bed, or you. But that isn't so. Inevitably, whether you like it or not, and more perniciously than the illness that has you in its grip, the world outside will infect you with its fevers and frauds, and you will have to face them, just as Kim and his friends did.

What drove those men who had sought to change the world to continue leading such dangerous lives, sacrificing their safety, the love of their families, and even in many cases their own self-respect, were a handful of ideals that nowadays are given little thought, and will soon be completely forgotten. Perhaps it's better that way: when all is said and done, to forget is one way to go on living. But now, added to all his usual worries, Kim has another concern: he cannot help thinking of his beloved daughter and his wish to see her well and happy.

I heard everything I'm telling you from Kim himself, one rainy afternoon we were drinking beer together in a grimy café on the Rue des Sept Troubadours in Toulouse. This was just before he left for Shanghai, and I came back to Barcelona. Were I to invent anything, it would be a few background details, some flourishes of memory, echoes and fragments I cannot explain or which I fancied I could make out in the midst of what he was telling me. But I'm not adding or taking away anything from his story, from the strange adventure that less than a fortnight later was to take him to the Far East.

What happened was that a week after handing over Carmen and her son to 'Denis', who wept for joy at seeing them, the arrest of Nualart and the others in Barcelona created all kinds of suspicion in the Central Committee, and Kim had to go to Paris to talk to a Spanish comrade who said he had inside information about it. That information came from unreliable sources, and was a load of nonsense. One suggestion was that I had given them away to the Police Headquarters in Barcelona in return for my own immunity. All this made Kim extremely angry, as he would not hear any talk of betrayal. He had been disgusted by what went on at the last CNT Congress in Toulouse, and this latest argument left him dejected, fed up with everything: the Communists' eternal mistrust and their unwillingness to support him because of his libertarian background, the way the Confederation committee kept turning down his initiatives, the splits in the different factions of the CNT, the unending struggle in which all the best people were dying . . .

That evening he was walking along the banks of the Seine wondering what to do with his life. The river resembled his hidden desire to be happy once more, a desire that was now threatening to burst its banks and wash away his wearisome past, so full of violence and death. But this trip to Paris turned out to be much less futile than he had expected. Soon he was to see himself leap from the Seine to the River Huang-p'u, for the first time in his life putting a great ocean between his political will to carry on fighting and his desire to return to some kind of private life with you and your mother, wherever and whenever that might be possible.

But let me tell you exactly what happened. On the last day of his stay at a colleague's flat in Paris, he got a phone call from the Vautrin clinic. It was from Michel Lévy, a French friend he had not seen since just before the liberation of Paris. Under the code name of 'Captain Croisset', Lévy had been Kim's leader in Lyons when they were both fighting in the Resistance. In March 1943 during an act of sabotage on a German patrol, 'Captain Croisset' saved his life, and Kim could never forget that. Lévy had more than enough reasons for hating the Germans, and he fought them with great ferocity. His father and two brothers, picked up by the SS in the big round-up of Jews at the Vél d'Hiv, had died in the gas chambers at Treblinka. The rest of his family had escaped by fleeing France. Lévy joined the Resistance, but shortly before the liberation he was arrested by the Gestapo and tortured. This left its legacy, and now he had to undergo two tricky operations. Kim decided to go and see him before he returned to Toulouse.

The Vautrin is a private clinic in the Paris suburbs. Kim was received by a shrunken man lying prone in a wheelchair, but with an alert and friendly smile. They embraced, joked and recalled the past. What are you doing in Paris, *mon vieux*? As you can see, Kim told him, nothing has changed, we haven't got rid of the scum in Spain yet . . . and I'm beginning to think we never will. I didn't really want to come to Paris, and in the end all I got out of the trip was another row. But now I'm glad, because at least it gave me the chance to come and give you a hug.

Lévy could see how dispirited Kim was. Don't imagine things have gone much better for me, he said to cheer him up, it looks as though the Nazis have finally managed to break me. Here I am – the doctors don't know what to do with me. And he told Kim all he had been up to since the end of the war: after the first operation on his spine, he left for the Far East to take over some family trading companies. Lévy was from a very rich French family, some of whom had been in Shanghai for many years, where they owned several businesses and concessions: the Tramway Company, a shipping firm, a textile factory and several restaurants. As soon as he saw it, Lévy fell in love with the city. Six months before his return to Paris, he had married a young Chinese girl called Chen Jing Fang, the daughter of an opium dealer from Tianjin. He was happily married, his business affairs were going well, he enjoyed a good reputation in Shanghai trading and banking circles . . . but now all that was hanging by a thread. The condition in his spine had got worse, and the doctors also wanted to remove a blood clot from his brain. That was why he had come back to Paris, to put himself in the hands of a famous neuro-surgeon. There was a risk to the first operation, and if that were successful, he had to face a second, still more dangerous one: even if everything went well, he would have to be in Europe for at least four months. In order to avoid causing her useless suffering, he had forbidden his wife to accompany him. He was to be operated on in two or three weeks, and was not afraid of dying in the theatre; he was, however, fearful for his wife Chen Jing Fang.

'That's why when I heard you were in Paris, I didn't hesitate to call you.' Michel Lévy pushes his wheelchair closer to Kim, looking anxiously up at him. 'I've got a favour to ask you, my friend. A huge favour, that only you can do.'

'You can count on me. What is it?'

'Do you remember Kruger, the Gestapo colonel who tortured me in Lyons?'

'How could I ever forget that criminal?'

'Did you ever see him face to face?'

'No. We once machine-gunned his official car but the bastard escaped by a hair's breadth, cowering in the back seat. All I saw of him was his peaked cap.'

'Well, he's in Shanghai,' Lévy says softly, as if trying to mitigate the effect this news might have on his old comrade. 'Helmut Kruger now calls himself Omar Meiningen. He runs a night-club known as the Yellow Sky Club, and several brothels. I dug out some information: he fled to South America before the war ended, trafficking arms in Argentina and then Chile, before he made the leap to Shanghai. He's very well-known in the underworld there, and I could swear he's protected by an ex-Nazi organisation that sells arms to the Kuomintang.'

He explains to Kim that he had met him by chance at a reception in the English consulate two days before his trip to Paris, when he was already confined to a wheelchair. He had recognised him at once despite his dyed hair, his moustache and his friendly smile. And Kruger had recognised him too, even though he pretended only to have eyes for Jing Fang.

'At first I thought I would denounce him to a Jewish Nazi-hunter I know in New York,' says the paralysed man. 'Even less than a year ago when I could still walk, I would have dealt with him myself . . . but given the state I'm in, I decided to wait and plan something carefully for my return, after my operations. Here in Paris though I've had all kinds of doubts. What if I don't come out of the operating theatre? The thing is, that bloodthirsty beast recognised me, and the next day sent me a threatening anonymous letter: if I am not wise enough to forget the past, my wife and I will pay for it when we least expect it, and she will be the first. Can you imagine?'

'You want me to finish him off?' says Kim.

'First and foremost I want protection for my wife. But of course it's better to be safe than sorry.'

'I agree.'

'You'll have to act alone,' says Lévy. 'You shouldn't even talk about it to Jing Fang, just do your best to protect her. Listen, my friend,' he says, leaning towards Kim from his wheelchair and gripping his arm. Kim can feel the despairing clutch of his fingers. 'If anything were to happen to Jing Fang, I'd prefer not to leave this clinic alive. I'm lost without her . . .' He gives an embarrassed smile, and goes on: 'Do you know what her name means in Chinese? Jing signifies calm, and Fang means fragrance . . . and that is exactly what this marvellous woman has brought to my life.'

'Don't worry,' Kim tells him. 'We'll take care of that damned German.'

'I knew you wouldn't fail me.'

He says he'll give instructions to his people for Kim to have all he needs as soon as possible. 'You must keep close to Jing Fang', Lévy adds, 'so you'll stay in my apartment, a penthouse in a skyscraper on the Bund, the most famous avenue in the whole Far East'. He will call his wife and tell her Kim is like a brother to him, and is on his way to Shanghai . . . looking for work, for example.

'You'll be well received,' says Lévy. 'But I still don't know how to convince Jing Fang of the need for you to be with her whenever she goes out alone or at night . . . and without mentioning Kruger and his threat to her, because I don't want to alarm her. Well, I'll think of something.'

Kim nods, then observes: what you say about travelling so far to look for work could sound a bit far-fetched, but what if it were true?

'What do you mean?' asks Lévy.

'I mean there's nothing I'd like better than to work in one of your businesses for you. You must remember I'm a textile engineer, though because of the war and my exile, I've never worked at my profession . . . With you there, I'd soon catch up.'

Michel Lévy studies his face silently.

'No doubt,' he says. 'But are you that disillusioned with the struggle?'

'I think the time has come for others to take over. They'll be able to do it better. And I want to get someone I love out of Spain so I can offer her a future.'

'I understand. But in Shanghai?'

'Why not? The further away the better.'

Lévy is delighted, and says Kim can count on him. They'll discuss it when he is cured and back in Shanghai, and they can celebrate together.

'For the time being, the most urgent matter is Kruger,' he adds, his voice suddenly taking on a vengeful, hoarse tone. 'But be very careful, and don't let him catch you by surprise. He's very cunning, and completely unscrupulous. To say it again: he calls himself Omar Meiningen, he owns the Yellow Sky Club, the most fashionable and *chic* night-spot in Shanghai. You can see him there any night . . .'

Kim listens intently, fascinated by the hero's broken, poisoned voice, as broken as the body it emerges from, poisoned like the memory of suffering that body represents. Faithful to a solemn debt of friendship and gratitude, in his mind's eye Kim sees fleeting images of violence and harsh treatment he would never have willingly summoned even out of a sense of solidarity with the victims. Overwhelmed, he does not notice the telltale sign at his feet, but I can see it, and so can you: a black scorpion crawling in concentric circles round the spotless white tiles, closing in on the two friends as it waves its raised sting, a scarlet, flaming fingernail. You might ask, how can you know this if you weren't there? Where did you get details like the poisoned voice and the scorpion from? What's an insect like that doing somewhere so antiseptic and bright as this room in a luxury clinic on the outskirts of Paris...? If you have ever watched a red sunset until the very end, when the last, most precious glow is snuffed out, and seen how the light flares before it finally dies, then you'll know what I'm talking about.

As Lévy pushes the wheelchair towards Kim, he crushes the scorpion. He has not seen the flash of the poisoned fingernail either, and asks anxiously:

'When can you go?'

'Whenever you say, captain,' Kim replies without a moment's hesitation.

'I'll see to your travel and money at once. You can board one of the company's ships in Marseilles. The captain is a friend of mine, so you'll have a good cabin... You may wonder why I'm asking you to travel by sea rather than by air, if not just to save myself a few dollars. It's not that of course. It's because that way you can do me another favour. The ship is the *Nantucket*, and there's something of mine I need to recover from the captain's cabin. It's a Chinese book by someone called Li Yan. It has yellow covers and beautiful illustrations; you'll be able to recognise it because there's a dedication on the first page written in red ink in Chinese characters, with a crimson blot next to it... It's very important you don't forget that: a crimson blot. I want you to remove that book without the captain noticing. Don't ask me why now, I'll tell you about it in Shanghai... if I survive. Can I count on you, *mon ami*?'

'Consider it done.'

'What will you take with you?'

'My toothbrush and a Browning with a mother-of-pearl handle.'

The Resistance hero smiles from his wheelchair.

'I see you haven't lost your courage or your sense of humour.'

'I've got more of the first left than the latter,' says Kim.

'Good. You'll need clothes and money. I'll make sure you have three thousand dollars available so you can buy whatever you like in Shanghai.'

'I thought the Japanese had looted it.'

'Not at all. You can find everything you can't buy in Paris, and cheaper and better. Once you're there, if you need more money or anything else, don't hesitate to ask my associate Charlie Wong; I'll give him instructions. I don't want you to go short of anything. And make sure you buy good clothes,' Lévy says with a smile that cannot quite disguise the painful grimace on his face. 'You'll need to be elegant to accompany Jing Fang, she's very beautiful . . . and one last thing,' he takes a tiny copper-coloured object from his pocket and shows it to Kim in the palm of his hand. 'Can you see this, comrade? Do you know what it is?'

'It looks like a bullet from a snub-nosed nine-millimetre.'

'That's right. It's the bullet Colonel Kruger put into my spine that's left me here in this wheelchair. I want you to place it in that murdering swine's mouth once he's dead.'

Kim nods silently, staring at the bullet as though to assess its cold, sleeping anger in the pink nest of Lévy's hand. But that is not what he is thinking of deep down, nor the risks and difficulties he will face. He isn't calculating the whirling trajectory of the unquenchable rage, the pressing demand for vengeance he is carrying with him across seas and continents. No, it's you he's thinking of, Susana, and this bed, this other lonely nest, and how he can get you out of it. How often since that day, certain in his mind that you would meet again in Shanghai, has he imagined you free of your fever, smiling as you stroll along arm-in-arm beneath the leafy trees lining the River Huang-p'u, looking so beautiful with jade pins in your hair and wearing a tight-fitting green silk dress slit up the side, like the most elegant young Chinese girls . . .

3

About once every fortnight, Doña Conxa called in at the villa to pick up the fine bobbin lace Señora Anita made for her and to leave a new order for more of the same simple patterns, usually for small mats or table centrepieces. She would often bring sprigs of elderflower for the sick girl, boil them up and then rub them on her chest and back. She joked with Forcat, and even helped Anita with some of her household chores. In mid-May, when the yellow broom was flowering on the slopes of the Pelada hill, Finito Chacón and his brother would come down with armfuls of it for Susana, and she would spread them all over the bed. After green, yellow was her favourite colour.

And every other Wednesday Doctor Barjau would come to visit Susana. The doctor was a plump, gruff sixty-year-old who lived near the Parque Güell and went round the neighbourhood with his threadbare jacket pockets full of sweets, dragging his feet as if they were made of lead. He brought Susana film magazines, then took her hand, sat heavily on the bed and put a thermometer in her mouth. He would dissolve Senocal powder in water for her and inject calcium intravenously, which almost always made her choke and feel dizzy. Doctor Barjau was completely bald, and as if in compensation a straggly mass of ginger hair poked out of his ears like a floral decoration. 'How is your cough today, child?' he would say, pinching her cheek. 'Lift your nightshirt and show me your back. And what about your temperature? Is it still thirty-eight point eight? Well, I suppose it always goes up a bit in the evening,' then he would suddenly press his flowery ear against her back to listen to the damaged lung. Sometimes he would amplify the sound by using two silver coins: he put one on her chest and struck it with the edge of the other, while he pressed his ear against her arched back, to catch the echo from the chest cavity. He would shut his eyes, grunt and mutter to himself, as if he were talking to the lung. But his rough gestures hid a concerned kindness which only surfaced when he saw his patient's eyes fill with terror at the sputum she brought up, or at the thought of death. As he placed the stethoscope on her chest for example, Susana's eyes would suddenly go helplessly blank, or would seek out her mother's or mine in despair. I could not bear it when she looked at me like that, but Doctor Barjau knew her very well, and all he did was give her a tap on the head and tell her: 'You're doing absolutely fine, and you're pretty as a picture.'

After that he always stressed the same thing: she needed a lot of rest, good steaks to eat, and most important of all, a happy atmosphere. Standing by the bed arms folded and with a glass of wine in her hand, Señora Anita would smile and tease him by saying she would love a prescription of that sort. Squinting at his thermometer, which confirmed his patient still had a fever, the doctor would cast a sly, sideways glance at her mother, starting at her legs and moving up to the gap in her mauve dressing-gown that revealed the shiny black slip underneath, until his eyes reached her breasts: 'You don't need any steaks or more fun, Anita, I can see from here how your liver is in top shape . . . and so are other organs I won't mention.' At that, Anita would wrap the gown round her body and laugh a tobacco-stained laugh.

'And I don't want you to smoke in here,' Doctor Barjau added.

'Who smokes in here?' Señora Anita replied. 'I never do.'

'Hmm. I'm only saying, just in case.'

I took advantage of their banter, which seemed to upset Susana more than the doctor's rough hands on her body, to lay aside my wretched drawing. It was turning out flat, lacking all perspective. But that was not the worst thing about it: what was most distressing was that it did not suggest anything at all. I racked my brains to try to find a way to show the frothing black and green smoke from the chimney. According to Captain Blay, that disgusting toxic slime covering the consumptive girl's bed was crucial. He had explained a thousand times how the smoke got into Susana's lungs, where it fed the Koch bacillus, ate into her bronchia and weighed on her heart, but all I ever asked myself was: how can you draw what you can't see?

I sat at the round table to work, a few feet from the bed near the stove. The strangely stuffy air around the patient, her mother's grating laugh, the steamy sweet vapour from the eucalyptus leaves, the needle in Susana's white skin, added to the smell of alcohol and the red sunset outside the window, all combined in a mysterious fashion to create a unique atmosphere that was somehow beyond time, an atmosphere impregnated with sensuality and microbes. I was convinced I would never be able to capture any of this in my drawing. More than a conviction, it was a physical sensation. In that voluptuous bubble, always so full of aromas, tastes and cloying moisture, I could sense the growing demands of my body, however clumsily and ineptly I sought to express them.

When the doctor came to call, Forcat stayed in his room. Doctor Barjau was aware of this, and I think he sometimes prolonged his medical examination out of curiosity and a chance to meet him. But it was not until his fourth or fifth visit that the house guest let himself be seen, and then it was unexpectedly, as he came into the verandah just as the doctor was putting away his stethoscope, and asked him to prescribe something for Susana's insomnia. 'There's nothing that's much good for that,' Doctor Barjau replied, looking him up and down and then adding curtly: 'Except a wish to dream. Get her to drink a lot of milk.' But when Forcat was presented by Señora Anita as 'a good friend of my husband's who's spending a few days with us', the doctor must have noticed the look of genuine concern on the face of this dapper, stiff man, and seen his affection for Susana, because he explained more fully and in a pleasanter voice: 'Don't think I'm joking when I mention milk. I had a patient about the same age as Susana who couldn't sleep, and I cured her thanks to a glass of hot milk every night before she went to bed . . . and the sermons of Father Laburu on the radio, of course.'

He cackled, and Forcat smiled, even though he did not have much idea who the preacher was. Susana felt dizzy so her mother took her to the toilet, leaving the two men to talk together for a while; or rather, Doctor Barjau talked and Forcat listened carefully to his recommendations as to how to look after the patient, a long list that Señora Anita and I knew by heart, and which all essentially came down to the same thing: we had to keep her cheerful, to stimulate her desire to eat and live; if we did that, the rest would follow naturally.

Doctor Barjau was aware of my adventures with the Captain in search of signatures, and although he approved of the idea, had no hesitation in describing it as a laughable waste of time. He thought the same of the drawing that was supposed to melt the heart of the city mayor. On his last visit, he studied my work and patted me on the back encouragingly.

'What about the gas?' he said jokingly. 'What colour are you going to paint that?'

'The gas is invisible,' I muttered.

'You don't say. Is that what that crackpot Blay told you? Well, well.'

Susana was another one who would not stop poking fun at the captain, the chimney, and its poisonous excretions. Whenever I was drawing it, she would hold her nose as though she could not stand the stench, then all of a sudden pretend to faint and lie with half her body dangling out of the bed, legs in the air. She never agreed with a single line of that drawing, and did all she could to discourage me and get me to put it to one side, so that I would start the other one.

'I have to finish this one first, to see how it looks,' I told her. 'Don't you see that the bed, the verandah and everything in here, including the cat, the chimney and the gas, will be exactly the same in both drawings? The only difference will be you: you'll be cured.'

In fact, I was deliberately taking my time. I could have made a good or bad job of it in a couple of weeks at the most, but I wanted to spend as long as possible with Susana, so I kept tearing up sheets of paper and repeating almost everything over and over again: the bed, the windows, the toy cat, the black smoke, and above all her, the poor consumptive finding it so hard to breathe on her bed of pain, just as the Captain wanted it. I found it difficult to get down the details accurately and to relate the different parts of the drawing to each other – her head slumped on the pillows and the threatening chimney in the background looking as if it was about to topple on her, the symmetry of the windows with the black hook of the stove – but if I had wanted to, I could have completed it much sooner.

4

Captain Blay reached the sunny side of the street, balanced on the edge of the kerb in his battered slippers, and turned back to look at me, hands on hips. In some bars they let him buy on the slate, and there were days when he got so squiffy he could hardly speak, but he never lost his balance.

'Come here and smell this,' he said, pointing to the drain. 'People don't want to know, and just keep on walking, but down there are at least a billion dead rats, and more than a dozen bodies of members of the sanitation and hygiene department...'

He described in great detail Barcelona's gloomy subterranean world. He told me that the sewage system and all the other tunnels were so full of an accumulation of gas from the leak in the Plaza Rovira that a spark from a tram wheel would be enough to blow the whole city sky high, with its port, its breakwaters, its Montjuïc mountain, its ever-crowded Ramblas, such a feature of Barcelona.

'It's a clear provocation,' he said, still staring at the open drain. 'And it's no use them pretending they don't want to know, or wallowing in it.'

To get him off this endlessly repeated topic, I asked the Captain how old he was. He said he was twice as old as that son of a bitch Franco, meaning somewhere around two hundred and seventy-one, according to his calculations.

'Here, hold this.' He passed me the folder with the signatures in, unbuttoned his fly and began to piss calmly into the drain. 'And there's no need to feel so sorry for the dead, because they're not aware of it anyway.'

'Please, not again,' I begged him. 'Don't do this to me in the street, Captain.'

'And besides,' he went on without paying me the slightest attention, 'things can't be all that bad in the other world, I reckon, because as far as I can tell no one has ever really come back, to keep on eating slops and shit, to live with the same woman under the same flag. No one.' His prick was as dark as a fig as he shook it and stuffed it back into his trousers. 'Whenever I put it away after a piss, I think of what that general said when he was sheathing his sword, but I can never for the life of me remember the exact words . . .'

I was furious because I hadn't been able to get into the villa that afternoon. When I arrived I saw the blinds drawn in the verandah, and at the front door Forcat told me Susana had a high fever and was asleep, so I shouldn't bother her, but come back the next day. He was holding a cup of chicory in one hand and held an open book pressed against his chest. Once again I caught the strange vegetable odour that always seemed to surround him. So then I went home, and as bad luck would have it, ran into the Captain on the stairs. He asked me to accompany him: they had promised him some signatures over in Travesera, he said, and he did not want to go alone. Either it was a lie or he had dreamed it; I discovered that he was even more incoherent in the afternoons than in the morning. He made me walk up and down the Travesera de Gracia from Cerdeña to Torrent de l'Olla; on the way up we knocked on all the doors with even numbers, and on the way back on all the odd ones. The only signature we obtained was from the boot-blackened hand of a drunken shoe-shine man in a bar.

As we were crossing Plaza Joanic on our way home that evening, the rubber band the Captain used to keep one of his slippers together snapped, so he sat on a bench, took a bit of string out of his pocket, and started to wind it round his foot. Shortly afterwards we were not far from the Civil Guard barracks when we saw a little man standing on a corner wearing a tight black overcoat. He looked furtive and was frantically rubbing the sole of his shoe back and forth on the edge of the kerb, as though he had trodden in some dog muck. All of a sudden his right arm shot out, and he stood there saluting with his back towards us. He was staring at something we could not make out until we drew level with him. Then we noticed another shrunken, timid-looking man standing a hundred yards further on at the next corner, saluting in the same fashion out of respect or fear towards the corner beyond him. There, like an optical illusion, we could spot a third tiny figure holding his arm out in a Roman salute that was a mirror image of the first two. He was standing motionless on the pavement facing the wall, and perhaps he was the one who could hear a military command or the notes of the national anthem: he was the one closest to the barracks.

'See that?' the Captain said, digging me in the ribs. 'The gas has got them. It's in their blood and has paralysed their nerves. Look at them, stuck there like fence-posts, gassed on the public highway.'

'No, it's not that, Captain,' I said, trying to stay patient with him. 'They must be lowering the flag in the barracks, even though we can't hear anything from here. That's why they're standing there like that, out of respect for the anthem.'

He was not listening. Hands clasped behind his back, he walked round the man in the black coat saluting on the kerb near us.

'What's the matter, my good man?' he inquired, looking him over curiously. 'Are you trying to make us believe you're shaking like a leaf at the sound of our glorious national anthem? Do you think it's right to make fun of our patriotic symbols? You've been well and truly gassed, my man, and it's no use trying to hide the fact.'

Keeping one eye on the other man who was his point of reference on the next street corner, our little man flung out his arm so forcefully it seemed it might fly off on its own. Out of the corner of his other eye he caught sight of the bandaged head and outlandish garb of the person talking to him, and positively quaked with fear: presumably it was even worse than he had imagined. There was a sickly pallor to our mouse-like friend's face, he gave off a strange odour, and had two bits of cottonwool sticking out of his nostrils, like a corpse.

'Be careful,' he warned in a virtual whisper. ' Just be careful.'

'Too late for that,' the Captain said. 'You're a goner. The best thing you can do now is die.'

The little fellow again glanced fearfully at him.

'Are you a sandwich-board man or something . . . ? If that's the case, be off with you and leave me alone, please. Don't you realise?' he implored the Captain, 'Somewhere up there they're lowering the flag . . .'

'What flag?'

'Which one could it be? Our flag.'

'Aren't you running a bit of a risk saluting a flag you can't see? What if it isn't ours? Or do you feel the way I do, that all flags are arse wipes?'

'Be quiet, will you?'

'No, I won't.'

'Don't you understand I'm doing this just in case? You never know. Look, that man down there is doing it.'

'That's because he's been gassed as well.'

'Are you an agent provocateur? People are looking!'

'Rubbish! What you should really be concerned about is that this drain is spitting out poison.' He cursed under his breath and turned to me. 'You see, Daniel? You're walking along minding your own business, you stop for a moment next to an open drain to say hello to a friend or watch an aeroplane in the sky, and pow! you've had it.' He paused to inspect the man's long black fingernails and yellow tobacco-stained fingers, then looked him full in the face and studied his tiny rodent's eyes, his pale ears and the small gobbets of green foam at the corners of his mouth. 'Do you need any help?'

'Clear off, you troublemaker, don't get me into trouble,' the man grunted. He seemed to have shrunk still further into the pavement as if he was afraid of being hit on the top of his head, but still he kept his arm flung out in front of him.

The Captain was not in the least worried about all the comings-and-goings in the street or the startled glances of the passers-by. I was tugging at the flaps of his coat to try to get him away, when he placed a hand on the shoulder of his hapless victim.

'You know what I think? I think you look a decent sort, compared to a lot of those you see around . . . So what are we doing here stuck in dry dock? Why don't we go and share a few glasses of wine together, eh?'

At that very moment, the man saluting on the next corner must have noticed that the third one, furthest away from us, whom we could hardly see in the encroaching gloom, had lowered his arm, because he did the same, then scuttled across the road and disappeared into a doorway. When he saw this, our little man dropped his hand to his side with a sigh of relief, muttered goodbye, I hope they sort you out, grandad, you're completely nuts, then pulled up his coat lapels and scurried away towards San Juan, skirting the walls.

'Poor devil, he's had it,' the Captain said, watching him go. 'Did you see his rotten teeth and see-through ears? The mark of the beast!'

CHAPTER FIVE

I

And so it is that one sunny Sunday in early summer that surely must remain forever in his memory, Kim takes the train to Marseilles, without saying goodbye to anyone or commending his soul to God or the devil. In Marseilles he boards the *Nantucket*, an old France-Orient Company cargo boat sailing under a Panamanian flag, whose captain, a fastidious and taciturn Cantonese by the name of Su Tzu, has already received instructions about his only passenger on this voyage.

The *Nantucket* is carrying fertilisers and tools for several ports in the Red Sea and the Indian Ocean, a cargo of cognac and French wines destined for Singapore, and spare parts for Lévy's own looms in his Shanghai factory. Captain Su Tzu, who speaks a measured and musical French, considers Kim a special guest, and shows him great consideration. He assigns him a steward to bring his meals to his cabin, make his bed, wash his clothes and keep him supplied with whisky and American cigarettes. Contrary to Kim's expectations, Captain Su Tzu does not show the slightest interest in why this odd passenger has chosen to travel to Shanghai by cargo boat when he could have done so much more quickly and comfortably by other means. A few hours after their departure, the two men watch night fall over Stromboli as they converse on the fo'castle. It does not take them long to discover they are both chess lovers, and from then on they play a lengthy game each night in the Captain's cabin.

Su Tzu is thirty-eight. He is tall for a Chinese; his features are not particularly Oriental, and he moves in an elegant Western fashion. Only his slow, heavy-lidded eyes, his thoughtful gaze and sensual mouth betray his Cantonese origin. His tact and politeness, even towards the crew, create a very good impression on Kim, especially since he has just left such a scorpions' nest behind him in France, the fraught tension and hidden violence of the Spanish exiles' endless debates.

The *Nantucket* crosses the Mediterranean uneventfully, calling at Tunis and Port Said before entering the Suez Canal, and then up the Red Sea to the Gulf of Aden. After a brief stop at Djibouti, the ship sails across the Indian Ocean, rounding Ceylon before entering the Malacca Strait, where she runs into violent squalls with winds of more than seventy knots with hail and rain storms. One stiflingly hot evening, she finally docks in Singapore. Two days later, leaving the coasts of Borneo to starboard, the *Nantucket* heads north through calmer seas and finally enters the South China Sea, where the nights are warmer and clearer, an open invitation to dream or play chess.

The old cargo boat lumbers on. To the idle curiosity of melancholy passengers on the ocean liner whose path it crosses, its battered prow streaked with rust and oil give it a ragged, antiquated look. But if you've ever been on the bow of a ship by moonlight, even an old rust-bucket like this one, leaning against the rail with the sea breeze in your face, you'll know you seen so much more than the vast mirror of silvery waters under the starry sky, so much more than the ocean and night . . . If you have ever been in love with the horizon, you'll know what I'm talking about.

The *Nantucket*'s sleepless passenger stares at the foam festooning the ship's hull as it ploughs through the waves. His mind reaches back through the darkness into his memory to try to recall a simple melody from a romantic tune we all took to our hearts during the war, an old song linking him for ever to this city, your mother and his friends. Later still, as he is smoking a cigarette leaning over the starboard rail, he sees distant lights flickering on the coast of Asia, and the dreams and scent of a new life. Yet again he fails to spot a portent of fate. A dark cloud slowly descends on the ship and threatens to engulf it. The cargo boat has just left the islands of Indonesia astern, the sea is calm and there is no hint of a storm, but this shadowy curtain is falling, blotting out the stars. According to Captain Su Tzu, it is a cloud of pollution that has been following the ship as like a faithful dog for several days, which Monsieur Franch, if I may be so bold – Su Tzu adds with a smile – has not noticed because not once since we left Marseilles, not once, has he looked back.

'I've spent too many years looking over my shoulder, Captain,' Kim says, smiling back at him. 'I'm convinced it does no good.'

'You may be right,' Su Tzu says in his strong Cantonese accent, perhaps with a touch of sadness. 'But your humble servant here finds that if he doesn't look back often, he can't go forward. Forgive me for confiding in you like this, Monsieur.'

He goes on to explain that the thick cloud which eventually does shroud the ship completely was probably formed off the coast of Somalia on the western shores of the Indian Ocean.

'By tomorrow morning it will have vanished without a trace, and apart from its sickly smell and the slight pricking it causes in our eyes and throats, it is more damaging to the spirit than the body.' And the Captain adds, with what by now is an enigmatic smile: 'some of our superstitious Malayan crew say it is the sign of a betrayal.'

Kim finishes his cigarette, throws it overboard, and stares the Captain in the face.

'Do you believe that too?'

'What your servant believes or does not believe is neither here nor there, Monsieur. Don't you find the heat up here on deck oppressive? What do you say to a game of chess by the fan in my cabin?'

Kim pauses for a few seconds, then asks:

'Forgive me for being indiscreet, Captain Su, but would you say your relations with your boss, Monsieur Lévy, were friendly, or strictly professional?'

All at once the Captain seems more concerned with detecting a missing beat in the noise of the engines rising from the bowels of the ship than in Kim's almost impertinent question. With frowning face, he listens intently to their dull throb, before finally relaxing and turning to his passenger again.

'Did you know this old boat has asthma?' he says, the friendly smile returning to his face. 'Well, how about a game?'

'All right. I'll give you another chance.'

For several days now, Kim has been waiting for the opportunity to get his hands on the book with yellow covers that Lévy wants. And it will take more than Captain Tu Szu's evasive words or the cloud supposedly heavy with the stench of betrayal to undermine his determination to look forwards, just as it will not alter the course of the *Nantucket* in any way.

So the voyage continues without incident, until one morning Kim wakes up in his cabin drenched in sweat: the thermometer on the wall shows forty degrees centigrade. The boat stops in Saigon to take on a cargo of rice and jasmine tea, then heads for Hong Kong, where thanks to Captain Tu Szu, Kim is given a visa for nationalist China. Then the *Nantucket* sails up the Southern Seas through the Formosa Strait and enters on the final stretch of the voyage, dropping anchor in the River Huang-p'u on the morning of 27 July.

But before then, as the boat is sailing past the coast of Taiwan, Kim unexpectedly gets the opportunity to recover Lévy's book. It's a warm, humid night with the threat of a storm in the air. Su Tzu and his guest have just finished a game of chess and have left the cabin to smoke a cigarette leaning over the rail, watching the rain and lightning coming towards them from the northwest. All at once the second mate appears. He says the Captain is urgently needed in the engine room: two Malay seamen have had a knife fight, and there are serious consequences. Su Tzu makes his excuses and leaves, just as a downpour hits the ship, forcing Kim to take cover in the captain's cabin. He will never get a better opportunity. He surveys the books on the shelves. He does not want to switch on a lamp, so the only light comes in through the porthole. He can see two books with yellow covers, and the first one he opens – almost by accident, due to the pitch and roll of the ship – is not the one he is looking for. It is not a Chinese book, it is a volume of Greek poetry. Once again, the sign he does not want to see, the sign revealing a change of course, another twist of fate, leaps from these pages. For fully half a minute, the dull thud of engines deep in the *Nantucket's* hull pounds along his nerves, and Kim thinks of Captain Su Tzu and his rare kindness, his eloquent silences. Without knowing why, in the broken-down boat's monotonous, hidden throbbing, he senses how time has slipped away from him, perceives the distant echo of the fragile hope that has brought him here, in the midst of a raging storm and crashing waves, and put in his hands a book open at page seventy-seven, thanks more to a sudden whim of the sea than any conscious decision on his part.

And if we had been there at that moment, my friends, if we had been able to slip unnoticed into the captain's cabin and stand beside Kim in the darkness with lightning flashing all around, surely our curiosity would have led us to glance over his shoulder for those thirty seconds – such a brief moment, yet somehow eternal in the heart of time and of mankind – to decipher together what chance placed in his hands that night:

> You said, 'I will go to another land, I will go to another sea.
> Another city will be found, a better one than this.
> Every effort of mine is a condemnation of fate;
> And my heart is – like a corpse – buried.
> How long will my mind remain in this wasteland.
> Wherever I turn my eyes, wherever I may look
> I see black ruins of my life here,
> where I spent so many years destroying and wasting.'
>
> You will find no new lands, you will find no other seas.
> The city will follow you. You will roam the same
> streets. And you will age in the same neighbourhoods;
> and you will grow grey in these same houses.
> Always you will arrive in this city. Do not hope for any other –

There is no ship for you, there is no road.
As you have destroyed your life here
*in this little corner, you have ruined it in the entire world.**

Limping slowly through the seas, as if towing shreds of its own rusty past through the rain, the buried memory of other itineraries through other more temperate zones, the *Nantucket* continues on its way to Shanghai.

2

'If you force me to eat all this, I'll be sick over the bed,' moaned Susana.

From being so long in bed and so spoilt by her mother, she had learnt to exercise a mild but capricious tyranny which she now employed on Forcat and the huge snacks he prepared for her, what seemed to her like trays filled with an impossibly big glass of milk, a boiled egg, or toast and jam.

'Eat the egg at least,' said Forcat. 'Look, I'll take the shell off.'

'I don't want any more eggs. I'm sick and tired of boiled eggs!'

They were always quarrelling like this, and I looked on in dumb astonishment, staring at the strange gentleness of her brow framed by her black hair, the mouth always half-open and taunting, the plump perfection of her top lip. She saw me and protested:

'What are you staring at?'

'Would you prefer it raw in a glass of Malaga wine?' Forcat suggested. 'Or would you like me to make you a lovely artichoke or aubergine omelette?'

'Shit and more shit! I don't want anything!'

'You know what the doctor says,' he says. 'Lots of eggs and milk

* From *The Complete Poems of Cavafy*, translated by Rae Dalven. The Hogarth Press Ltd. London 1961. p.27.

. . . lossa milk an' lossa eiggs, as the Chacón boys say. Susssana, eat loss and loss if you wanna get betta, nise an' plump an' pretty . . .'

Forcat often managed to make her smile, but not always to eat. Sitting on the bed beside the tray, his stained fingers still plucked at the shell while he patiently employed every argument he could think of to get her to swallow something.

The first time I really noticed Forcat's hands was not so much because I was intrigued by their patches of different colour, but because he had laid them on Señora Anita's knees in a way that somehow did not surprise me, even though I was proved wrong. It was one Sunday midday while I was keeping Susana company but had to leave because I was supposed to go with Finito up to Parque Güell to get eucalyptus for the pot and some broom to decorate the verandah with. As I was passing the open door of Señora Anita's bedroom, I saw the two of them sitting by the bedside table. Forcat was in a chair and she was sitting on the edge of the bed, with no shoes on and her crossed legs appearing through the folds of her dressing-gown. Forcat's hands were resting on her top knee. I barely had time to see it, but even in this first fleeting glimpse there was something about their attitude that did not fit in with the ideas I had been having about them: Forcat's solicitous hands did not seem like those of a man caressing a pair of pretty legs, and Anita's behaviour as she filed her nails, apparently completely oblivious to what his fingers were doing, did not suggest she was allowing herself to be stroked. But the whole thing was over too quickly. I thought they had not seen me and I carried on down the corridor, but her voice brought me up short:

'Daniel, sweetheart, are you leaving?'

'Yes.'

'Come here a minute would you?'

I made my way back to the bedroom doorway. Anita's knees glowed faintly in the gloom, and Forcat had lifted his hands off a short way, before replacing them again with a calm concern, a strange fervour. I thought there was the smell of raw artichoke in the room, though I had no idea where this impression came from. Señora Anita asked me if the Chacón brothers were still out in the street, so I told her

95

they were waiting for me. She asked if we could please bring her some eucalyptus leaves, and I said Susana had already told us to do so, and that was why we were going to Parque Güell.

'Daniel in the lion's den!' she said, smiling contentedly. 'I don't know what I'd do without you.'

I could see that Forcat's hands were barely brushing Señora Anita's knee. It was more as though the gesture were aimed at protecting it from something, the light or the atmosphere or who knows what; or as though his own raw, suffering hands were seeking some kind of relief from her bare knee. Whatever the reason, they did not look as if they were being used to caress, and if they were, this was something new and disturbing, because they were not even touching her skin. Bent forwards in the chair and apparently totally absorbed in his task, Forcat did not look even once in my direction. I felt bewildered: this was nothing like the torrid scenes I had imagined whenever the two of them disappeared and left me alone with Susana in the verandah. At that moment I was suddenly convinced that this was something far worse.

'And on the way can you buy me a peseta's worth of ice and a flagon of wine?' she added. 'The empty one and the money are on the dining-room table.'

'I'll leave it at the bar and pick it up on the way back.'

'You're a sweetheart, Daniel.' Still filing her nails, she turned to look at Forcat. 'Isn't he wonderful?'

Forcat said nothing. As I was leaving, Señora Anita uncrossed her legs, but he was still cupping his hands round the left one, and seemed so patient and absorbed he looked like a knife-grinder bending over his humble task. For days afterwards, I was still wondering whether this had been a strange form of caress, a game, or a secret rite, or perhaps all three things together.

That Sunday Susana's mother had done a swap with the other box office assistant, so she did not go to the Mundial and had the afternoon free. About five o' clock, while Susana and I were waiting for Forcat on the verandah, we heard the rapid tapping of high heels.

'Susanita, we're going out for a while.' Señora Anita appeared, tightening the broad white belt that made her look so slender. She was wearing a loose-fitting dress with a pattern of white buds all over it, white high-heeled shoes and a coral necklace. She had on fine silk stockings, had put on lipstick and looked lovely, with her blonde curls cascading down. I stared at her open-mouthed, and she smiled: 'Will you keep my daughter company until I get back?'

'Yes.'

'Where are you going?' asked Susana.

'For a walk down the Ramblas and along by the port, I think.'

'On your own?'

'Of course not. With Señor Forcat.'

'Señor Forcat? What are we supposed to do then?'

'Oh, I'm sorry. He's devoting this afternoon to me.'

She kissed her daughter and disappeared down the corridor. We soon saw her going through the garden gate with Forcat, who had on his dark glasses and was wearing a baggy grey suit that must have been very hot. Señora Anita leant on his arm and, turning quickly to look over her shoulder, lifted one of her legs and straightened her stocking seam, laughing as she did so. Supporting her arm, Forcat stood stiff and serious as he waited for her to finish.

Behind the verandah windows, Susana burst out laughing and said she had never seen such a ridiculous, old-fashioned couple.

This was the first time they had left the house together. The Chacón brothers had not appeared all afternoon. Susana was clutching her toy cat, and asked me to go and fetch a silver-plated lipstick in her mother's bathroom. When I brought it, she threw down the cat, cast off the bedclothes, and kneeled up on the bed. She grabbed the lipstick with both hands, and when she bared her teeth I could see how her mouth suddenly became adult as she started to apply it to her lips, which grew redder and redder with each stroke. When she had finished, she turned down the volume of her radio, got back between the sheets, and went to sleep. I got bored drawing and wasting my time studying her, so I started to play patience on the table.

Night was falling by the time Forcat and Señora Anita came back.

They were very lively, and her mother did not scold Susana when she saw the thick layer of cherry red lipstick. Instead she looked at her handkerchief to see if she had been spitting any blood, then went to change. When she came back, she was carrying a glass of wine which she drank straight off, filled a second time, then took to her room with her bobbin lace cushion. In the meantime, Forcat was preparing something for supper. Shortly afterwards he came into the verandah smiling, his hands concealed in the wide sleeves of his kimono, and said in a mysterious stage whisper:

'Susana, guess what I've brought you.'

'A bottle of cologne. No, a lemon ice lolly.'

Forcat sat on the bed.

'We visited a French liner in port. It was all dazzling white,' he said. 'The captain is a friend of mine and your father's. While an officer was showing your mother the ballroom, he gave me this for you.'

'Captain Su Tzu?' asked Susana.

'No. Another captain,' Forcat smiled and went on: 'Our Captain Su Tzu is sailing off the coast of Taiwan, remember?'

'Yes . . . so what is it?'

'Open it and you'll see.'

It was a brown envelope without a stamp, and written on it in handwriting that made her eyes suddenly gleam, was Susana's name. Inside was a postcard depicting an ancient Chinese pagoda in yellow, red and black tones. On the back was Kim's cramped, nervous writing:

Dear Susana, keep your dream alive. As I write this card, in Barcelona it will be six in the afternoon and here in Shanghai it is one in the morning. I'd really like it if every day at exactly six o' clock you thought of me, and I'll think of you at the same moment. Isn't it a great idea? That way our thoughts will unite across seas and continents, until the day we can stroll together in the Garden of Happiness. Remember: at six o'clock precisely. Imagine your father seated at the bar of the Silk Hat, Shanghai's most elegant night-club, a glass of champagne in hand, listening to a song your mother loved. And raising it in a toast to you. For reasons I'll explain to you some day, I'm still incognito in this marvellous city, so for the moment I prefer you not to write to me. A thousand kisses, and eat lots so you'll get better. *An mías!* (In Chinese that means: sweet dreams). Your loving father, Kim.

3

Susana wanted a map to follow the *Nantucket*'s course, and one day the Chacón brothers arrived with a brand new atlas they could not explain how they had come by. Susana asked me to draw the ship's path in red pencil on the deep blue of the sea, from Marseilles to Shanghai. It crossed two pages of the atlas, taking in the most important ports in the Mediterranean, the Indian Ocean and the China Seas. We learnt later that Finito had stolen the atlas from a schoolboy who had given him his bag to look after while he tried to find his mother in the street market, and Susana forced him to give it back. Finito said that was a pity, and suggested tearing out the two pages showing the *Nantucket*'s voyage before he did so. After thinking about it, Susana finally decided against the idea, arguing that the boy would be sure to see there were pages missing. Instead, she suggested I copy the route on tracing paper, colouring in the coasts, ports and islands with different pencils. I did as she asked, and she put it in her bedside table drawer along with her cinema programmes, her cuttings, hairbrush, hand mirror, and the nail polish.

When we showed Forcat the map, he pointed out a mistake I had made. As I peered over it, his long, stained finger traced the west coast of India, and he reminded me that the *Nantucket* had never called in at Bombay. His finger was so close to my face I could again smell its strange odour: this time it made me think of the sharp fragrance of fig leaves.

Later that evening, when he came over to have a look at the

scribbles I had made that were supposed to represent Susana in bed, I was able to study his hands from close up:

'Why don't you try to sketch in the bed first? Do you really like drawing, Daniel? Or are you doing it to keep that lunatic Blay happy?' Then, in a lower voice: 'would you like to be a draftsman when you grow up?'

His thin smile encouraged me to tell him my secret.

'I don't know . . . I think what I'd like to be,' I said naively, 'is a pianist.'

As soon as I said it, I regretted it. I was ashamed he might discover my secret romantic streak, my confused fascination with certain dark images of Anton Walbrook playing the *Warsaw Concerto* as the bombs fell all around, and searchlights swept the sky . . .

'A pianist? Why, that's a great idea!' Forcat stood watching me struggle with my pencil as I tried in vain to capture the light-blue bedcover. I was drawing it drooping over the edge of the bed, because like that it seemed to me to offer more aesthetic possibilities, but I kept on trying to make a faithful copy of the folds, and they escaped me. All of a sudden, Forcat's hand seized the pencil from me. Drawing rapidly and with incredible skill, he conjured up in front of my eyes a series of long, magnificent folds that had little to do with the original, but gave the bedcover in the sketch such a weighty elegance, so real and convincing a texture, I could scarcely believe my eyes.

This was the first and only time we ever saw him demonstrate his skill with a pencil. He ruffled my hair, then went back to the kitchen to have a cup of chicory and prepare something for Susana to eat. In my mind's eye for a few moments I could still see his hands wielding the pencil, so close to my face I could feel the warm pulse of his blood through the thick, dark veins. And it confirmed for me the faint smell of raw artichokes I had first noticed in Señora Anita's bedroom, even though I had never really been aware of their smell in my life before, and of course I have no idea why his elegant hands with their badly damaged skin should have suggested the smell of artichokes in the first place. It is a conviction held deep inside me, a kind of special homage to my own childhood garden. There are several aspects of that man's personality and my behaviour towards him that I have never been able to explain to myself. In all my life, I have never known anyone capable of arousing such expectations, who responded to challenges with such a sense of complicity and gentleness as he did by simply resting his hand on your shoulder and looking you in the eye. Almost as soon as I had noticed the odour which I could only define in my rough-and-ready, provisional way, I noticed that the hand moving the pencil so skilfully a few inches from my face also gave off a gentle but persistent warmth. I could sense waves of a strange effluence like burnt vegetables coming from the stained skin itself; as if he had just burnt his hand on the stove.

Later that afternoon, Susana lay back on her cushions with the radio turned up loud, and seemed to be dozing with a magazine open on her lap and surrounded by the armfuls of broom that Finito and Juan had brought that morning. It was a sunny afternoon, but very windy, and she was finally awakened by the jumbled branches of the willow in the garden whipping against the verandah windows. She sat up in bed, and while we were waiting for Forcat to appear I passed the time half-heartedly sketching the outline of the ever-present chimney and its lethal smoke, the sinister shadow threatening the sick girl's life for the drawing which according to Captain Blay's optimistic forcecast was sure to melt the authorities' hearts. Both of us were feeling impatient, because that afternoon Forcat was taking a long time over his chores and had not come to continue his story for us. Soon though I witnessed something I do not know whether to describe as a small miracle or cheap sleight of hand.

What happened was that Señora Anita's house guest came in from the kitchen ceremoniously bearing the tray with Susana's snack on it. Wrapped in his silk kimono, he carefully placed the tray on the bed, and sat down next to Susana. As usual, she had no appetite, and grumbled at the sight of the big glass of milk and the ham and tomato roll she knew she could not force down. The truth is that Forcat always prepared these rolls with great care, and he was so good at it they almost cried out to be eaten – I can vouch for that as I was often invited to share them with Susana – but she almost always turned up her nose at the food. This particular afternoon she seemed even more tired and irritable than usual; she had difficulty breathing and kept dozing off without meaning to. In spite of all Forcat's entreaties, she refused to eat and would not try the milk. The tray was left untouched on the bed while she started to brush her hair, then stopped that and began looking for another music station on the radio. Sitting on the edge of the bed, Forcat tried another tack:

'If you don't eat, you'll never know how your father reached Shanghai or why his friend Lévy asked him to steal the book back . . .'

'Why was that?'

'You'll never guess. It's a real surprise.'

Susana lowered her chin, protesting all the while. Then she thought about it and asked:

'Why didn't he come here first so we could have gone together? Even though I was ill, I could still have travelled . . .'

'No you couldn't. And he set off on a very special and dangerous mission. He had to go alone.'

'I've never been on a boat, but I'm sure I don't get sea-sick . . .'

'I'll tell you what happened if you drink the milk and try at least one slice of bread, just one. And some ham, because that's very expensive and your mother isn't exactly well off. Go on, there's a good girl . . .'

'That's enough,' Susana interrupted him. 'There's just one thing I want to know.'

'What?'

'Is my father tall?'

'Don't you remember?'

'That night he came to see me he was crouching down the whole time . . .'

'Well, yes, Kim is quite tall.'

'How was he dressed when he boarded the boat that took him to Shanghai?'

Forcat hid his hands in the kimono sleeves, put his head to one side and smiled:

'Oh no, that's not fair. That makes two things you've asked me. You'll have to pay. Either a mouthful of bread or a sip of milk, you choose.' He turned to me. 'Danny, don't you agree she has to pay if she wants her curiosity satisfied?'

'Yes,' I said. 'She'll get really fat, but she has to pay. Yes, let her pay!'

'You can shut up, you little sniveller! When are you going to finish that crappy drawing anyway?'

She picked up a pair of scissors and threatened me with them, but soon calmed down and started to cut out a photo of Judy Garland following the yellow brick road in a magazine. Then she flung the scissors down on the bed and screamed at Forcat, eyes blazing:

'I couldn't give a damn about that stupid boat and the people on her! Do you think I give a stuff about anything to do with my father? Do you think we don't know how to get on without him here?' Forcat said nothing, so she went on: 'As far as I'm concerned he can go wherever he likes, by boat or plane or motorbike, I don't need him anyway!'

'All right, calm down,' said Forcat. 'What gets into you sometimes? Usually you're such a sweet, well-behaved child . . .'

'I don't want to be a sweet, well-behaved child; you can keep your sweet well-behaved girls, get it?'

'Got it.'

Susana fell quiet. She cuddled her toy cat for a few moments, then asked him:

'Have you been in lots of places with my father? Were you in Shanghai?'

'I was there long before he was. As a young man I was a steward on a boat, and travelled a lot. I know the city like the palm of my hand.'

Susana looked at me and then down at the tray of food.

'Ask your mother if you don't believe me,' said Forcat.

'I already did,' she murmured. She shut her eyes, and added: 'But you can stick the milk and all this food Doctor Barjau says I have to eat up your backside. If I have to force down that bread roll I'll be sick, I promise you.'

'Don't talk nonsense. You'll be sick some day on a boat, there's no doubt about that, and I'd love to see it . . . but for now, drink the milk at least, while I tell you something that will interest you.'

Susana clutched her cat and said nothing. She stared down at her polished nails, plumped the pillow behind her back and then very slowly and reluctantly stretched out her arm to pick up the glass of milk. But it had gone cold, so she put it down again, and I could not tell from her face whether she was annoyed or relieved.

'Grrr . . . cold milk is what I most hate in the world.'

'Let's see.'

It was then that it happened. Picking up the glass, Forcat cupped it in his hands very gently, as if he was afraid of dropping it but at the same time did not want to touch it – as if despite what Susana had said, it was boiling hot – and sat like that silently for two or three minutes. I remembered how he had placed his hands on Señora Anita's knee: it was the same intense concentration, the same tension in his body.

When he handed the milk back to Susana, it was hot. Susana could not believe it, and nor could I until I touched the glass. I've often been led by the nose in my life, but I swear on my mother's grave that this time I was not: both Susana and I dipped a finger into the milk and found it was as hot as if it had just been taken off the stove.

4

If I'm not mistaken, we were in Captain Su Tzu's cabin, at the moment when Kim, realising it is not the right one, puts the first book with yellow covers back on the shelf, and opens the second. He immediately sees the beautiful illustrations Lévy had mentioned.

The rainstorm has passed and is vanishing to starboard. The sky clears and the stars come out once more. Kim needs more light, so he goes over to the porthole and flicks through the book's pages. Just as Lévy had said, there is a crimson blot on the first page right next to the personal dedication in red ink in Chinese characters. It is too dark in the cabin for him to make it out properly, but he knows the book in his hands must be the one his friend wants. At that moment, he thinks he hears a sound behind him, and spins round: there's no one to be seen. The half-open door bangs against its frame as the ship pitches to and fro; outside the porthole, where the sea is moving gently in the moonlight like a huge silver eyelid, flits an unseen shadow.

Kim takes the book back to his cabin. Lying on his bed he opens it again and looks more closely at the crimson blot. He sees in fact it is two shapes: they were made by female lips, and are the perfect imprint of a lipsticked mouth which has planted a scarlet kiss on the page next to the dedication and signature. Who was that kiss for: Michel Lévy, Captain Su Tzu, or perhaps neither of them . . . ? The printed lips are smiling and plump, slightly open and furrowed. They emerge out of nothing like some fantastic obsession. Their outline is so strong and perfect it gives an immediate impression of intense, burning life, the passion and fire that for a fleeting moment inspired that mouth and left it displayed on the page. From now on, the same image will remain fixed in Kim's memory: ghostly and insubstantial, staining the pale white cloud of the page like a wound.

He wraps the book in a jersey and hides it in his case. According to Kim, the rest of the voyage across the South China Sea seemed endless. The following evening, out of curiosity he times how long it takes the sun to set, and discovers it lasts longer than the night itself, even running into the next dawn. For several days a harsh east wind blows that burns the skin. For his last night on board, Captain Su Tzu invites him to eat in his cabin. Kim finds him more withdrawn than usual, but as polite and friendly as ever.

At eight the next morning, the *Nantucket* enters Hangzhow Bay, and soon after sailing up the muddy, slow waters of the River Huangp'u, prepares to dock at the pier, surrounded by a swarm of launches, barges, fishing boats and junks. A small, plump, impeccably dressed

Asian man is waiting for Kim on the jetty in front of a brand-new black Packard. This is Lévy's business associate, Charlie Wong: an animated hybrid of French and Indo-Chinese, who has already seen to all the customs formalities. As Kim stands by the rail waiting for the boat to finish docking, for the first time we can hear the distant hubbub of Shanghai, and our astonished eyes can scarcely believe what they see: beneath the deep blue of the sky, a line of imposing skyscrapers stands guard over the legendary city.

'I'm very grateful for all your kindness,' Kim says, as he shakes hands and takes his leave of Captain Su Tzu. 'Perhaps we'll meet again, and then I'll be able to explain certain things to you.'

Su Tzu smiles softly and bows.

'Good friends make poor liars,' he says. 'Just like in Li Yan's poetry, some things are there without having to be mentioned.'

'I'm sure you're right. But they say that to lie can be a form of respect. It's been a pleasure to meet you, captain.'

'Good luck, Monsieur.'

'And to you.'

The jetty is bustling with activity, and sing-song voices ring out. As he is about to step into the car sent for him, Kim suddenly feels himself caught in one of those mysterious moments when the heart senses things the mind cannot comprehend. A certainty overwhelms him: what awaits him in Shanghai after such a long voyage, what he can sense in the air — because in some way the feeling rises from the foul-smelling river, and floats in the damp, stifling atmosphere of the city — is not at all what he has come looking for. It is not an act of revenge or a settling of accounts with history, it's not the well-aimed bullet meting out his just deserts to a criminal, or compassion for an invalid friend, it's not even the desire or hope of having Susana with him some day soon. No, it is a far deeper and more desperate secret: the unconfessed desire, the painful need to use that last bullet to wipe out all traces of his own haunting past, finally to erase all remaining evidence of a humiliating, never-ending personal defeat. To kill himself by killing Kruger, that is why he has come: one bullet for two people.

Michel Lévy's wife, Chen Jing Fang, receives Kim on the garden-terrace of her luxury penthouse apartment in one of the Bund skyscrapers close to Nanking Road. She is friendly but reserved; she will follow her husband's instructions and offer him hospitality, even allow him to keep an eye on her day and night, but she does not share his concern or see any need for protection.

'I don't feel threatened by anyone or anything . . . Are you listening, Monsieur?' Chen Jing adds, noting his absent gaze.

Kim appears to recover, still staring at her.

'I'm sorry,' he says. 'I'll do all I can not to disturb you, but your husband has his reasons for what he's asked me to do. The danger is real enough, Madame, and we cannot take too many precautions.'

Lévy's wife is a twenty-four-year-old Chinese woman. She is strikingly beautiful, in a proud, constrained way. She is wearing an elegant sleeveless, sky-blue silk *chipao* with a high collar and slit up the sides. Her jet-black hair is rolled up in a chignon and kept in place with several jade pins. Faced with this beautiful woman, just as he did when he first caught sight of Shanghai, Kim again suddenly feels the need to redefine the fragile reasoning behind his coming here. Slowly, as if recognising one by one the features of someone he thinks he saw years earlier or has perhaps only dreamed of, Kim takes in her fine, pearly forehead, the well-defined arc of her brows, her honey-coloured eyes, the gently receding chin and, above all, her mouth and its sudden gleam of scarlet. As soon as he sees her, Kim knows it is this mouth with its full lips that is the same ghostly, mysterious mouth burning in the pages of the book he has stolen from the *Nantucket*. Why was the imprint of that mouth kept prisoner in the remote cabin of a dirty old cargo boat, as if someone were trying to preserve its ancient fire . . . ?

As Kim details the security precautions he thinks she should take, Chen Jing smiles faintly. She may accept, but her smile is cold and enigmatic. Then she tells him his room is ready, and summons an old Chinese servant by the name of Deng. The others in the household are a Siamese maid, a male cook and the *Ayi*, a sort of confidante of Chen's, as Kim is soon to discover. Educated at the lycée français in

Shanghai, Chen Jing speaks a fluid and gently melodic French with no guttural effects, in a refined, clear voice. She comes from a rich trading family based in Tianjin who made their fortune in the twenties when they settled in the heart of the French concession in the Rue du Consulat and started opium trafficking.

Before withdrawing, Chen Jing tells Kim that her many social commitments mean she has to go out almost every evening. Tonight she is due to attend a cocktail party at the Cathay Hotel.

'I suppose you will want to go with me,' she says, casting a brief glance at her guest's crumpled suit. 'But I'm sure what you want most of all right now is a nice bath and a rest. Deng will provide you with all you need . . . Welcome to my home, and I hope you will feel comfortable here, Monsieur Franch.'

'And I hope not to get in the way too much, madame.'

While Deng is preparing his bath, Kim unpacks and hides Lévy's book in a safe place. He repeats her name to himself: Chen Jing Fang, and thinks how good it sounds, like a soft caress on his ears, a reminder of the sombre promise that has brought him here, his vow to keep her from all harm, Jing meaning calmness, Fang fragrance. His room is spacious and light, with the gentle, tranquil scent of lacquered furniture and objects. The big sliding door leading out onto the terrace is open, and the perfume of flowers wafts in. Kim goes outside, and stands looking down at the river snaking beneath a blue-tinged mist towards the east of the city.

5

As the drawing of Susana advanced, I could sense inside me a growing feeling of desperation. I could see myself becoming more and more trapped in a cheap, fake setting, an artificially theatrical creation that in no way did justice to Captain Blay's delirious hopes or to the gripping stories Forcat told us every evening. The Susana I was colouring in would never be the deathly spectre that the Captain wished for, nor the delicate china and silk doll Susana herself wanted to send to her father. I was not even capable of depicting the background. I had tried to make the verandah look like a glasshouse, which was how I saw it, but in my glasshouse no flowers could bloom. I had tried to portray on paper Susana's smooth forehead and the velvety red rose that glowed brighter by the day in her cheeks, but all I produced was the pale reflection of a lifeless rag-doll. The Chacón brothers and I were agreed: as the days went by, her illness made Susana more beautiful and brought her closer to us, to our feverish imaginings: she oozed a sort of warm, moist and contagious sensuality. That was what I was trying to capture with my pencil, but I failed utterly.

This was the drawing for the Captain that Susana mockingly referred to as 'the portrait of the poor ugly consumptive and the slimy chimney'. I had hardly even begun the one for her father, which I thought would be much more difficult. One night I dreamt I had torn this drawing into a thousand pieces and was embarking on a China ink sketch of the battered outline of the *Nantucket* as it headed for the Far East with Susana and me as stowaways, curled up together in a corner of the hold.

6

'Would you like to hear the sounds my sick lung makes?' asked Susana.

'Can you hear them . . . ?'

'Of course you can, you dolt. Come over here. Sit next to me. Don't be afraid, I'm not going to infect you with my microbes . . .'

She threw her head back and instructed me to place my ear against her chest. I did so very carefully, holding my breath. She took my head in her hands, pushed it slightly lower down, then started to move it gently but forcefully round her left breast.

'Can you hear it?' she asked. I could not avoid a sharp expulsion of breath. 'What's the matter, ninny, are you going to sneeze . . . ?'

'I don't know, I think I can hear something in there, but I'm not sure . . .'

'Can you, yes or no? Press your head against me properly, like this . . . They say it's like a buzzing sound in a cave. Can you hear it . . . ?'

'A buzzing sound?'

Now I could clearly hear her heart. And mine. I persisted:

'Did you say it was like buzzing . . . ?'

'Yes, that's what I said. Are you deaf or something?'

'Well, what I can hear at the moment isn't a buzzing. Hang on, wait a minute . . .'

'I'm telling you it's a buzzing sound. Listen carefully, dummy. Have you got it or not?' She continued moving my bewildered head with her hands, placing my cheek directly on her breast, which was burning like ice. 'What's wrong, have you got ear-plugs in, or are you deaf as a fence-post?'

My face flushed hotly, and I felt increasingly desperate, as if Susana's decayed lung were about to infect me with its malignant fever through her hardening breast. I could feel its soft firmness and the erect nipple, and shut my eyes, but she did not seem to notice what was going on, and did not push my head away. When she spoke, her voice was cold and disdainful:

'Can you hear anything or not? Come on, get a move on. What about over here . . . ?' As she shifted my head once more, the increasingly hard nipple was quivering under the thin nightdress. 'Can you hear it now? What about here . . . ?'

'Something, but it's not clear. Not yet.'

I snorted again, and she said:

'What are you doing, sleeping or something?' She took my hand and placed it on her forehead. 'Can you feel my fever? My temperature's always high . . . Can't you hear anything?'

'Yes, I think I can now . . . Wait . . .'

'That's enough, don't try to take advantage!'

She pulled my head away roughly, and when she saw me blushing and could tell from my eyes how excited I was, burst out laughing, picked up her felt cat, turned her back on me and switched the radio on.

Then she got up to tidy the bed and smoothe down the bedcover, while I went back to my post at the table.

'Daniel,' Susana said after a while, lying back on her pillows. 'Do you know what I was thinking?'

'What?'

'I was thinking that in the other drawing, the good one, to give my father a surprise you should put me in a dress like Chen Jing's . . . it's such a beautiful dress, tight-fitting and with slits up the sides. I want you to draw me lying on the bed in a dress like that, as if I were half-asleep, like this, look . . . Are you listening, dummy? What a stupid kid!'

'I'm sorry . . . what colour would you like the dress?'

'Green,' she said. 'Or black, completely black in raw silk . . . No, green, it has to be green. Sleeveless and with a high collar. What do you reckon? Can you hear me, or are you away with the fairies?'

I could still feel the soft, springy firmness of her breast on my cheek. I could not think of anything else, even if I had wanted to. She did not insist, and lay back as if lost in thought. A short while later she seemed to have fallen asleep holding the cat, but at a certain moment I could see her half-closed eyes laughing at me from behind the cat's ears, level with the bedclothes.

As the days grew warmer, Forcat stopped lighting the stove, but he still heated the pot with eucalyptus leaves in the kitchen and left it in the room to keep the atmosphere in the verandah humid as Doctor Barjau had recommended. One afternoon when I was late getting to the villa I met Señora Anita just leaving for work. She told me Señora Conxa was with Susana, and that Forcat was still sleeping his siesta. As I entered the verandah I saw the Captain's wife bent over Susana, rubbing her bare back with a cloth she dipped in a bowl of boiled water with elderflower. 'Bettibu' insisted these massages were wonderful for strengthening pulmonary fibre, improving the circulation and for the delicate skin of pretty young girls. She was facing away from me and did not see me come in, but Susana, who was lying flat on the bed with her nightdress pulled down to the waist, did notice me, and watched me all the time her pink, wet back was being rubbed. When 'Bettibu' tapped her on the backside and said: '*Ara el pitet, maca*', she kept staring at me with ridicule in her eyes as she turned slowly round, barely bothering to cover her breasts with her arm, and poked out her tongue. Doña Conxa must have realised something was going on and looked round, but I dodged back from the doorway and went to sit and wait at the dining-room table.

The massage session went on and on, so I opened my folder and from memory sketched the felt cat sitting upright on the bed as if standing guard over Susana's drooping head. It came out quite well, except for the mouth. The weather was very warm, and 'Bettibu's' herbs made the atmosphere even more intoxicating. Then the Captain's wife came out of the verandah, took the bowl to the kitchen, and came waddling back on her fat legs still without realising I was there. She left behind her a rarefied atmosphere, a strange mixture of sweat and crushed flowers.

When I entered the verandah, Susana was lying on her back, her feet bare and close together, her eyes closed and her hands folded across her chest. I tiptoed over to the bed and said hello, but she did not reply. She lay there without moving, playing dead, so that for several minutes I could gaze openly at the disturbing swelling of the nightdress across her groin, then stare at her long white neck, with the Adam's apple moving stealthily beneath the skin. With her eyes closed, the dark lines under them seemed more pronounced and purple-coloured, the skin more tender and vulnerable. Her half-open mouth showed a red stain on her upper teeth. Then I noticed a piece of paper she was holding upright between her fingers on her chest. It was written with her mother's lipstick, and was for me:

SILLY PRINCE
GIVE ME A KISS
AND I'LL AWAKEN

I read this a couple of times, looked down at the half-open mouth of the sleeping beauty, the teeth with their bloody stain, this mouth offering me the stuff of my dreams all mingled with deadly microbes. By the time I finally made up my mind I had lost a few decisive seconds: all at once Susana opened her eyes and gave me one of those mocking smiles I knew so well. She slipped her hand under the pillow and pulled out a handkerchief spattered with red stains, which she waved frantically in my face. I immediately caught the perfume of cologne, and along with it another fruity, greasy smell I should have recognised, but all I could see were the macabre spots of blood, and instinctively I drew back. I quickly realised it was a joke, but once again I was too late, and she laughed, waving the deceitful handkerchief in front of my face:

'It's only lipstick, you idiot. Nitwit. Dummy.'

CHAPTER SIX

I

Kim spends the afternoon buying clothes in the Wing On department store on Nanking Road, and visiting the centre of the city. The streets of Shanghai's commercial district are crowded with people rushing to and fro. They look like constantly flowing rivers of black-currant, mint, lemon, of gold and rubies. He had never seen such a multi-coloured crush of people, such frenetic activity in public places, such an abundance of goods in shops and on street stalls. One tall, luxury store window decorated with a never-ending cascade of purple stars, is displaying a range of pink wedding dresses. With an unerring sense of direction, coolies speed their clients through the crowds and dense traffic. To the north, near the River Suzhou, there are still traces of the Japanese bombardment of seven years earlier. Endless lines of tricycles pass by piled high with flowers, leaving behind them in the damp air the fragrance of flowers starting to rot. Kim hails a rickshaw and asks to be taken to Shantung Road so that he can take a look at the Yellow Sky, Kruger's night-club. It is shut at this time of day, but its name figures in yellow letters on a big, red, glass lantern hanging over the door.

As night falls and the first city lights come on, Kim is back in his room adjusting the straps of the shoulder holster for his Browning, on top of a newly-acquired white dress-shirt. He slips on the safety catch and checks the magazine. He does not want any surprises.

Shortly afterwards, stuffed into an impeccable dinner-jacket, he is driving Lévy's black Packard to the Cathay Hotel, at the corner of Nanking Road and the docks. He does not have far to go. The lights of Bund Avenue are reflected in the river. Looking very elegant in her black silk *chipao*, Chin Jeng has got in beside him to be able to talk. What is this terrible danger she and her husband are in? How long have they been threatened, and why? Remembering Lévy's advice not to mention Kruger/Omar so as not to alarm Chen Jing, Kim gives only evasive answers.

'I'm a good friend of Michel's; we've shared many dangers and a few ideals, and that's why I'm here,' says Kim. 'He asked me to come, and to stick as close to you as a shadow, and that's what I'm going to do. But don't ask me anything more, Madame Chen, because that's all I know.'

He wants to change the subject, so he tells her he really likes the city and is thinking of staying on, working in one of Lévy's businesses. He says he would like to discuss the possibility one of these days with Charlie Wong, her husband's business associate, but Chen Jing does not seem in the least bit interested. She has taken the hand mirror out of her bag, and is staring intently into it as she uses the long lacquered nail of her small finger to tidy the red lipstick at the corners of her mouth. When she is satisfied, she puts the mirror away and says with a smile, staring out through the front windscreen: 'So you're not going to let me out of your sight for a minute.' Kim casts a sideways glance at her delicate profile, with its one slanted, falsely sleepy-looking eye beneath a heavy, unblinking lid. 'That's not what I said.' She replies: 'I suppose you'll let me go to the ladies' toilet on my own.'

Kim laughs and thinks: her sense of humour is too western, it does not suit a Chinese woman, but she is so young and beautiful she must like to flirt and make jokes, she probably learnt that from Michel . . . But as we shall see, Chen Jing is not flirting or joking. Just as they are reaching the hotel, she remembers she has some good news for him: her husband has phoned from Paris to tell her the first operation was a success. Kim is genuinely pleased, even though he detects a sense of barely-controlled impatience in her voice, as though Chen Jing wants to get her report over with and move on to something else.

The cocktail party in the Cathay Building has been organised by the leading industrialists and financiers in the French concession to honour the police and other officials of the sector. The police are well-known to be up to their necks in corruption, and the man who really gives the orders is a ruthless Chinese gangster by the name of Du Yuesheng, nicknamed in French Du 'Grandes-Oreilles' . . . but we'll hear more of him later. As I was saying, the party is being held in the luxurious Green Room on the eighth floor, and it has attracted the cream of the foreign colony in Shanghai. The intense fragrance of jasmine wafting in from the balcony mingles with a vast array of the most expensive perfumes worn by the ladies present. In one corner of the room is a small platform with a microphone. A young, slightly wall-eyed Chinese woman dressed entirely in green, and holding a long green cigarette holder with a green cigarette in her green-gloved hands, is singing 'I Get a Kick out of You' in a squeaky voice, accompanied on the piano by a negro in a white suit. An obese North American the worse for wear for drink staggers over to the singer and to general merriment offers her a glass of peppermint.

Chen Jing is obviously liked and admired by everyone. She replies politely to the enquiries after her husband's health, and presents Kim to some groups of people as Joaquim Franch, a Spaniard who is a close friend of Michel's, who has just arrived from Paris. Kim does not want to burden her too much with his presence, so he leaves her with her friends and goes off to the bar in search of a drink. He bumps into Wong and takes the opportunity to bring up the question of working in the textile business. Wong knows about his wish to do so, and suggests it will be best to wait for Lévy to return so they can discuss the matter together. There should be no problem, and he says Kim can count on him: 'Michel told me you have studied engineering, but that above all, you're like a brother to him.'

Some time later on that stifling July night, after noting that Chen Jing is on the far side of the room talking to two eastern dignitaries, and perhaps himself admiring her cold, distant beauty through the crowd, and while he is listening with half an ear to a song that brings back happy hours spent with your mother, we can imagine Kim making his excuses to Charlie Wong and going out onto the terrace, glass of whisky in hand, to look down on the Bund and the rest of this beautiful city beneath the star-filled sky, the port and the silent river where the reflections of neon light shine like bright glow-worms. He can feel the light pressure of the shoulder holster rubbing against his chest in a way that links him with a violent past and his solemn promise: to kill a man who does not deserve to live, and then rebuild his own life in this distant city. With a single shot, to rid himself of the pressure on his chest, and with it the sorrow weighing on his mind. This is a good place to do it, he tells himself, clutching the whisky in his hand as he leans against the window-frame in the magnificent Cathay tower. Encouraged by the music and the scent of jasmine, he thinks how good he feels, how young and full of life, how pleased he is with this latest twist of fate. He is sure his luck will change, and perhaps even sees himself as good-looking and elegant in his dinner jacket. This is a good opportunity, Kim, for you to pause and look back along the road we have travelled, that poor road of ours beset by traps and lies, at the end of which you have been fortunate enough to meet up with your old comrade Michel Lévy again. If you do that, you'll see that what you've left behind is not only one defeat after another, and untold lost illusions, not only all your dead comrades, but also all those who are yet to die, those intrepid and daring youths in Toulouse and elsewhere in the south of France who will cross the frontier once more, weapons in hand, with that same crazy determination that once drove you on. You'll see blood spilt in the past and in the future, the noble blood already coursing through the veins of others. You'll think of 'Denis' and his Carmen trying to find happiness in some corner of France, and remember Nualart, Betancort and Camps rotting in jail or perhaps already shot by firing-squad. You'll think of all the unrecorded, futile sacrifices, all that generosity and courage which in the end will not change anything or benefit anyone. And who knows, perhaps he will even remember me and all my hard work as a forger, poor Forcat, whose fingers are always stained with ink, a dead man who has returned to the city of dead men . . . But there are others who are even more desperate, Kim tells himself, those who have surrendered and now hope for nothing more than for time to pass and for the day to arrive when they are finally swallowed up by nothingness, they and all their future generations. Because if, like me, you knew what Kim was thinking that moment, you would realise he is thinking above all of those waiting for another chance: from the far side of the world, what Kim is trying to tell us is simply that we should not give in to despair, bad luck or illness, not even to the black smoke of that chimney. Life can sometimes be a heavy burden, but we have to deceive ourselves a little by nourishing some secret hope . . . All this is going through Kim's mind as he stands on the terrace of the Cathay Hotel, whisky glass in hand, peering down at Shanghai in darkness, and feeling the warm, damp breath of the city rising like steam from some sleepy tame beast, when suddenly he realises he has not seen Chen Jing for some time.

He thinks it unlikely that Kruger is at the reception, and even if he were, he would not be crazy enough to attack her with all these people around.

At that moment, he feels a hand on his shoulder, and hears a friendly greeting. It is Lambert, the garrulous French owner of several silk factories and stores. The two men were introduced earlier, and now he has come to strike up a conversation. They are soon joined by four other guests, one of whom cannot help commenting ironically on how devilishly lucky Michel Lévy is, being married to his golden-eyed Chinese wife who is not only young and beautiful but is also related to the Red general Chen Yi, said to be organising for a push with his Communist troops across Manchuria, then up the Yang-tze river to Shanghai. Kim realises a lot of the foreigners are worried about their firms and businesses in Shanghai: defeat for the Kuomintang and victory for the Communists could well mean all foreign concessions were abolished. But although the subject is of great interest to him, it's not that which captures his attention as much as a commentary that has nothing to do with this. It's made by one of the group, the North American who has had too much to drink and who earlier had been making fun of the Chinese singer. Sweaty and with a heavy cold, he digs his neighbour, an angular-faced man with straight black hair, in the ribs and says in a slurred voice from between curling lips:

'I bet while Lévy's in Paris to see if they can straighten his spine, and . . .' he adds with a cackle, 'his prick while they're about it, the little whore Chen Jing Fang is consoling herself in the arms of that sea captain, that damned Cantonese fellow, Su Tzu, or whatever he calls himself . . .'

This unexpected rudeness brings all other conversation to a halt. Kim is about to challenge him when the black-haired man to his right seizes the Yankee by his jacket lapels and growls at him:

'Stapleton,' he says, 'you're a liar and a drunkard. Either you take back what you said about that lady right now, or I swear I'll give you reasons to be sorry.'

Visibly quaking, Stapleton quickly mutters an apology and leaves the group, holding up his glass of whisky to the light and grimacing, as if he has seen a strange insect inside it. Shortly afterwards, the conversation lags and the group disintegrates, leaving Kim alone once more with Monsieur Lambert. For several minutes, he politely satisfies the other man's curiosity about the political situation in Spain, but he cannot get the drunken Yankee's insult out of his mind. Captain Su Tzu and Lévy's wife? Was their relationship public knowledge? Did Lévy know? As discreetly as he can, Kim tries to find out. The Frenchman tells him he has no idea whether there is any truth behind the rumour, but that it has been going the rounds of Shanghai.

Kim then hastens to ask Lambert who the man was who came so stoutly to madame Chen Jing's defence, although in his heart of hearts, thanks to the strange empathy he feels for the dark side of other people, he already knows what the Frenchman is going to say:

'His name is Omar Meiningen. He's a German who owns the Yellow Sky Club and two of the most select brothels in Shanghai,' Lambert tells him, adding in a friendly, conspiratorial way: 'They say he's a very determined and dangerous man, Monsieur, although they also say – especially the women – that he's a perfect gentleman. But I reckon he's a communist.'

2

I am not sure when Forcat's walks and visits to the port and Barceloneta became more frequent. Although Señora Anita sometimes accompanied him, he usually went alone, and I have no idea whom he met or how he managed it, but he never reappeared at the villa without some kilos of flour or rice, or a few litres of black market oil.

In early July, almost three months after her guest had installed himself in the villa, Señora Anita stopped drinking and smoking. At first she was very irritable and quarrelled with Susana all the time, and it seemed to me she was constantly avoiding Forcat's steady, cross-eyed gaze, but it was not long before her mood improved, and she was very affectionate with her daughter, attentive to Forcat, and even laughed at all the tricks the Chacón brothers employed to steal food from the market stall holders. It did not take us long to realise that this change was thanks to Forcat's good influence; shortly beforehand she had acquired the habit of buying a very cheap white wine she bought by the flask from the bar. Forcat called it 'rat-poison', and had refused to use it in the special stews he occasionally made for Susana. Then one fine day, the flask that always had pride of place on the dining-room table, and which the Chacón brothers and I were constantly being sent to refill in the Calle Cardoner bar, disappeared. We never saw it again. Forcat also helped her with the household chores; he changed the sheets on Susana's bed, raked the ashes from the stove and did the washing up, and whitewashed the garden walls. He encouraged Señora Anita to water the plants and look after them, and taught her to enjoy making a few cheap, simple meals. She seemed much happier, her behaviour more restrained: she was more ladylike, and took a lot more care over her way of dressing and walking. Despite this, whether she was drinking or not, she was still a target for the neighbourhood gossips, and a sarcastic comment was going the rounds that was said to have started with Doctor Barjau. Captain Blay loved it, perhaps because it infuriated his wife so much: 'Señora Anita may have stopped drinking, but the whore in her still likes a good suck'.

One afternoon I arrived at the villa earlier than usual. Susana was taking her siesta, and her mother had not yet got dressed for work. After looking outside and seeing that Finito and Juan were not there yet, she turned to me and asked:

'Daniel, sweetie, can you do me a favour?' She looked so nervous I was sure she was going to send me to the bar behind Forcat's back. 'I've run out of aspirin . . . the chemist won't have opened again yet. Could you go to the bar and see if they have any . . . and bring me half a litre of brandy while you're there? . . . No, no, just the aspirin.'

When I got back, Forcat was on the verandah, and Señora Anita was ready to go out. She was dressed in her old, provocative way: purple high-heeled shoes, fine black stockings, one of the soft-coloured pleated skirts she liked so much, a low-cut white blouse with a wide apple-green plastic belt. Her thick blonde hair, cut short and always tousled, emphasised her youthful appearance and her body's provocative vitality. There was a fleck of tobacco ash on her cheek close to her mouth, which made me think she must be smoking in secret, and Forcat would say something to her, but he didn't. She kissed her daughter on the forehead, picked up her bag and, before leaving, took two aspirin with a glass of fizzy water.

'Ever since I've stopped drinking I get headaches,' she said. 'My knee doesn't hurt any more, but my head does. What a bore! Do you think it's the water?'

Seated on the edge of the bed at Susana's feet, Forcat smiled faintly as he watched her drink. His long, stained hands lay on his knees as though he were a prisoner in handcuffs, but even so they did not look helpless or pathetic. There was always some force burning in them. He waited for her to finish, then said in his usual persuasive manner:

'You don't have the slightest headache. Your head thinks you've got one, that's all.'

Susana burst out laughing, then started to cough. Her mother, who had been just about to leave, put the glass and her bag on the round table and muttered: 'bastard'. Then she took off her shoes, pushed Susana over to the far side of the bed where Forcat was sitting, and lay down with her feet towards the top of the bed and her head in his lap. She took his right hand in hers, and pressed it to her forehead. She lifted it, pressed it down again, and gently repeated this movement several times, as if she were applying hot compresses. She closed her eyes and sighed with relief. Susana and I glanced at one another.

'I don't think this is the moment, Anita,' said Forcat.

'If I can't get rid of it, I won't be able to go to work,' she said. 'You've no idea how much it hurts.'

'It doesn't hurt, you'll see.' Forcat raised his hand and held it a few inches from her forehead. She tried to pull the hand down, but he fought her off. Since then I have often thought that his treatment depended not so much on the direct contact of his hands but in the current that flowed from them, the controlled heat or whatever his damaged skin transmitted to remove or ease the pain. This went on for about ten minutes, until it looked as though Señora Anita had fallen asleep. I opened my folder and checked my pencils, or at least I pretended to, because I did not want to miss a thing. I was intrigued above all by the space of an inch or so beneath the palm of Forcat's hand; I was trying to see if I could detect the current leaping from it, some spark or God knows what, because there was no doubt that this was the spot, the tiny gap between his hand and her forehead, where the miracle took place. Susana refused to look at her mother and made as though she was not interested, but deep down she disapproved of what was going on.

But after about ten minutes Señora Anita sat up, completely restored, and not in the least bit surprised; this could not have been the first time. 'You see,' she said, 'I feel much better.' She smoothed her curls down, put on her shoes, and picked up her bag. Then she reached over and quickly and spontaneously ruffled her guest's hair. She kissed Susana once more and sighed, and then suddenly, standing there in the middle of the verandah, with her bag over her shoulder, and staring into space, she burst into tears, even though she still had a smile on her face. At that moment I had no idea what was going on, but now I know she was overcome by one of the few moments of fullness that life can have offered her.

'Why are you crying, ma?' Susana said, kneeling up on the bed. Then she pleaded anxiously: 'Please, don't cry! Please!'

Señora Anita soon got over it. She said goodbye to us all and left in a hurry. But before she reached the corridor she came back, took Forcat by the hand and made him get up and quickly follow her through the dining-room. They rushed along the corridor until they reached the front door where – I think, I've always liked to think – she gave him a farewell kiss. I never saw it, but my memory of the scene is so vivid I usually forget I was not actually there: their mouths seeking each other out and colliding as the two of them stood entwined in the darkness of the hall.

A few hours later, after Susana had been served her big glass of milk and a roll and the Chacón brothers had called in, their pockets full of eucalyptus leaves and carrying bundles of comics and dog-eared novels tied up with string, we were led hand-in-hand by Forcat's cross-eyed gaze and bewitching voice out of the magical, silent verandah bathed in evening sunlight, up towards the bright terrace of Chen Jing Fang's penthouse apartment high above the quays and the River Huang-p'u.

3

Kim has been in Shanghai for three days when Michel Lévy rings from the Vautrin Clinic in Paris and has a lengthy conversation with his wife. Then he asks to speak to Kim, and Chen Jing passes him the phone out on the terrace. Kim is idly reading a newspaper under a parasol, and waits for her to withdraw to the living room before he speaks: *Bonjour*, old friend, how are you feeling? Excellent, says

Lévy, how about you? OK, no news as yet. I've got very good news, Kim: the first operation was a success, and I'm very hopeful. The second operation will be trickier, but my luck is in and I'm convinced everything will be all right and I'll soon be home. So tell me: how's that business of ours going? Did you do as I asked?

'Only partially,' says Kim. 'I have the book you wanted, but so far I've only got Kruger identified. I can't finish the business without being very careful.'

'You need to hurry,' Lévy says. 'Kruger is smart, and could smell a rat.'

'I'll run that risk,' Kim says. 'I'll tell you what the problem is, captain. Now more than ever I have to be sure of what I do. I have to stay in the shadows and leave no traces, because as I told you, once I've got rid of that fiendish torturer, I want to stay here and bring my wife and daughter out here too . . . That was what we agreed, remember? It would be very different if after I gave Kruger his just deserts I caught a plane and said goodbye to Shanghai forever. But I don't want to compromise my future or that of my family. I have to think up a plan, seize my chance, and then make sure no one suspects me, right?'

'You need to be cautious but quick,' replies Lévy. 'This can't wait. And keep a close watch on Chen Jing, because I don't trust that son of a bitch with her . . . I'll phone again. Goodbye and good luck.'

'To you too, captain. Good luck.'

As he hangs up, Chen Jing emerges onto the terrace once more, followed by her faithful servant carrying a tray of drinks.

'Would you like some jasmine tea, Monsieur Franch?' the young Chinese woman asks with a smile. 'Or would you prefer a dry martini? I'm very good at making them. My husband says mine are the best in all Shanghai . . . apart from a very special one he himself prepares, that is.'

'I'm sure Michel prefers the ones you make,' says Kim. 'By the way, are you going out tonight?'

'I'm afraid I am, Monsieur. Sorry.'

'Don't say that. It's always a pleasure to accompany you.'

Chen Jing's golden eyes smile discreetly, her eyelids opening and shutting at a calculated, almost mechanical, rate. This measured movement, the sensuality and the silkiness of her eyelids, fascinate Kim.

Escorting Chen Jing is taking up much more time than he had imagined, and in little more than a fortnight he has come to know Shanghai's genteel night-life, and the whole gamut of picturesque Western and Asian figures represented there. The society pages of the *North China Daily* and the *Shanghai Mercury* regularly report the presence of Mrs Chen Jing Fang and Mr Franch at parties and receptions. Chen Jing also likes to meet her friends at fashionable night-clubs such as the Casanova, Del Monte, the Little Club or Ciro's. Occasionally she gets a call from a married couple to have dinner together and then go to the cinema or dancing, but she almost always prefers to go out alone – invariably escorted by Kim, with whom she jokes about a couple that is already being talked about in Shanghai more than her husband would have liked.

One night, during a crowded reception on the shores of the Western Lake in Hangzhow, Kim is chatting with Charlie Wong and his wife. He has lost sight of Chen Jing for several minutes when all of a sudden over a sea of heads he spots Kruger talking to her beneath an illuminated silver fir. Kim pushes his way forcefully through the guests, and as he draws near notices Kruger has seen him too: unhurriedly but deliberately, the German bows and takes his leave, kissing the beautiful Chinese woman's hand, then turning on his heel and vanishing into the crowd.

'Do you know that man?' Kim says offhandedly, offering her a cigarette. 'He seems a pleasant sort.'

'Who doesn't know Omar in Shanghai?' she says. 'But I've only spoken to him a couple of times. He came over to say hello and ask after my husband ... Why do you ask? Have I been in great danger without realising it?' There's an ironic gleam in her eyes.

Rather than get caught up explaining, Kim prefers to make excuses.

'I'm sorry, but since you are alone, anyone who approaches you rouses my suspicions.'

'You're afraid of leaving me alone in the midst of all these people,

Monsieur Franch?' the young Chinese woman says with a smile. 'You needn't worry, I'm surrounded by friends . . . And now perhaps you'd be kind enough to go to the bar and bring me a glass of champagne?'

Kim smiles back at her, and gently touches her elbow.

'It will be a pleasure to accompany you to the bar and make all the men jealous . . . Look, there are Wong and Soo Lin with the Duprezes.'

'That'll be fun,' Chen Jing sighs. 'But you're in charge. This empty-headed Chinese girl solemnly swears not to move so much as a yard away from her guardian angel . . . unless that is, Madame Duprez insists on telling me for the millionth time about her famous night of passion with Jean Gabin and his little dog Lulu.'

'You're a wicked woman,' says Kim with a smile.

'Do you really think so? I take that as a compliment.'

'Why's that?'

'Because I've always wanted to be a wicked woman.'

In her frequent visits to nightclubs, Kim is relieved to note that Chen Jing has not once been to Omar's Yellow Sky Club. He wants to get to know the ex-Nazi's lair on his own, if he has a free evening.

He gets his chance one stifling Sunday evening. He is about to sit out on Chen Jing's terrace when Deng comes up and says that Madame sends her apologies for not joining him at dinner: she has had to lie down because she has a dreadful headache and is not thinking of going out, so she begs the gentleman to use the time as he thinks best.

And so after dinner, ceremoniously served by the Chinese servant, Kim hires a coolie to take him to the Yellow Sky Club on Shantung Road. The club is full of people, and is decorated in yellow and red, with a gleaming dance floor and a gaming room. Kim orders a whisky, and stands at the bar observing the customers while the orchestra plays 'Siboney' and a few couples dance wrapped in each other's arms. On each table bordering the dance floor there's a red lamp and a long-stemmed yellow rose in a slender glass vase. Kim is also struck by the sight of a very elegant young Chinese woman, with slanted eyes and pretty legs, sitting on her own. She is dressed entirely in red, in a tight-fitting *chipao* with a high collar and slits up the sides. She sits looking down at her bright scarlet nails in a bored fashion, smoking a red-coloured cigarette and has a redcurrant drink in front of her. From behind her at the roulette wheel in the gaming room there come shouts of joy, a gentle explosion of delight and surprise.

Then he sees Omar standing calm and smiling by the dance floor, talking to some customers at a table. Kim can get a better view of him here than at the Cathay Hotel or in Suzhou. The man who now calls himself Omar must be thirty-eight or forty years old. He is very tall, with a thin, aquiline nose, and a searching gaze; beneath the empty smile there is a bitter twist to his full, well-defined mouth. His manners are gentle and courteous. As he passes by the Chinese girl dressed all in red, Omar picks up the yellow rose on her table. He smiles as he lifts it to his nose, kisses her on the cheek, and bows goodbye to her, carrying off the rose in both hands. He glances at his watch and makes for a small blue door inlaid with ivory and lacquer at the far end of the bar. In the second before Omar shuts the door behind him, Kim glimpses the bottom steps of a well-lit staircase.

Kim thinks Omar has not seen him, or has not wanted to, but that he must know who he is. He has accompanied Chen Jing to so many receptions and public events in Shanghai he must have realised he was acting as her bodyguard.

When half an hour goes by and Omar does not reappear, Kim asks the barman if the night-club owner is coming back, because he has an important matter to discuss with him. The barman, a moon-faced Chinese man with a straggly moustache, tells him his boss has retired to his rooms and given an order not to be disturbed. His rooms? Kim asks. Does Monsieur Omar live here? Yes indeed, Monsieur, his apartment is above the club . . . That's very practical, says Kim, although I suppose he must have a separate entrance from the street. Of course, Monsieur: in King Loong, a back alleyway. But your glass is empty, Monsieur, would you like another whisky?

Kim is about to reply when from behind his back a falsely cordial voice pre-empts him:

'Perhaps monsieur prefers company.'

Kim turns slowly around and finds himself face to face with a short fat Chinese man wearing a light-blue suit, black shirt and white tie.

'I prefer whisky,' says Kim.

The barman serves him, but the stranger insists:

'I am sorry to bother you, but are you the honourable Monsieur Franch?'

'Yes.'

'My boss Du Yuesheng would like a word with you. It would be an honour if you would accept a drink from him.'

'Talk about what?' says Kim. 'I don't know him.'

'Have you never heard of Du "Grandes-Oreilles?"'

'I have heard something of him. All right, what do you want?'

Still smiling, the Chinese man bows and says:

'Follow me, please.'

He walks round the dance floor and crosses the gaming-room, with Kim close behind him. Du 'Grandes-Oreilles' is sitting at a table with his back to the wall in a part of the club between the gambling tables and another crowded bar. He is wearing a spotless white suit, a white hat, and a salmon-coloured tie. His prominent, aggressive chin contrasts vividly with sly, hooded eyelids and his thin-lipped mouth. He is holding a glass of champagne frosted with cold. His hands look like two large hot-water bottles. Seated next to him, hat brim pulled down over half his flat, expressionless face, a Filipino bodyguard is busy plucking the petals off the yellow rose from the vase on the table. Kim sees at once he is a professional *tufei*, a hired gunman. The first man sits on the other side of Du Yuesheng, but Kim remains standing, glass of whisky in hand.

'It's a pleasure to meet you, Monsieur Franch,' says Du. 'Will you not sit at your humble servant's table? You look tired. Perhaps you haven't had much sleep lately.'

'Perhaps.'

'I understand it was Monsieur Lévy who invited you to Shanghai, and that you came on one of his boats.' Du 'Grandes-Oreilles' smiles thoughtfully then goes on: 'That's rather strange, don't you think? You could have travelled much more comfortably by plane...'

'I get airsick.'

'Is that so, Monsieur?'

'I could swear to it.'

'Are you aware that some of your honourable friend Monsieur Lévy's boats are used to traffick arms to the communists who want to take over Shanghai?'

'I have no idea what you're talking about.'

'Oh, I'm so sorry. Perhaps I'm not making myself understood, I have such poor French,' says the Chinese gangster, lowering his gaze. Kim guesses that beneath his fine clothes, his refined manners and his smooth pink skin, Du 'Grandes-Oreilles' is probably a lot older than he looks. 'But your French is not perfect either, is it, Monsieur? I've heard you aren't French, is that right?'

'Yes, that's right. I am Catalan and Spanish, but believe me I am heartily sick of being both those things. So you see, I have little patience left, especially when it comes to a thug like you, dressed up like an old turtle. What do you want?'

The insult has no effect on Du Yuesheng's porcelain smile. He sips his champagne and replies:

'Don't be so impulsive, my friend. May I ask you a question? What brings you to Shanghai?'

'If I say I've come to buy a hat, like Shanghai Lily in 1932, you won't believe me.'

'You have a strange sense of humour,' says Du 'Grandes-Oreilles', still smiling broadly. 'But we ought to understand each other. Come now... won't my honourable friend sit at my table and share a glass of champagne with me?'

'I like to drink alone.'

'We will overlook your lack of courtesy. But anyway, I would like to do you a favour.'

'What kind of favour?'

'I want to tell you to leave Shanghai.'

'Don't even dream of it.'

'Why not, Monsieur? What kind of talk is that?' Du is still beaming. 'It's good to dream. I recommend it.'

'I never daydream.'

'I don't believe it. You wouldn't be in Shanghai otherwise. Well, at least you'll dine with me, won't you? We have snake soup, lotus shoots and *ju lai*. Do you know what that is?'

'Pig's tongue. No thank you.'

'I can see you've made great progress with our language ... Well then, would you at least accept a word of advice, monsieur?' His voice has suddenly become harsh.

'Don't bother.'

'I should warn you: you are looking for trouble, Monsieur.'

'I never look for trouble,' Kim replies coldly, 'but if I find it, let me warn you I don't let go.'

The orchestra has launched into 'Poppy', and all of a sudden, from the distant reaches of his mind, Kim recalls your mother dancing in his arms, spinning round slowly, her head resting languidly on his shoulder as if asleep. This was her favourite song, which she used to hum like a magic charm against adversity and ill omens. Du is watching him closely and when he speaks his voice is soft once more:

'I'll tell you what you are going to do, Monsieur Franch. Tomorrow you are going to board a plane and return to France via Japan.'

'I've already told you, planes make me feel sick.'

'Take a boat then. There are a thousand ways to leave Shanghai monsieur, the important thing is that you take the first step, and not have someone push you,' Du smiles so broadly his eyes almost disappear. 'Do I make myself clear?'

'Why are you so keen to see me go, Du?'

'Let's just say there are too many communists in Shanghai.'

'Is that what Omar thinks?'

'I have no idea what that honourable gentleman thinks,' says Du, his smile wiped away. 'He is not my friend.'

'Is that so?'

'You can ask him.'

'In that case, I've been misinformed.'

'That's right,' says Du. 'Well, Monsieur, what do you say? Will you take heed of advice?'

'I have other plans. And they don't include wasting my time with people like you,' says Kim. And he adds: '*Jia xi zhen zu.*'

This is a phrase used in China when someone is trying to 'pull the wool over your eyes'.

'*Chang shou,*' says Du. 'May your life be a long one, monsieur.'

Kim gives the gangster's two bodyguards a last, hard look, turns on his heel and goes back to the bar through the gaming-room and round the dance floor, where he enjoys the last few bars of 'Poppy' and imagines the elusive, indelible perfume of your mother's blonde hair. He pays for his drinks and leaves the Yellow Sky Club.

He decides to walk home, and by the time he arrives it is half past two in the morning. Chen Jing has already given him the key, so there is no need for him to awaken Deng, who as he does every night has left the lights on in the living-room and the terrace. While he is undressing in his room, Kim thinks about what Du 'Grandes-Oreilles' had said: what did his threat mean? Who and what was behind it?

It is still very hot, so before he goes to bed Kim decides to take a shower. Then he puts on a dressing-gown and goes out onto the terrace to smoke a last cigarette. He hears a noise behind him, and when he turns round sees Deng standing there silently and respect-fully, uncertain of whether to speak.

'Does Monsieur need anything . . . ?' the faithful servant eventu-ally says.

Kim studies him. He asks after his mistress, and Deng tells him she has been asleep ever since he went out.

'Did she have dinner?' Kim asks.

'No, Monsieur, she did not want anything to eat.'

Deng still has his gaze fixed on the floor. It seems as though he wants to speak further, but in the end withdraws without another word.

Kim sleeps badly, and wakes at dawn. From his window he sees a huge red sun rise out of the sea. He drinks tea in the kitchen, then thinks he must have left his cigarettes on the terrace the night before, so goes out to look for them. They are not there, and are not in his room either. As he comes and goes, he crosses the spacious living-room four times. Each time, he stops a few seconds to look round at the plush sofas with their silk cushions, the grand piano, the big display case with its collection of fans, and jade and glass figurines, the shiny green plants and the tall curtains. He has a vague notion that there is something new in the room, a furtive presence lurking close by him that he has not yet been able to uncover, a definite sense that there is a new object somewhere. The piano lid is open, and the keyboard is uncovered, its eloquent silence seeming to promise to reveal the secret . . .

Kim's heart senses it before he is conscious of it. He has not yet discovered the exact focus of his concern, but he knows intuitively he will not miss the sign, perhaps because this time it is more than simply an omen or a danger signal, it is the expression of a feeling. Then there it is, on the piano – the long-stemmed yellow rose which was not there when he came in the night before. The beauty and dazzling colour it displayed on the table in the Yellow Sky Club is fading, as it droops over in the slender crystal glass as though to gaze at itself in the polished surface of the piano, the last drops of its fragrance and mystery about to fall.

4

The night and the fragrance of the rose had infiltrated into the verandah without us realising it, so I got up to switch on the light. It was not the blue rose of forgetfulness, friends, if only it had been. No, it was the yellow rose of disenchantment . . . all at once Forcat interrupted his story, as if the bright electric light had cut the thread of his recollections. He got up from the bed, and paced head down for a while with that Fu Manchu look of his, hands hidden in his kimono sleeves. Then he patted Susana's head and disappeared into the garden.

It was not long before he returned. He stood in the doorway, hands behind his back, and told me to switch off the light. I did, and then he came in, hands held high with his palms bathed in a white glow, suspended in the darkness as though they were someone else's.

'I want it too!' Susana cried. 'Me too!'

'Open your hand.' When she did so, Forcat carefully placed three glow-worms on her palm. 'Do you want to be a ghost? Rub them very gently on your face like this, and you'll become a ghost for a few minutes.'

'Only for a few minutes?'

'All good things must come to an end.'

A short while later, Susana's face emerged from the darkness like a luminous mask, and Forcat went out into the kitchen, leaving the two of us together. Señora Anita was about to return from the cinema, and he wanted to surprise her with another of his special dishes.

'Come here,' Susana whispered, kneeling on the bed. 'Bring that silly face of yours over here. Come on, don't be scared, sit next to me...'

I sat on the bed and she rubbed the glow-worms quickly on my face, then she undid my shirt and I could feel the cold worms tickling as she pressed them against me. She unbuttoned her nightdress, and held her strange phosphorescent fingers over her heart, leaving fleeting traces of light. She was still looking at me as she pushed her knees forward on the bed and arched her back as she continued to rub her own chest under the material. My face was next to hers, and as the ghostly phosphorescence faded it was as though I was being spurred on to act under cover of some kind of disguise, anonymity or impunity. I could hear her rapid breathing and my own, as I stared in fascination at her luminous breast, but could scarcely make out what she said:

'Would you like to kiss me...? If you weren't so worried about my microbes, you could, you know. I'm sure you'd like to, dummy that you are. But just a quick one... Answer me! You're such a dolt!'

A thousand times I have relived that phosphorescent moment, that passion in the darkness, with its morbid combination of suppressed sexuality, mortal illness, fervour and timidity, and I am always filled with the same remorse, the same doubt: I am unsure whether it was Susana who would only let me brush her lips, or if it was me who was afraid to go any further. Of course I wanted to kiss her, to strip her naked, to caress her breasts and her burning thighs; I was even willing to be infected with the microbes in her saliva and her hot breath . . . But as all this rushed through my mind I again lost precious seconds, and I held back. She noticed at once, and pushed me away.

'Fine,' she said. 'Now go away.' She dodged back under the sheets. The few remaining streaks of light on her face and hands soon faded altogether.

'How little it lasts,' I said, to say something.

'Yes, hardly at all.'

'Tomorrow, if you like, I can look for more glow-worms in the garden and we can paint ourselves again . . .'

'Yes, tomorrow,' she interrupted. 'But for now switch the light on and go home.'

5

Occasionally I had heard Captain Blay speak of his true, frustrated ambition: to be an expert pickpocket, one of those who ply their trade on trams and in the metro with such stealth and skill they make a real art of it. He said he still felt he had a certain tactile memory in his fingers, a dormant nostalgia for leather wallets or sateen linings, because when he was a young man he had received theoretical and practical lessons from Doña Conxa's first boy-friend, a sly youngster from Murcia who lived in the neighbourhood for a while, until in the end the Captain pinched his girl-friend rather than his wallet.

As so often, I only half-believed his story, but one hot, windy morning as I was wearily trudging after him around Can Compte with the signatures folder under my arm, I suddenly had the chance to see him demonstrate his capabilities. That day the Captain was wearing fresh bandages, and his high, pointed head, with its stiff hairs poking out of the crown, looked like a huge parsnip. I do not know why, but perhaps to add a romantic touch to his ramshackle disguise as an accident victim, for a couple of days he had been wearing one arm in a sling made from an old silk scarf. Thanks to this deception, his calamitous figure regained a semblance of the decorum and elegance he must have shown on the Ebro front, in the days when his intelligence, sense of responsibility and gallantry were all still intact. We had reached the far end of Calle de la Legalidad, where the streetlamps had been smashed and the street sign was illegible. The Captain waited for me to catch up with him, rested his hand on my shoulder, and stood there silently for a while listening to the sound of the wind in the palm trees. At that moment, a car braked sharply alongside us. The driver stuck his head out of the window, and once he had recovered from the shock of seeing such an outlandish figure, asked the Captain if Calle de la Legalidad was anywhere near. He was a tubby, snub-nosed fellow with thick lips and black hair slicked down with brilliantine. He was wearing an extremely elegant jacket that looked more like a military tunic, with square shoulders and big buttons. His shirt was undone, and revealed a hairy chest, together with a gleaming row of fountain pens in his inside pocket. The Captain said we were in the street the driver was looking for, but I was surprised to hear him say this in Catalan. It was the first time I had ever heard him use his native tongue:

'*Justament ens trobem en el carrer que busca, senyor, és aquest...*'

The man cut him short:

'I don't speak that mongrel language ... speak to me in Spanish, won't you?'

'*Què diu, senyor?*'

'Reply in Spanish when you're spoken to!' He looked at the Captain's arm in a sling, the threadbare pyjamas and the raincoat, the bandages and the dark glasses, and asked mockingly:

'Where on earth have you escaped from looking like that? An operating theatre or an asylum?'

'*No n'has de fotre res, gamarús.*'

Both the Captain and I had realised we were talking to someone who did not and would not understand a word of Catalan. The driver pulled on his handbrake and rolled the window down the whole way. He insisted:

'Speak to me in Spanish, I tell you! Or you'll soon see what's what! Come on now, where is that blasted Calle de la Legalidad?'

Captain Blay smiled through the bandages in a friendly way, and leaned respectfully into the car window. I soon realised what he was up to. It took me a few seconds, but then I recognised the alarm signals: a nervous twitch of the head, a clearing of the throat that usually preceded a moment of deep thought, then a tensing of his muscles or even a creaking of bones I sometimes thought I could detect, as if when the old lunatic straightened his back, the sound of his vertebrae popping warned me he was about to commit another of his follies. I never really knew what got into the Captain, especially in the most difficult situations. Was it a strictly irrational impulse, the devil he had inside him, or some kind of mental hangover from defeat, the last angry gasp of a spirit of revenge that no longer made any sense? Whenever it happened, I merely stood by him, silent and expectant. Protected behind his glasses, the Captain was concentrating on the man's chest: if there are all these pens in one pocket, he must have been thinking, then his wallet has to be in the other one.

'Yes, sir, you're quite right,' the Captain began in a humble tone. 'The thing is, I speak Spanish so badly. And I don't just mean the accent, because I could never speak it like a gentleman from Madrid . . . It's the syntax that fools me, the natural fluidity of the language . . . But what an idiot I am! Pay no attention . . . !'

'That's quite enough of that! If you know, tell me where Calle de la Legalidad is for heaven's sake, you old fool, and then go to hell!'

'Of course I know! Take this street here on the right until you come to a square. Then it's right again until you reach the Avenida General Franco, what used to be called the Diagonal, right again and you'll see the statue to Cinto Verdaguer – he was a separatist poet who wrote in Catalan, of little merit as you know . . .'

'Come on, come on, don't make me waste any more time!'

'Well from there it's straight on. Don't stop until you're beyond Pedralbes, where you'll see a sign for San Baudilio, in other words Sant Boi, then carry on another couple of miles and you'll be in Calle de la Legalidad, you can't miss it . . .'

While he was giving these directions, the Captain propped his arm in a sling on the car window, and rested the other on the bonnet. Then he started to drum his fingers on the bodywork. It was like the sound of raindrops, and the driver looked down to see what was going on. That was enough for the Captain. The lifeless hand in the sling suddenly shot out to the right side of the driver's jacket. His first and middle fingers were like a bird's beak, and in the blink of an eye they removed a smooth brown leather wallet and transferred it to his deep raincoat pocket. The Captain insisted:

'No, really, you can't miss it.'

'You see how you can speak properly if you want to?' The driver joked, turning the key in the engine. 'The problem is you're so ungrateful you refuse to, dammit.'

'The problem is I'm so absent-minded, your honour,' the Captain cravenly apologised. 'Who wouldn't want to speak the glorious imperial tongue? I love languages anyway: English, French . . .'

'We have more than enough with our own!' the man said, struggling to get the car started. 'You still talk it like a foreigner, but with time you'll lose the accent.'

'With time Sir, yes, that's what I hope,' the Captain agreed in all humility. 'We do what we can, Sir. With time. And don't forget: straight on until you reach Sant Boi. You can't miss it.'

'You seem like a smart fellow, grandad. Before I go I'd like you to do me another favour,' he said, making fun of the poor man. 'Yes, I really like you, you idiot. So come on, repeat after me in Spanish: "sixteen judges are eating liver . . ." Got it? Go on, as fast as you can.'

'It's a patriotic verse by Joan Maragall.'

'I don't know about that. Go on, say it.'

'It loses a lot in translation. It's about a man who was hanged up in Montserrat, where the Black Virgin is . . .'

The driver gave an impatient laugh. The car engine finally started.

'Come on, say it in Spanish for me, you clown!'

'Yes sir, whatever you say. "Sixteen judges are eating the liver of a hanged man." Maragall has another good one. It goes: "*elàstics blaus suats fan fàstic.*" It's dedicated to the glorious German army.'

'Translate it into a proper language, ninny.'

'Sweaty blue braces fan . . . tastic.'

'You're really funny for a Catalan. Remember to keep practising, you old fool.'

He laughed asthmatically, lifted his foot from the brake, and the car sped off. Before he had reached the end of Calle de la Legalidad and turned the corner, Captain Blay had seized my hand and we scurried off in the opposite direction. 'We've sent him to the back of beyond,' he chuckled.

There were 150 pesetas in the wallet. After making me promise I wouldn't spend it all at the pictures or the billiard tables, the Captain gave me fifty. 'Buy some more drawing paper,' he said, 'and give the rest to your mother, she needs it.'

That evening I told my mother what had happened. She said she felt sorry for the Captain, and that she would pray to the Virgin to give him good health, a clear mind, and a long life. She also said she disapproved of what we had done. Sending the poor man so far out of his way, that was cruel. But she kept the pesetas.

CHAPTER SEVEN

I

I was tormented by the memory of the glow-worms rubbed on Susana's skin and the scarlet stain on her teeth, by the way the poisonous flower of her mouth opened the day she had pretended to be dead. I felt a growing sense of shame and regret. Then a fortnight later I got the chance to put things right.

That summer, Forcat could only have left the villa five or six times on Sundays, always with Señora Anita and always, apart from the first time, in the morning. On Sundays they would go to the matinee performance at the Roxy, and during the week they would often go to the Baños Orientales on Barceloneta beach. They would return with a watermelon or a kilo or two of mussels or fresh pasta, and Forcat would make a mayonnaise and then appear ceremoniously on the verandah carrying a huge dishful of steamed mussels. Susana would call to the Chacón brothers out in the street, and we would all sit round the bed for the feast.

It was Forcat who insisted her mother should never leave Susana on her own in the house again. Whenever they were going out, they would tell me the evening before and I would stay with her, making my excuses to Captain Blay.

One Sunday when just the two of us were in the villa, after tearing up yet another of my drawings because she did not like it, Susana kneeled up on the bed and suggested we go and search Forcat's room.

'You should put some shoes on,' I grumbled as we made our way up the spiral staircase to the first floor.

Forcat's room was small and dark, but it was scrupulously clean and tidy. He made his own bed, and cleaned the tiny bathroom we could see through an open door. On his bedside table were a glass of water covered by a coffee saucer, aspirin, a clean ashtray, and a packet of Ideales. We had never seen Forcat smoking in the house or garden, much less on the verandah in front of Susana. His old cardboard suitcase was under the bed.

'Should we open it and see what's inside?' asked Susana.

I pulled the case out, and Susana squatted beside me and pushed open the catches. A strange vegetable perfume, the unmistakable smell of Forcat's hands, filled the air. Inside was a jumble of cuttings from French newspapers, maps and travel agency brochures, cheap music sheets, a dog-eared book that has lost its covers called *The Fight for Bread*, record sleeves with songs in English and French. And tucked in one corner, wrapped in a yellow shammy leather cloth inside an old black jersey, was a small, snub-nosed revolver, so new and shiny it did not look real.

'It's a toy,' said Susana.

'It's not,' I said, weighing it in my hand. 'I wonder if it's loaded?'

Susana snatched it from me, wrapped it quickly in the leather cloth and jersey, and put it carefully back in the suitcase. Then she started examining the newspaper cuttings, most of which were in French, from Paris or Shanghai. There was one of a cyclist with an enormous nose – Fausto Coppi. It showed him reaching the top of a mountain pass, struggling through a blizzard with two inner tubes across his chest, his face streaked with mud. He loomed out of the mist like a ghost. Then beneath a moth-eaten scarf we found a passport with a photo of Forcat, but bearing the name José Carbó Balaguer. Inside it there was a folded piece of paper with a note signed by Kim: 'I owe my friend F. Forcat the amazing sum of one hundred and fifty francs (150F), a glass of brandy and a kick up the arse for having lent money to a rogue like me, Joaquim Franch. Toulouse, May 1941'. There was also an old, stained pencil box with a few foreign coins and a Paris metro ticket. No letters, no photographs apart from the exhausted cyclist . . . We were disappointed and a bit confused. Hadn't Forcat told us he never carried a gun? Could these be the only belongings of a man who had travelled the world, a cultured and well-read man like him? Forcat the transatlantic adventurer, as Captain Blay had called him. All he had was one book, and that looked as if it was from the year dot.

What we found most extraordinary were three small vermouth bottles in a corner of the case. They had corks in their tops and were full of a cloudy, greenish liquid. Susana pulled the cork out of one, and as we both sniffed at it, our cheeks almost brushed each other. The warm fragrance of her hair and her feverish breath mingled with the unmistakable smell of Forcat's hands.

'What can it be?' said Susana, grimacing with distaste as she quickly put the stopper back in the bottle. On a sudden impulse I had put my arm round her waist, and when she turned to look at what I was doing, she saw something behind my back that she had not seen until then, but which completely changed her expression: through the open bathroom door she could see her mother's frilly dressing-gown hanging on the wall next to Forcat's black kimono and his pyjamas.

For a few seconds she stared at her mother's bath-robe without moving.

'Put them back and let's get out of here,' I said, to make her return the other bottle she was still holding. 'They'll be here soon, and they'll catch us . . .'

'So what?' she said. 'I couldn't care less.'

She started to rummage in the bottom of the suitcase, then all of a sudden screamed and pulled her hand out as if she had been bitten by a hidden insect. A thick jet of red blood spurted from the tip of her little finger.

'Suck it,' I said while I searched the case bottom. I found a razor blade that had come out of its wrapping. 'Look, this is what did it. I'll put some alcohol on it.'

'What for? I just wish I could bleed to death,' Susana said, squeezing her finger as though to get all the blood out. 'I wish I could.'

'Don't say that.' I quickly wrapped her finger in the hem of her nightdress; we were both still kneeling on the floor by the bed, and she turned to look again at her mother's dressing-gown in the bathroom. The blood was seeping through her nightdress, so I took her by the hand, unwrapped the finger and put it in my mouth before she had time to react. It was only a moment: she glanced at me in surprise and while I was sucking the blood, ran the other four fingers of her trembling, feverish hand gently down my cheek, in what I desperately wanted to see as a caress. My fear of contagion made me close my eyes, but I began to taste her warm, sticky blood more and more in my mouth and my mind: I did not care if I died of tuberculosis just as long as she looked at me like that, and I could feel her burning fingers touching my skin. All too soon though, she pulled her hand away and said:

'What are you doing? Do you want to get infected?'

'I couldn't care less.'

'Liar.'

'I swear it.'

'Well I care . . .' She stood up and rushed out of the room. I shut the suitcase, pushed it back under the bed and followed Susana down the stairs, with the faint taste of her hot, sweet blood still in my mouth, together with the benign fever of desire, her need of affection, my own terrors and fears.

2

She is lying on her back in bed, with her left arm behind her head. Her pale face is turned towards me but her eyes are indifferent, distant. She is wearing a yellow carnation in her hair, and the black felt cat is sitting upright, on guard behind her. The sky-blue eiderdown hangs with studied, romantic carelessness off the edge of the bed and reaches the foot of the cast-iron stove where the eucalyptus leaves are steaming. In the middle ground is the huge verandah window, with beyond it the weeping willow in the garden, and even further off and higher up, looming over this cluttered and crowded scene, the murderous chimney is spewing out its black, pestilential cloud over the glass house where the sick girl lies prostrate . . .

This was the naïve, ghastly drawing I finally completed, which Forcat approved after suggesting a few changes: the carnation went from yellow to red, and Susana's deathly brow, her colourless cheeks and bare feet took on a delicate ivory sheen. I had not succeeded in showing fear in those pretty, sometimes so lively, eyes of hers, and I was glad of it. Susana barely gave the drawing a second glance.

The Captain however was very pleased with it, and quickly put it in his folder along with the protest letter and the signatures. So far we had only managed to collect fourteen, but he was confident that my drawing showing the poor, suffering, consumptive girl would stir people's hearts and appeal to their solidarity.

I started work at once on the second drawing. I saw it as very similar to the first one except for the figure of Susana in bed: she insisted on being portrayed with a dreamy, faraway look on her face, and wearing the tight-fitting green *chipao*. But I could not get her posture or the exotic dress right; I would start the drawing and then tear it up, either because she did not like it, or because I didn't. And yet as I drew the first hesitant outline of this silk tunic, without adding much colour, with its high neck and somehow untidy shape, with stitches missing and folds in the skirt, Susana began to look like a real Chinese girl. There was something indefinable about the drawing that pleased me, more the result of a chance combination of colours than any talent of mine as an observer, or any manual skill. Now the slimy froth pouring from the mouth of the chimney, the greeny-black smoke hanging over Susana's head really looked as though they were threatening the dreams of far-off lands and oriental silks suggested by the posture and dress of the consumptive girl.

'The folds of the skirt aren't right,' she protested yet again when I showed her the drawing. 'You're spoiling the dress, idiot. They should be a bit rounded at the ends . . .'

'No they shouldn't,' I said. 'I've seen them in films and that's how they are. Ask Forcat.'

She threw the sheet of paper at me, soaked her handkerchief with cologne and rubbed her chest and face with it. Then she picked up the pack of cards and started a game of solitaire on the parcheesi board on her lap.

'He's taking his time,' she said after a while. 'The hotter it gets, the longer he sleeps his siesta. Don't you think we should wake him? Why don't you go up and look?'

'One day he'll get annoyed.'

'Go on, leave your pencils and fetch him,' Susana insisted. 'It's very late, he's probably still flat out . . . Please, Danny.'

Forcat's bedroom door was never closed, but I always knocked and waited outside. Sometimes he was sleeping stretched out on his back in his underpants, his mysterious hands calmly crossed on his stomach. But on this occasion, he was already up and just out of the shower, wrapped in his amazing black kimono and wearing his wooden-soled sandals as he slowly brushed his lank black hair and contemplated himself in the wardrobe mirror.

'We thought you must still be asleep . . .'

'Who thought that?' he asked. 'Susana or you?'

'Well . . . both of us.'

'That's good.'

He threw the brush on the bed, turned to me with a smile, and put his big, warm hand on my shoulder to guide me towards the spiral staircase. I walked down in front of him, then we crossed the dark corridor towards the sunny verandah. When we came in, Susana was lying back plucking her eyebrows with a pair of tweezers, and staring into a hand mirror. At that moment the clock in the dining-room began to strike the hour, and she sprang upright in bed, threw down the tweezers and the mirror, and stared intently at the photograph of her father on the bedside table. Before Forcat took us back to the flaming dawn staining the river Huang-p'u and the windows of the Bund with blood, and illuminating a small yellow rose in Chen Jing Fang's living-room, Susana closed her eyes and sat completely immobile for a few seconds in front of Kim's portrait. As the six chimes of the clock died away, our cross-eyed storyteller cleared his throat to speak, then also sat for a while in silent contemplation of the rose.

3

Standing by the piano, Kim picks up the rose and stares at it, as if he could find the key to the enigma in its sagging petals and dying fire. The night before, this rose had been adorning one of the tables in the Yellow Sky Club, and it must have been left here in its glass when he was already asleep.

He questions the *Ayi* without success. Deng also claims to know nothing, but he cannot meet Kim's gaze, and replies timidly and hesitantly that perhaps it was the Siamese maid who put it there . . . Kim suddenly seizes him by the lapels.

'Listen to me, Deng. I am responsible for Madame Chen's safety, and I'm going to do my job whatever you or anyone else may think, even her. For your mistress's sake, tell me what you know, or I'll throw you to the crocodiles, you lousy chink . . . I'm not joking. Last night Madame went to bed with a headache and said she was not going out. But she did go out, didn't she? Answer me!'

Terrified, Deng nods in agreement.

'Yes. Almost an hour after you did . . . She made a phone call, dressed and went out. She made me promise not to tell you . . .'

'What time did she come back?'

'It was very late. After five in the morning . . .'

Deng tells him he saw her arrive because he had been unable to sleep, and that he had got up because he was afraid something might have happened to her. He says he had realised from the outset that Monsieur Franch had been sent from France by Monsieur Lévy to protect Madame Chen from any harm, and he wished to help in any way he could, but last night madame ordered him not to say a word about her going out, and he had to obey, although he later regretted it. When he got up and saw how late it was, he had been about to wake up Monsieur to tell him what had happened, when just as he was crossing the living-room Madame arrived carrying a rose. She asked him for a glass with water, put the rose in it, and placed it on the piano. Deng says he was relieved to see Madame again, and would never have forgiven himself if anything had happened to her.

Kim insists Deng must realise that Madame Chen's safety is paramount: her every movement, and in particular those she herself wants to keep quiet about, should be immediately conveyed to him.

'I promise it won't happen again,' says the servant. 'But please don't tell Madame I've told you . . .'

'That's all right, Deng. You can go now.'

Kim stares again at the fading rose on the piano. He is disturbed by what has happened, and decides to go on the offensive. But for three nights running, Cheng Jing stays at home. A few women friends visit her, and each evening, shut in her bedroom, she has lengthy telephone conversations with Paris. In the mornings she busies herself with running the household and the servants, and in the afternoon spends hours reading on the terrace.

Charlie Wong knows Kim wants to buy a couple of kimonos, so one afternoon he arrives at the apartment to take him to his wife's shop in the old city, near the Great World Theatre. Chen Jing tells him she does not intend to go out that day either, but even so Kim gives Deng precise instructions: 'If your mistress leaves, call me at Madame Wong's shop.'

Wong's wife, Soo Lin, helps him choose the kimonos and happily charges him for them at full price; but then she makes him a present of another one – this one I'm wearing, which Kim gave me some time later. As they are leaving the shop, Wong suggests in a discreet, roundabout way that if Kim ever feels alone in Shanghai and wishes to relax with a pipe of opium and some female company in pleasant surroundings, he should not hesitate to suggest it . . . Kim thanks him but rejects the offer. At that very moment from the busy street corner where they are standing he sees Kruger get out of a white convertible and disappear into a doorway over which hang a big glass lantern and red silk banners. Kim points him out to Wong.

'Isn't that elegant gentleman over there the famous Omar?'

'Quite right,' says Charlie Wong. 'And no doubt he is going in to try out one of those pleasurable pastimes I was offering you a moment ago, my friend.'

'Is that one of the brothels he runs?'

'No, it's an opium parlour, although . . .'

'Wait,' says Kim, coming to a halt on the pavement. 'Do you and he have dealings?'

'Well . . . sometimes,' Wong says with a sly smile. 'He's an excellent fellow, and can be very useful.'

'Does he own that place?'

'I think so. Do you want us to go in and have a look round?'

'I'd like to meet Omar. Can you introduce us?'

'By all means,' says Wong.

The opium den is a kind of beehive lit by coloured candles. Everything in it, from the couches and lacquered screens, the pipes and trays with tea sets on them, the servants gliding about, to the smokers lying in corners, seems to be floating in a shadowy, perfumed atmosphere that caresses the temples and eyelids like a woman's warm, knowing fingers. An old Chinese man offers them somewhere to lie down and a pipe, but Wong tells him that first they wish to talk to Omar, and then perhaps they would like some tea . . . Kim has advanced into the room. Some customers are lying fast asleep on mats, on their sides or with their hands behind their head. Others are drinking tea, or cups of mulled wine.

Omar Meiningen is lying propped on one elbow, watching with apparent boredom while a young Chinese girl prepares a pipe, heating it in the flame of a candle.

Wong catches up with Kim and presents him to Omar, who holds out a hand but does not get up.

'If you require any special service,' Omar says, looking at Wong, 'all you have to do is ask . . .'

'That's very kind,' says Kim. 'I just wanted to meet you. I've heard you can't get to know Shanghai if you don't know Herr Meiningen.'

'I also wanted to meet you, Señor Franch.' To Kim's surprise, Omar speaks a more than adequate Spanish. 'As you see, I speak your language.'

'I know you lived in South America for some years.'

'That's true. And what else do you know about me, my friend?' asks the German with a smile. 'Do you know, for example, that I am jealous of you? You're the man of the moment. Ever since you arrived in Shanghai you've been seen everywhere with Madame Chen Jing Fang. You won't deny that is a rare privilege, a gift from the goddess Fortune.'

'The truth is, I don't deserve such good luck,' Kim says, smiling back at him. 'I've simply been friends with her husband for many years. I suppose you already know that.'

Omar stares at him for a moment, then takes the pipe the young Chinese girl is offering him with both hands.

'In that case,' says Omar, looking down at the pipe, 'our friend Lévy is doubly fortunate. By the way, Wong, when are we going duck shooting at Hangzhow?'

'Whenever you like,' says Wong.

'Do you like hunting, Señor Franch?'

'Duck shooting isn't my favourite,' Kim says, noticing how refined and neat the German's hands are as they raise the opium pipe. 'Although when it comes to hunting, I enjoy all kinds. I think there's a Chinese saying which goes: it doesn't matter if the cat is black or white, so long as it catches the canary.'

Omar settles back on the divan and smiles faintly:

'It's not a canary the cat in the proverb catches, Señor Franch, it's a mouse. A common mouse. And now, gentlemen, you must excuse me . . . I hope to see you one evening in my club, Señor Franch, it will be a great pleasure to offer you some drinks.'

'I'll be there.'

After five days and nights without stirring from her home, one suffocating Friday evening as they are finishing dinner Chen Jing decides to go to the Metropol cinema, and Kim goes with her. They see a Chinese film shot in Shanghai with Chinese actors called *Spring River Flows East*. Kim cannot not follow a word of what is going on, but enjoys the harmony of the actors' expressions, and he gets some impression of their feelings as they waft over him. When they leave the cinema, Chen Jing suggests they have a drink in the Silk Hat, an elegant night-club where you can dance beneath the stars, and where she hopes to meet Soo Lin with her husband and other friends.

Half an hour later, while Chen Jing is sitting at a table in the Silk Hat with Wong's wife and a gaggle of her staunchest admirers, one of the group leads Kim to the bar, where he introduces him to a Spanish engineer who has been working in China for twelve years with an English cotton firm that has factories in Hong Kong and Shanghai. This man turns out to be Esteban Climent Comas, a friendly, well-built fellow who is about the same age as Kim. But when they are introduced their greatest surprise is to discover that not only had they both studied at the School of Textile Engineering in Terrassa, but that they were in the same year. Kim wants to celebrate this encounter and offers him a drink. Climent is onto his third martini, Kim orders a whisky for himself, and they launch into their memories of the school. Kim then mentions his friendship with Michel Lévy and his hopes of finding work in Shanghai.

Climent's eyes stray to Chen Jing, whose table is close to the bar.

'What an extraordinary woman, and what strength of character,' he says admiringly. 'Did you know that at sixteen she was raped by the Japanese and made to serve in a brothel set up for their troops? When I first met her two years ago she was crazy about a merchant navy captain who now works for her husband . . .'

'Captain Su Tzu,' Kim interrupts him. 'It was his boat that brought me to Shanghai.'

'It's a strange story. Your friend Lévy literally tore her from this sailor's arms and married her. I've always wondered how on earth he did it.'

A few minutes later, Chen Jing comes up to the bar and suggests to Kim that since this is such a special night for him as he has met a fellow-countryman and is having such a good time, he should stay as long as he likes. She can get a lift home in the Wongs' car . . .

Even before she has finished speaking, Kim has noted the evasive gleam in her honey-coloured eyes. He makes a quick decision:

'Do you want to go home now?'

'Yes, I'm tired,' says Chen Jing. 'Charlie can leave me at the door.'

'Promise me you'll go straight to bed.'

'I promise,' she says, pouting as she looks at Kim's friend. 'Señor Franch thinks that the behaviour of this poor lonely and bored Chinese girl is not worthy of a proper lady . . . he's worse than a jealous husband!'

She laughs as she moves away, and shortly afterwards leaves the night-club with Charlie Wong and Soo Lin. Kim orders a second whisky and another martini for Climent. He lights his friend's cigarette and glances down at his watch: he needs to let a couple of hours go by until he goes into action.

Esteban Climent, who seems well-acquainted with the social life of the foreigners in Shanghai, goes on to give him a brief outline of his own personal history. In 1933 he left his father's textile factory in Sabadell to go to work for a firm in Manchester which was very interested in a new kind of shuttle he had invented, and it was not long before the English firm sent him to the Far East to modernise their looms. First he had been in Japan, then in Hong Kong, and when the Japanese bombarded Shanghai he was just getting settled there. He was in the Peace Hotel can remember the orchestra was playing 'La Cucaracha' when the first bombs began to fall . . . those were hard times, my friend, he says, but what we're in for now is no better: when General Chen Yi's Communist troops force their way to the Yangtze and then spread out along the river, Nationalist China will have lost the war in the north, and even if the final battle is still some way off, the end of the foreign concessions is in sight. The big foreign entrepreneurs in Shanghai are already trembling . . .

'Take a look around,' Climent goes on, 'look at all these people going wild until dawn, the people wandering about in the moonlight soaked in champagne, look at all the Americans and Europeans crowding the dance floor, spinning round and round and drinking like sponges to avoid thinking of all they are going to lose if God and Chang Kai-Shek don't come to their aid. There are Americans and French people here who have taken T.V. Soong, Asia's most important banker, the brother of Madame Chang Kai-Shek, for trips up the Yangtze on their fabulous yachts . . . now all that will count for nothing. Take a good look, my friend, at these elegant couples dancing lost in each others' arms, blind and vain in their dreamworld: it's a unique, wonderful spectacle that will probably never be seen again in Shanghai.'

'It makes me feel a bit giddy,' Kim says with a smile.

But it is worth looking at. Under the dazzling spotlights, the dance floor is like a writhing, sinuous flame. Standing out in front of the orchestra, the beautiful, fragile Chinese vocalist is singing 'Goodbye Little Dream, Goodbye' in her nasal little girl's voice. Screened by the smoke from his cigarette, Kim is at first uninterested, but then becomes increasingly fascinated by this glittering, unreal scene; the garden lit by torches under the stifling star-filled night; the sharp smell of the burning resin as it launches its silver darts up into the sky; couples clasping each other and kissing while they stroll against this lighted backdrop; elegant, solitary men in their white dinner jackets standing motionless on the lawn, drink in hand, stunned by this fierce leaden glow, as still as plaster statues reflecting on their abandonment in this forsaken landscape. But Kim merely receives these impressions on his retina. He feels little sympathy: this chaotic splendour, this glittering light and music simply mask the same old tale of surrender, renunciation, farewell. There is nothing in all this that he has not already seen here with us before the war, absolutely nothing worth saving from the revolutionary flood about to engulf them, nothing except love, friendship and the heart's eternal truths. And for a fleeting moment Kim gets a glimpse of a devastated future, a posthumous world. Fragments of broken glass, or perhaps melting ice cubes, sparkle in the grass like tiny fallen stars.

'You, though,' the man from Sabadell says, interrupting Kim's thoughts, 'have nothing to fear or lose.'

'No? Why not?'

'Because Lévy's wife is a relative of the Red general Chen Yi, and when he takes over Shanghai, your friend is bound to use his influence to obtain privileges. I think your wages are safe for a few years at least, Franch.'

Kim sips his whisky and thinks this over. Then he asks:

'Do you know Omar Meiningen, the owner of the Yellow Sky?'

'Not very well.'

'What have you heard about him?'

'He has a dubious reputation. But that doesn't mean much in Shanghai. Someone told me he had a brilliant career as an officer in the Wehrmacht, but was clever enough to get out in time.'

Kim asks him if he thinks that Michel Lévy trafficks arms for the Communists. Climent considers it possible:

'I've already told you of his links to General Chen Yi.'

'And what can you tell me about that charlatan they call Du "Grandes-Oreilles?"'

'Be careful with him. He's one of the leaders of the Triads. Do you know what they are?'

'I can imagine. Some sort of mafia.'

'He's the head of the Quing Bang, one of the most powerful and influential secret societies. Although I suppose his little game will soon be up too . . . The Communists will get rid of all that trash, I hope.'

'Do you think he works for Omar?'

'No, I don't. Du Yuesheng has used his sect to help well-known industrialists and financiers, the cream of the foreign concessions, and in return they've turned a blind eye to him. The police know he controls the drugs trade, and do nothing about it; he probably uses your friend Lévy's dollars for it too . . . Listen, I wouldn't venture into that quagmire, if I were you. As for Omar Meiningen, he's a sharpshooter, an outsider working on his own. I've heard he's thinking of selling up here and moving to Malaysia to grow rubber.'

Climent downs his martinis in quick succession, his nervousness showing in the way he looks down at his watch every few minutes. At a half past two in the morning, after telling Kim he can count on him for anything he needs, he suddenly wishes him the best of luck and takes his leave.

Kim finishes his whisky slowly, then walks alone up Peking Road and then the Kokien Road. He feels depressed by what Esteban Climent has told him; he can sense the alien city all round him, and its uncertain future; but tonight at least he knows where he is going and what awaits him. He walks quickly and his spirits soon lift, not because he has drunk too much or even because he has decided to take action, but from a deeply-felt need to overcome Climent's cynical disillusion: he cannot and will not believe in his dire predictions. He is not going to be dragged down with all those collapsing dreams.

By the light of a streetlamp on Canton Road, he checks his Browning – the butt feels colder than usual – and lights a cigarette. He turns down Shantung Road. The neon lights blink in their ghostly fashion in the night. Kim enters the Yellow Sky Club.

4

Only once did I succeed in climbing through the fake wardrobe and into the hideout where the Captain now sought refuge less and less frequently – I could swear more to escape from his wife than to feed his personal demons. It was a cubby-hole that had once been a bathroom and was now filled with flowerpots and wooden boxes full of geraniums and carnations, as well as a camp bed, and a chair. There was also a small bedside table on which stood a wooden contraption sprouting cables and wires and rusty batteries that looked like some huge dangerous beast but was in fact nothing more than an old cat's whiskers radio. The toilet and the bidet had been filled with earth where several bright green climbing plants were growing, and fronds of flowering honeysuckle hung down from the cracked wash-basin to the floor.

This profusion of flowers was doubtless thanks to 'Bettibu's' plump green fingers. A tiny window let in a fitful, bright sunlight whenever it managed to pierce the clouds. From it was a view over the flat roofs of the neighbourhood, the spires of the Sagrada Familia church further on and, in the distance, the sea.

I sneaked into the Captain's den that day because his wife asked me to help him bring out the unused camp bed so we could get rid of the bugs and disinfect it. I found the Captain sitting on the chair talking into a microphone as large as a bowl. He was holding it up to his face despite the fact it had no cable and was not connected to anything. He did not seem surprised to see me, and simply put this antiquated relic back on the table. Doña Conxa had emptied the wardrobe of clothes, and shouted instructions to us from the far side, so the Captain and I hauled the bed out into the dining-room and onto the balcony, where we shook it until we got rid of all the insects. 'Bettibu' carefully burned them with bits of newspaper. The effort left the Captain so exhausted that I was hoping he would for once postpone his search for more signatures, but I was mistaken.

By the time we were out in the street, later than usual, the sky had clouded over and despite the oppressive heat there was a slight drizzle. I could not convince the old fool we should go back home. After a couple of failed attempts to collect signatures from people in Calle Congost, the Captain took pity on me and offered me a lemonade in a bar where a radio was on at full blast on the counter.

'Good day, gentlemen,' the Captain said as he entered. 'By chance did any of you hear the most interesting, timely and well-documented political commentary just broadcast on EAJ Independent Health Radio?'

There were four customers, three at the bar and one sitting by the wine barrels. They answered his greeting, but not his question, so the Captain repeated it, singing the radio journalist's praises.

'All right Blay,' one of them said. 'We all heard it.'

'And what do you think, gentlemen? A magnificent speech, as far as I could judge.'

'A load of drivel.'

'Come off it, I enjoyed it,' another of them said jokingly. 'That fellow has the gift of the gab.'

'Don't get him started,' the landlord warned them in a whisper.

'A real bolshie that speaker, Captain, but he has style.'

'I'm glad you liked it,' the Captain said.

'Well Blay, I still reckon it was a load of tripe,' insisted the first man.

'I suggest you reconsider your opinion,' the Captain persisted, 'because it was a lucid and valuable analysis of the national and international situation. No other radio station, and much less any of our gagged national press, will give you a more precise, accurate and bold comment on the current political and military state of this Europe in ruins . . .'

'You tell them, Blay,' the other drinker said, trying to stir up trouble in a bored sort of way. 'What do this lot know?'

The barman, nervous at Captain Blay's radio mania, suggested they all changed the subject. I went on drinking my lemonade. The bar was a den of shadow, and over by the barrels there was a faint smell of sulphur. A little man who was swaying in front of a glass of red wine gripped the edge of the bar with red knuckles and blurted out:

'What I like is the Taxi Key programme.'

'And I don't know what on earth you're complaining about, Blay,' said the seated customer in his sly manner, winking at the barman. 'The truth is there's never been such peace or prosperity as we have now in this country.'

The little fellow nodded thoughtfully and murmured:

'Prosperity. Ah yes, prosperity.' He pronounced the words as if he were talking about a very special vintage wine, whose bouquet and taste he had just recognised with his eyes closed. 'On that score, this gentleman here with the bandaged head is right.'

'How would you know, with the skinful you've had?' the fat man said.

'What d'you mean? . . . I drink my wine with water, you ass.'

'You're the one braying.'

'Gentlemen, calm down please, that's life,' said the Captain, and added: 'I get drunk on life, and who knows what she will do . . .'

'Don't start with boleros, for God's sake,' the fat man moaned.

'It's not a bolero,' the little man protested. 'It's a very beautiful, very sad poem.'

'Yes, and you're still an ass.'

'Gentlemen, please!' the Captain said, taking the folder from me and turning to the little man, who had gulped down his glass of wine. 'You're new around here, aren't you? Might I ask you to sign this important document intended to put right an act of injustice?'

For some reason, the little man felt pleased and honoured, and he signed straightaway, looking nervously over his shoulder all the time at the fat fellow. 'Let's be off,' the Captain said, digging me in the ribs. 'Their bellies are all full of gas that's going to explode at any minute.' He paid for my lemonade and his white wine, and we went out into the street, leaving the customers staring at their glasses or perhaps talking about what they always talked about, with the same well-worn phrases.

Something strange, a kind of blind sense of urgency, drove the Captain on that day, and we roamed a long way from home, across grey, ashen waste ground, past heaps of smoking rubbish. We passed the bullring and all at once, in a bare empty place that sloped down to a pool of black water, we came across a railway carriage, its splintered sides still full of bullet holes. The two bits of track it was on could no longer take it anywhere. They emerged from the ground like twisted black snakes: all that was left of a railway line that in the distant past must have crossed this dusty plain dotted with bushes and withered broom. It was an old third class carriage with wooden seats. One or two windows were still intact. The rain started to beat down, so the Captain suggested we take shelter. Nettles and thistles were growing out of its wrecked platform, and when we pushed our way inside the carriage we found a blue-eyed tramp with filthy skin sitting by a window. His forehead was pressed against the glass, his chin cupped in his hand. He could have been asleep or dead. He seemed to have been there forever, staring out as the devastated, barren world turned around him.

'Where is this train headed, my good man?' Captain Blay asked, sitting down opposite the tramp, who didn't even turn to look at us. I stared at his fine young lips, smooth and bright in the middle of his encrusted face. As usual, the Captain was not going to miss out on a conversation if he could help it, so he gave the man a friendly pat on the knee and went on: 'I could swear it's the train that used to go to Toulouse via Port-Bou. If it is, we're on the right track, you can sleep soundly . . .'

The shower had finished and the sun came out again. I was anxious to get the Captain home, when all at once the carriage suddenly went dark as if we had just gone into a tunnel, then tilted over slightly towards the pond, its wooden struts creaking and a low, grating metallic sound coming from beneath us. I told the Captain we had arrived, and he stood up and followed me without a word. He looked so beaten and exhausted I was suddenly frightened.

'He looked like a dead man,' I said as we were walking away from the carriage.

'So what?' said the Captain. 'The dead learn to live quickly enough, and better than we do.'

'Let's go home, Captain, we've come a long way.'

He stood there quiet and thoughtful for a moment, then said:

'The thing is, that poor man is hungry. You should learn to look more closely.'

In Calle Argentona he came to a halt once more, asked for the folder, and examined the list of names. We continued on our way, but instead of giving it back to me, he kept it under his arm. On the corner of Calle Sors and Laurel he started to say he felt weak and complained his knees were hurting.

'I don't know what's wrong today,' he growled, leaning on my shoulder. 'I'm not too good. My joints are liked barbed wire, and my head is spinning. That bed was so heavy I think I've put my back out . . . Maybe we should have a rest in this wine cellar.'

I was lost in thoughts of my own, and felt crushed by the heat.

'And also,' the Captain went on, 'I've got that feeling again that this city is built on tunnels full of mines, and that we could all be blown sky high at any moment . . . yes, I'm really doing well today, dammit.'

'I think we should get home, Captain,' I said as we entered the bar. 'You don't look right.'

'It must be premature ageing.' He stood next to a man drinking on his own at a table, and went on: 'A lot of people say I'm prematurely old. Yes, I know I'm crazy, but it's not that. I've always been premature. The problem is that recently my premature old age has got mixed up with my retarded youth, and there are days when I don't know what I am. And besides, I've got no one to scratch my back.'

We had a bit of a rest. The Captain smoked half a cheroot and had a small glass of red. I did not want anything. When we left the bar we crossed the road to shelter under the acacias, and the Captain sat on the edge of the kerb next to the open drain, to tie up the string round his battered slipper. Then he realised he had left the signatures folder in the bar, and told me to go back and get it. I left him sitting where he was, and went into the bar, but neither the barman nor the only customer in there at that time of day had seen any folder. The barman swore that the old lunatic had not been carrying anything when he came in. I thought about it, asked for a glass of water, and stood there for a while, secretly glad we had mislaid the notorious folder: that meant I wouldn't have to knock on any more doors, or have to go up and down all those stairs making a fool of myself to complete strangers by reading the ghastly protest letter out loud . . .

When I came out into the street again, the Captain was still sitting there, head lolling between his knees, the fingers of his right hand caught up in the twine that had come loose from his shoe. A stream of foamy, dirty water swirled round his feet and down the drain, carrying with it a scattered bunch of wilted white roses. Even before I reached him, I knew he was dead. I could tell just by looking at the way his lifeless hand was caught up in the string, and how the rebellious crest of his grey hair was being ruffled by the breeze which brought a sudden moment of relief from the heat, an eddy in the air that neither his skin nor his heart could feel.

I ran to tell the man in the bar, who came out to look then went back inside and called the Red Cross. Next to the bar was a convent school for poor girls, and two nuns came out. One of them made the sign of the cross on the Captain's forehead, the other, who was very young, said that perhaps he was not dead yet, but I knew he was. Seeing him doubled over like that, his head tilted carefully towards the drain as if his acute hearing could catch the silent underground spreading of the gas, the same ghostly, lethal gas that many years before had seeped into his brain on the banks of the Ebro, the Captain seemed more absorbed than ever in his own thoughts, while at the same time he appeared to be sniffing the rotting smell of the roses and the drains, a fragrance of faded roses and death that no doubt would have given him cause to denounce fresh abuses and confusion. Nowadays I realise that there was only a tiny gap between the phantom gas pouring from the drains to put us all to sleep, and the valiant belief the old man had that this gas truly existed. He once told me that all the nonsense he was accused of, all the crazy things he had done in his life were nothing more than rehearsals for one single act of lunacy . . . that he never managed to commit because he was never quite sure what it might be.

As usual, I did not know what to do, so I sat beside him and did up the string round his slipper. Then the ambulance arrived, he was put onto a stretcher and taken to the Clinic, while I ran to tell Doña Conxa.

As for the lost folder, it never reappeared. If he had lived, the Captain would have been convinced it had been stolen and would have raised hell. I imagine he dropped it in the street, and if someone found it and opened it they might have smiled indulgently at the protest letter, the few signatures of support, and my clumsy drawing, then tossed it away again.

Yet something was not lost. In some way, after roaming the streets for so long with him and having to put up with all his craziness – and despite my sense of shame, my reproaches and my desperation to get away and run to Susana's villa, her realm of dreams, the sweet warm hive of microbes I could escape to every day, fleeing the lies and misery of the world outside – the old fool had succeeded in infecting me with a dose of the virus that had eaten away at his mind, so that sometimes I also felt I could smell the stink from the gas in the drains and was swallowing the black slime from the chimney that dried up Susana's lungs. That was why, during the last two weeks I spent wandering the streets with him, I tried as hard as I could to help the brave foolish old veteran fight his lost cause.

So it was that, over time and without my realising it, the setting of my childhood adventures gradually became a moral landscape, and that is how it has always remained in my mind.

5

The mourners at the funeral included several pale phantoms I knew quite well, wretched shadows from the bars who had silently and stoically put up with the Captain's harangues as they sipped their harsh wines clinging to the counters and old barrels in the wine cellars of Gracia, La Salud and Guinardó. Also in the church were Forcat, accompanying Señora Anita, the Chacón brothers, and a few of Doña Conxa's neighbours. She herself was assisted by my mother. A chiropodist from Extremadura my mother knew from the hospital, a man by the name of Braulio, who had been to dinner at home a few times, took care of all the papers at the Clinic and the funeral parlour, and was also very attentive to Doña Conxa. My mother was very grateful to him for that, and from then on felt a special affection towards him.

One night when I got home she was not in. Next to my dinner was a note saying she was at the Roxy cinema with Braulio and Charles Boyer. I laughed at the joke, but I am not sure I was very pleased. At that stage of my life I was irritated by the way she robbed past and future of any value, and insisted only on the needs each day presented. I was also annoyed at her increasing need for religion and the warmth she derived from friendships in the neighbourhood or from Braulio himself. I switched on the radio and sat down to eat. All of a sudden I thought of Captain Blay sitting there hunched up on the kerb in Calle Laurel, with the wind playing with the tufts of white hair on his vanquished head. I wondered if in those last moments he was fortunate enough to think, if only for a fleeting second, not of his house which had been a prison to him, nor of his patient, hardworking Conxa, not even of his dead sons who never finished falling or dying in his recurring dream of mists over the Ebro, but of the only thing he really owned and saw as being entirely his – that scruffy folder he was hoping to recover and which he thought was such a worthy denunciation against injustice and submission – which in fact was nothing more than the expression of his rage, an affliction of memory, the shattered sense of a greater ignominy that others preferred to forget.

CHAPTER EIGHT

I

Kim is ready to meet his fate.

Once inside the Yellow Sky Club he moves unobtrusively to the far end of the bar. He stands there for a while in the shadows, leaning back against the yellow dragon entwined round the lacquered column, near the blue door leading up to Omar's private rooms. The club is crowded, and he cannot stand next to the bar, but it suits him that the barman does not see him. He notices a waiter with a drinks tray who heads for the door, pushes it open with his elbow and then disappears upstairs. Kim moves closer to the door and waits. At the far side of the throbbing dance floor lit by shafts of red light, the orchestra has just finished 'Bésame mucho' and is launching into 'The Continental'. All of a sudden, when he hears the cheerful tune which many years before had sheltered his and Anita's dreams, all their hopes for true love and adventure, he remembers another cabaret, a dance hall on the Rambla de Cataluña by chance called the 'Shanghai', in that Barcelona winter of 1938 as the bombs fell. One night there, when Kim was on leave, he bought a fake Manila silk shawl for Anita from a saucy, lying gypsy who was going from table to table, and exchanged his brand new military leather jacket for a glass-bead necklace . . . which he had thought was very valuable.

The waiter reappears with the empty tray, and Kim takes advantage of the opportunity to slip inside the door and silently climb the narrow, carpeted staircase, dimly lit by a violet light. He finds it odd that no one stops him, that there is no guard. He reaches a landing with two doors. One of them is shut; the other gives on to a small entrance hall with beyond it a number of small rooms painted light blue and crammed with etchings, lithographs, scrolls and silk screens painted in soft colours with Chinese characters on them. There are untidy piles of books, ivory and jade figurines, screens and couches . . . Close by he hears a kind of incessant clicking noise, which reminds him of the bobbins used by his grandmother to make lace during his happy childhood days in Sabadell, although this sound is more delicate and fleeting. As he walks through the rooms, with his hand inside his jacket on the butt of his Browning, he reaches a shadowy living-room that leads on to a smaller, scarlet-painted room, separated by a bamboo curtain with the head of a tiger showing its fangs painted on it. Kim can detect the sweet smell of opium in the air, and as he progresses he rips through bluish clouds floating like perfumed gauze. The noise comes from the strands of bamboo curtain as they are blown gently by a ventilator, which makes the tiger head seem to move and leap towards him. Suddenly, a clawed hand appears in the centre of the animal's head and pulls it apart. It is Omar, dressed in a kimono, but barefoot and with tousled hair. There is more controlled fury than surprise in the way he stares at Kim.

Behind the German, in the red shadows someone gets up cautiously from a heap of satin cushions, crumpled sheets and lingering smoke rings. Even before the figure moves into the light, Kim knows who it is: Chen Jing Fang.

2

I don't know if I'm telling this properly. These are the facts and the fate that drove them on, the feelings and the atmosphere their adventure was steeped in, but who knows if I have got the details and the different points of view right. Forcat had the gift of making us see what he was talking about, but his story was aimed not at the mind but at the heart. First came the account he had received – doubtless in haste – from Kim himself. Then came his own recreation of that story, in lonely reclusion in Toulouse, and later here in his guest room, or perhaps even in Señora Anita's bed. Time and again in his mind he would go through episodes and details in order to offer Susana day after day what had become his own sad version of events, with its geographical precision and its loving attention to names, settings and emotions. The fact is that the hazardous mission which took Kim from his refuge in the south of France to this scarlet bedroom in Shanghai, burning with opium and betrayal, had undertaken such a long, treacherous and uncertain journey that it was impossible for the imagination not to have infected memory, and confused the lived experience with the invented one.

That is why, now as then, this is Forcat's story.

3

Kim told me of his anger when he saw them together, and his wish to kill the two lovers on the spot, but I know he was exaggerating, that this was simply a blind impulse: Kim is no murderer. What he really wants is to explain why he is doing what he is doing, why he has come and in whose name, in remembrance of what almost buried ideals, in solidarity with what shadows and ghosts. Then he will act accordingly. But seeing the German's untroubled appearance, the disdainful yet resigned look on his face, as if he knew Kim were coming that night and was expecting him, Kim realises he must be on his guard. Behind Omar, Chen Jing is still rising from the bed; she wraps herself in a kimono with a lotus-flower pattern, and her unpainted mouth opens like a wound in the darkness, as if rising from the pages of the book Kim stole.

'Very well,' Omar says calmly but bitterly, 'So now you can inform Lévy.'

'Not yet, Kruger. First . . .'

'My name is not Kruger.'

'First I have to finish a job I began in occupied France in April of 1943. In Lyons, to be precise.'

He undoes his jacket and, with a gesture that is no more than a reflex, lifts his hand to his shoulder holster, but does not draw his pistol. Omar seems to understand anyway:

'A job that involves killing.'

'That's the only kind we've had for the past ten years,' says Kim. 'Just like you, colonel.'

'What colonel are you talking about? Why on earth do you call me that?'

Chen Jing pushes forward, clinging on to Omar as if to protect him with her body. She stares terrified at Kim and says:

'What do you want? Who is this Kruger?'

'Get him to tell you,' Kim replies. 'Come on, Colonel, now's your chance.'

'I don't know what you're talking about,' says Omar.

Kim cannot take his eyes off Chen Jing:

'Ask him who he really is, Madame.'

The young Chinese beauty looks first at Omar, then back at Kim:

'It's you I'm asking, Monsieur Franch. Who is Kruger?'

Kim senses there is something wrong; this may be a time of betrayal, but who is betraying whom? When he answers his voice is flat, devoid of emotion:

'He's the man who tortured your husband. Helmut Kruger, a Gestapo colonel. He committed atrocities in a cellar in the Place Bellecour, in Lyons. That was where his headquarters was. He was unable to finish Michel off then, and so it seems he's determined to do it now . . .'

'You're off your head,' Omar protests. 'Where did you pick up such nonsense?'

But Kim is not looking at him. Instead he is studying Chen Jing's face, anticipating an insult or denial. His own mouth is pursed thoughtfully. His nerves are jangling, but he needs to keep a cool head. Omar perceives this odd mixture of determination and doubt in Kim's attitude, and stares him in the eye before replying in Spanish with a slight Argentine accent:

'I don't have a very clean past, if that's what you want to know; few people come out of a war with a clear conscience. But I swear to you I'm not the man you say. My name is Hans Meiningen: I've never hidden it, and that's what it says on my Argentine passport. Here in Shanghai I'm known as Omar. In forty-three I was a Wehrmacht soldier in Warsaw, and I have no wish to tell you what the German high command ordered us to do there . . . I was transferred to Casablanca as part of a colonel's personal bodyguard, but by then I'd seen enough, so I deserted. I am a deserter, my friend, and I've never been in France. I lived in Buenos Aires for two years, and then in Chile, before I came out here. I'm not the man you're looking for. You're mixing me up with someone else. You're making a big mistake . . .'

'It's no mistake, my love,' says Chen Jing, pressing herself against him. Then she gazes up imploringly at Kim. 'We already suspected my husband had sent you to keep an eye on me, but I didn't lend it much importance . . . Now I realise that wasn't his only intention, that he was in the grip of something much worse than a fit of jealousy, something much more terrible . . . Michel told you Omar is that hateful torturer simply to justify his death. But Omar is not Colonel Kruger, Monsieur, he is only my lover, and my husband was well aware of that when he asked you to kill him, claiming he was a danger to me . . . He wanted to kill Omar, not Kruger – that's how far his mad jealousy has led him. Do you understand now?'

The muffled echo of the orchestra and the reedy, nasal voice of the Chinese singer drifts up to the room. Kim stares grimly at Chen Jing. He does not so much as blink, or move a muscle of his face.

'Repeat what you've just said,' he says. 'I want to hear it again, Madame.'

'It's quite clear,' she replies. 'Omar is the target, the one who's meant to die. There's no Colonel Kruger here.'

Kim finds he cannot take his eyes off Chen Jing's distraught

features. Her voice is calm and firm and shows her love and devo-
tion to the man she is still clinging to as if to protect him. Kim makes
no reply, but then turns slowly and appears to be looking for something behind him, perhaps an ashtray, because he has taken out his
cigarette case and lit a cigarette. His attitude is hard to judge: he
might seem cool and restrained, as if nothing he has heard has any
effect on him, but inside he is seething with rage. In his mind's eye
he tries to recall the gleam of despair in Lévy's elusive gaze during
their talk in that white, spotless room in the Vautrin Clinic. He tries
to imagine a mask of betrayal on his comrade's face, but cannot see
beyond the image of an invalid in a wheelchair, in the grip of pain
and hate, hounded by fears of solitude and death.

'And that is why,' Chen Jing goes on, 'he asked you to secretly
recover a book I gave to Captain Su Tzu when our affair was over,
before I got married ... I know you took the book, because the
Captain told me so. There is a very special dedication to Su Tzu in
it, a very frank statement more of passion than love,' the young
Chinese woman says with fierce pride. 'My husband always wanted
that book, because the idea of it tortured him ... All this is rather
sad and ridiculous, but that's how it is. It's not just Michel's body
that is sick, but his spirit too. I know he was a brave patriot and an
idealist, a man of honour in his own country, and at the start of our
marriage he was a kind and generous husband, but as his health failed
and he became crippled, his jealousy and his obsession with a dreadful
event that happened in my youth gradually poisoned his mind ...
Now do you understand, Monsieur?'

Omar takes her gently by the shoulders and makes her sit down
to regain her composure. Then he turns to Kim and says:

'And don't get my intentions wrong either. I've bought a rubber
plantation in Malaysia, and I want to take Chen Jing with me. There
is nothing to keep us here: everything is going to change soon, and
neither she nor I want to see those changes. Tomorrow's Shanghai
is not for us.'

Kim is still staring at Chen Jing, who meets his gaze without
blinking or looking down. All at once he turns his back on her, or

rather, he turns in on himself to question a credulous shadow from the past, the phantom of loyalty that went by the name of Kim Franch, which brought him here from the other side of the world, but whose blind faith he now curses and rejects. It is true then that the man he admired and respected so much had been using him for his criminal ends, taking advantage of him to conceal what was merely an emotional, domestic problem – when all was said and done, nothing more than a cheap story of marital betrayal? Kim does not know whether to laugh or cry. What hurts him most is that Lévy, whether consciously or not, has done this in the name of the ideal that bound them together in their fight for freedom and justice, the dream Kim had believed in all his life, the dream that had given meaning to all his actions, and had even sent him here to Shanghai, risking his life and putting his future in jeopardy, only to find himself plunged into this ridiculous farce with two extraordinary lovers confronting him determinedly and resolutely; and all three of them aghast at Lévy's desperate stratagem . . .

Let's just pause again at this point, friends, and observe Kim's reaction to adversity, his laconic, austere response to defeat, his disillusioned shrug when he realises life has cheated him, when his ideals have yet again been trampled on. He will not reveal the slightest flicker of surprise, his eyes will not give away his hurt and bitterness, despite the lifelong tussle he felt already coiled inside his breast, the moral battle between heart and mind he has never been able to avoid, not even in the zealous years that forged his beliefs, and his ideas of solidarity, when his hopes for the future were so much higher, when he was convinced he was fighting the good fight, when his mission to Shanghai was still far-off, and the fiery sting of the scorpion of revenge had not yet been created. Now, certain that this is no time for words, especially not from him, as if at last freeing himself from some ghastly imposture, he pushes up his hat on his forehead, leans thoughtfully towards the ashtray on the lacquered table, carefully stubs out his cigarette, glances at the lovers with a sad, cynical smile directed not so much at them as at himself, then turns on his heel and leaves the room.

The night has still another surprise in store for him. Forty minutes later, when he enters the lit but deserted living-room of Chen Jing's home, the telephone will ring. The call will be from the Vautrin Clinic in Paris, where it is seven in the evening. The message will be a short one: 'We regret to inform you that Monsieur Lévy died in the theatre while undergoing a delicate operation . . .'

But as he walks through the stifling heat of the night along Kiukiang Road towards the penthouse apartment, Kim does not yet know this, and his thoughts are far from Paris and his Machiavellian friend's predicament. As he strolls along the Bund, he stops to lean over the edge of one of the darkened quays and peer down at the slow, silent Huang-p'u flowing by. He does not see what he is looking at, if indeed he really is looking. He does not see right in front of his eyes how a sudden whirlpool opens like a sleepless eye in the dirty sluggish waters, a tiny vortex caused by some deep, violent river current that swallows up anything and everything floating by. Kim dimly perceives that he has little time left, except possibly to return home . . . but what home? Which is my home, where is it? He hears the persistent lazy slap of water against the pier, and smells the heavy sickly smell of oil and decomposing flowers, the forgotten urgencies of the day. Dancing serpents of light flicker over the surface of the river, their wavy lines reflected on the greasy ships' hulls. Deep down in the water, carried off on the slow, muddy current, Kim sees a procession of the faces of companions who have died or disappeared in the bloody turmoil of the past ten years, first in the trenches or the jails of the last days of the war in Spain, then in the ranks of the Resistance or the concentration camps at Mauthausen and Buchenwald. On the submerged monument of memory, he reads their names once more, and once more senses in his blood the heady roll-call of promises that life had whispered to them in the not too distant past, none of which were kept. The dark silence of the drowned rises from the river, and in solidarity Kim tries to see himself in the muddy waters, to become one of them, to drown and disappear forever, but he feels nothing. Through all his desperate exile, Kim has viewed himself indulgently in the mirror of the past. Then one day he decided to smash that mirror, and to see himself in the one the future offered him, together with you, your mother and a few unforgettable songs – so few things, so light is the baggage of hope he carries with him – but now he wonders if it's not too late even for that . . .

What fresh defeat has he suffered, and how did he not see it coming? He gazes down again at the river of time, and asks himself: Where did we go wrong? When did we miss our way, when did we lose utopia? Why did all that faith and moral courage have to turn into mere selfishness and deception?

It starts to pour with rain, and the leafy trees of the Bund give off an intense aroma that mingles with the stench from the Huang-p'u. Before he sets off again, Kim lifts his hand to his heart and then to the pistol in his shoulder-holster, perhaps intending to throw both of them into the river's dark waters, although I could swear it's only the gun he wants to get rid of . . . So don't worry child, this isn't the end of the story, Forcat said with a laugh, winking his wall-eye at Susana and taking her affectionately by the hand . . .

CHAPTER NINE

I

A smell of wet earth invaded the verandah from the street or the garden, or perhaps from nearer still, from the very heart of spring that Susana was imagining in her dreams, or from the stormy centre of the adventure that kept us bewitched in that distant, phantom city. Wherever it came from, the fact is that a scent of wet earth suddenly filled the room, and Forcat fell silent. It was a Wednesday evening, the last day in August, and the impression was all the stranger because it had not rained and Señora Anita had not yet begun to water the garden, but was still busy in the kitchen. It was then that the door-bell rang.

The blinds were drawn, so we had not seen anyone come into the garden. We heard a man's voice talking to Señora Anita. When he became aware of it, Forcat's expression changed visibly. He dropped Susana's hand and got up from the bed to go over to the round table. He sat there without moving, staring down at the drawing I had almost completed. I had been sitting on the far side of the bed, but I also stood up, though without quite knowing why.

'There's someone here who says he knows you,' Señora Anita announced from the dining-room as she showed the visitor in. Forcat did not respond, but seemed determined to keep his eyes fixed on the drawing. Anita added hesitantly: 'He says he's called Luis Deniso and that he's come from France . . .'

Forcat leaned forward over the drawing. Before the newcomer had even entered the room, he placed his hands on it as though trying to protect the sheet of paper from a sudden gust of wind or shower of rain, or to shield it from the visitor's prying eyes, from the hatred and despair that had driven him to our room.

'Hello there, Forcat.' With his left hand placed casually in his jacket pocket, Kim's lieutenant from Toulouse strolled across the room and patted him on the shoulder. Then he greeted Susana, asking after her health in a friendly way, chucking her under the chin and telling her she was every bit as pretty as her father had made her out to be. Fanning herself with her silk fan, Susana stared at him with open curiosity. He hardly seemed to have noticed my presence, until Señora Anita introduced me as a friend of her daughter's and wound up the blinds quickly and nervously. The last rays of the August sun were lingering in the garden.

The first thing I noticed about 'Denis' was that he smiled with his eyes, not his mouth. His eyes had a dark, unsettling glint to them, and set off his well-defined, full lips in a strange but powerfully sensual way. I suppose I did not really pick up on these details – the most striking in his generally distant and cold manner – until some time later, when the personal drama that had brought him to the villa had become public knowledge; they were the eyes and mouth of a man possessed, someone eaten away by a fever of suffering. Ever since Forcat had painted us such a vivid picture of his limp, and his eloquent farewell to Kim in Toulouse, greasing his gun and wishing him all the best, this good-looking figure with his intriguing name had held a strange fascination for both of us.

'Denis' was wearing a double-breasted navy-blue suit with a dark green tie that shimmered like snakeskin. He was younger than I had imagined, or perhaps he just looked that way, tall and handsome and with romantic dark lines round his eyes. The only slight failing in his elegant manner was an obvious desire to charm, to be well-liked.

Forcat still did not say a word, and 'Denis' noticed his Chinese kimono with its wide sleeves and flower design.

'Just look at our Barceloneta house-painter,' he said. 'My, hasn't he come a long way? I heard you were here, on the scrounge as always, but I never thought you'd be so well set up, and so refined.'

'And what about you?' Forcat said in a thick, throaty voice, still without looking up. He cleared his throat and went on, as if he had suddenly decided to change subjects: 'When did you arrive?'

'A couple of weeks ago.' 'Denis' leaned back against the window, both hands now thrust in his trouser pockets. He looked over at Señora Anita, who had sat down on the bed, but his words seemed aimed at Forcat: 'Don't tell me you're surprised.' A few seconds later, he added: 'Well, let's get down to business. What do you know about that bastard Kim? Have you or his family here heard any news?'

Señora Anita and her daughter glanced sharply at Forcat, expecting him to answer back or protest, but he did not react. It was Susana who responded first, eyes glittering as she threw the fan on the bed, seized her felt cat, and said with all the ferocity she could muster:

'What right have you got to talk of my father like that? Don't you know he's a long way away?'

'Yes, a long way away. But where exactly?'

Susana looked him up and down warily before replying:

'He's in Shanghai.'

'Is that so?' 'Denis' pretended to be surprised, and opened his eyes wide. 'My, my, that really is far away! And why not in Peking, or Baghdad, or Cochin-China? Who told you that story, pretty one?' He paused to weigh up Forcat's continued silence, then addressed Susana's mother. 'What do you say? Do you think that son of a bitch has run off to the far side of the world to hide? You know, I reckon that Carmen . . .' As he mentioned her name, 'Denis's' voice went suddenly husky. He seemed shaken, as if he had lost his authority, but he shook his head and went on as firmly and evenly as he could: 'Well, she scarcely knows how to read or write, and I bet she couldn't even point Shanghai out on a map, but I'm sure she knows it's on the other side of the world, and I'm sure she wouldn't want to live so far away . . . No, it's got to be a joke. What's the matter, Forcat: cat got your tongue? Or do you prefer to play the innocent? He's a real character, you know ...' By now he had regained his composure, and was staring directly at Señora Anita. 'You might not think it to look at him, but he knows Latin and Greek ... you'd be amazed by all he knows!'

Susana's mother stared at 'Denis' with fear in her eyes.

'What are you talking about?' she said in a barely recognisable voice. 'What are you doing in my house?'

'Denis' raised his eyebrows and smiled a half-smile.

'So it's true then,' he said. 'You don't know anything yet.'

'What should I know?'

'Ask Forcat. He can tell you why I'm here, what ill wind and what treachery have brought me here.'

But Forcat still did not react, and so 'Denis' told his story, without a trace of bitterness, in an expressionless tone that had already accepted its fate. He had come for news of Kim, to see whether in this sweet home of theirs they had heard or expected to hear from him, whether his wife thought not so much that some day she would be re-united with him — that had always been unlikely, and by now was downright impossible — but that at least he might remember his daughter and come to visit her, or perhaps write to ask after her; to see whether Forcat or anyone else knew where Kim was living, in Catalonia or some godforsaken town in the south of France, in some bolthole he had been sharing with Carmen and 'Denis's' son for almost two years now. As he slowly told us all this, he was staring at Forcat, but his words and his deep resentment were aimed at Señora Anita and her daughter. He said he had no idea when the treachery had begun, how his best friend had proved so disloyal and deceitful, but he had gone crazy imagining it a thousand times on a thousand endless nights. It must have been during Kim's last trip when he brought money for her and 'Denis's' parents: 'Money they never received, but I suppose you didn't know that either,' he went on, peering down at Forcat; but he reckoned it could have started much earlier, because Kim always spent the night at his parents' house in Horta whenever he was on a clandestine trip to Barcelona, and Carmen lived there too and cooked for him and made his bed ... Since when had the two begun their affair, or fallen in love? Was it from the first time they met? Who took the first step, which of them seized the opportunity and provoked the passion that had led them astray and driven them heaven knew where? Had Kim taken the lead, and seduced her with the dark despair that had become so typical of him? Or was it her, so much in need of warmth and affection, if only for one night . . . ? Or had they fallen helplessly in love without meaning to, and suffered for the hurt they were inflicting on a comrade . . . ? What the hell did that matter now anyway? Now that Nualart, Betancort and Camps had been arrested – also betrayed by Kim, who knows? Oh, you didn't know about that either? Well that same night, Kim and Carmen hurriedly packed their bags and crossed the frontier with the boy, just as I had begged and pleaded him to do, only they never reached Toulouse, and I never saw them again . . .

'Denis' moved around the room in a relaxed way. He seemed very sure of himself, knowing he was attractive and coolly in control of the situation. Every so often though, he could not avoid a sudden start, and his eyes went cold in the way of those who have lived for years in exile and have had to learn to accept a bitter past that condemns them to a lonely present.

'But God knows, I can't get used to the idea that I've lost her,' he went on, thrusting his hands back into his trouser pockets as though they were freezing. 'I've searched the Midi from Marseilles to Tarbes, from Toulouse to Perpignan, but it's as if the earth had swallowed them up. The fact is I don't even know whether they crossed the border . . . They might have stayed in some village or other in the Pyrenees, or perhaps in a town large enough for them to vanish without trace. My only hope is that he gets in touch with you, little one,' – saying this he cast a sad, appeasing glance at Susana: 'Yes, that he writes to you or comes to see you. I know he will some day, and when he does, I'll be close by . . . He loves you. He was always talking about his precious little child. Although the truth is,' and for the first time he smiled a melancholy smile, 'you're not such a child any more. But my son Luis is still a little boy, and I've only ever seen him in photographs . . .'

Forcat had been watching Susana closely for some time. She was sitting bolt upright in bed, clutching the fluffy cat to her and staring down at the bedspread. While 'Denis' was talking, I tried several times to get her to look at me, but I failed. I imagined what she must be feeling at that moment and was horrified. Her mother was pacing up and down, arms folded. When 'Denis' at last fell silent, she came to a halt in front of Forcat and asked him beseechingly:

'Did you know all this? Tell me, did you know about it? Come on, explain yourself.' She put her hands on the table and leaned over him to repeat the question, this time in a more violent, almost hysterical tone of voice, but she soon relented and went to sit in the white rocking-chair, eyes fixed on the floor. She whispered once more: 'Please tell me . . .'

Forcat said nothing. He was still staring at Susana, with his hands still covering my drawing, where the chimney's naively writhing, threatening smoke seemed to be trying to slip through his stained fingers while he desperately attempted to hold it back. He sat there tense and withdrawn, as though still listening to voices echoing in their make-believe world, helplessly trapped in a situation he had not foreseen, caught up in a snare of his own devising somewhere on the distant, unreachable shore where the lies and deceit of this world live and multiply. His penetrating wall-eyed gaze roamed everywhere, only occasionally alighting on the sick girl, but rather than remorse or shame it displayed nothing but sadness. As I write this I wonder what could have been going through his mind, now that I too have become convinced that everything passes, and it is all exactly the same, masks and the faces beneath, sleep and waking.

We all held our breath as the shadows of night crept into the room and the deepening silence pointed its accusing finger at him. Increasingly hurt and bewildered, Señora Anita again begged him to explain.

'Let him be,' said 'Denis', all tension drained from his voice. 'What can he say, the poor devil?'

As I looked at his hands apparently shielding Susana's drawing on the table, I was convinced they had lost all the inner fire that had brought them to life and lent them their strange power over Señora Anita's mind and body. Nowadays I think that in his heart of hearts the great enchanter must always have known that his hold over this credulous, unhappy and vulnerable woman would last only as long as his flickering flame could light Susana's dreams, the time it took her to discover that the *Nantucket* had never really existed, or if it had, had never been anything more than a decrepit, rusting hulk which even now was rotting against some stinking quay in the Barceloneta docks. I like to think he saw the ship by chance one misty winter night as he wandered through the port, at a loss about what to do with his life and his memories, and that it was right there, sitting on a capstan alongside this phantom craft looming out of the mist, that he began to weave the threads of his peaceful assault on the villa, the sentimental spider's web he would use to ensnare mother and daughter. I can picture him in the days before he came to the house that spring, wiping glasses and serving behind the bar of his married sister's tavern down in the port, glancing through the window at the prows of ships moored outside, and dreaming up the *Nantucket*'s voyage through the seas of memory. I like to think he bought the kimono and the presents he gave Susana from some slant-eyed Chinese sailor who got drunk in the bar one night, or who in his greasy vest attracted his attention from the rail of a ship, and with a smile offered him a fountain pen or American tobacco, a collection of exotic postcards of Shanghai and Singapore or the pretty silk fan, in exchange for a bottle of rum or brandy, which Forcat would steal from the bar . . .

Señora Anita had not finished reproaching Forcat for his stubborn silence when 'Denis' realised how unhappy all this was making Susana:

'What's wrong?' he asked, clacking his tongue. 'I bet you were still expecting him to turn up, weren't you? . . . Do you still think he'll come to fetch you and take you away? Do you really believe that, pretty one? I'm sorry to have to say it, but I'm sure Kim never really thought of taking you or your mother with him, even though he often talked about it. He had already forgotten your mother by the time I met him: he never so much as mentioned her. All he thought about were Franco's dictatorship, Catalonia and freedom, that's all . . .' He fell silent and rubbed his tired eyes, but then I saw his vengeful stare roaming the room again. 'But that was before. Perhaps these days he thinks a lot about his daughter.'

I sat on the far side of the bed away from the others, and I soon felt Susana's hand searching for mine under the covers. 'Denis' loomed over us as he lit a cigarette, and his eyes betrayed a sudden cruel, mocking curiosity when he asked what on earth she thought her father could be doing in Shanghai, what a rootless and desperate refugee like Kim or he himself could possibly hope to find there, and finally whether she wanted him to come back to her. Susana did not answer any of his questions. She refused even to look at him; I realised she found it impossible to talk. But when 'Denis' insisted: 'Come on, let's have a laugh, we all need it, go on child, spit it out,' I could not bear to see her so cowed and forlorn, so I decided to speak on her, or our, behalf. My voice may have been weak and unconvincing, but in a manner I am still proud of today, I was determined to tell him the story. I told him of the pact Michel Lévy and Kim had made in Paris, the voyage of the *Nantucket* and Kim's special mission in Shanghai, his attempts to protect Chen Jing and her husband's double game. 'Denis', who was listening amused to all this with one foot up on the bed-frame and hands folded across his knee, questioned me about some details and facts and made me repeat the names of Captain Su Tzu, Kruger, Omar, Du Yuesheng, Charlie Wong . . . As I reluctantly complied, I had a strange feeling I was betraying them, breaking their trust. I felt I was turning the knife in Forcat's wound, and I looked across at him several times imploring him to come to my aid, but he seemed not to be there in the room with us any more. When 'Denis' did laugh, it was a strange, stifled guffaw. Then Susana shouted that's enough! You can all go to hell, and flung herself down on her pillow with her back to him. Still clutching her cat, she now lay facing me with her eyes wide open, but she could not see me: she was gazing deep into a world that had lost all transparency and possibility of communication.

Contrite, 'Denis' leaned over to stroke her hair and say he was sorry. Señora Anita had calmed down, and was asking Forcat in a pained voice: 'What about the letter, the postcards . . . ?' It was the newcomer who explained that as well: 'That was the easiest thing in the world. He faked Kim's handwriting and signature. He was always very clever with a pen or pencil. A real artist.'

By now there was very little daylight coming in through the window, and as he continued to pat Susana's back and whisper in her ear all I could make out of 'Denis's' features were the parts lit by the glowing tip of his cigarette. Without waiting for Forcat to tell me to do so, I went over and switched on the ceiling light. Forcat at last took his hands off the drawing and rose slowly from the table. He walked past Señora Anita and stood in the doorway, then turned and stared at Susana's back. Standing there with head held high and hands stuffed in the sleeves of his kimono, he seemed on the verge of saying something – I desperately wished he would, even if it was only to say good night to her – but instead he turned his head slightly towards the intruder and gave him a weary but friendly smile, the last tiny spark of their former friendship or the fraternal bond they had once shared. He glanced down at the smoking cigarette in 'Denis's' hand:

'There's no smoking in here,' he said sternly and decisively, then disappeared into the house without another word.

Standing there with her arms folded, Señora Anita thought about it for a few seconds, then followed him out. A few moments later we could hear her shouting and insulting him. 'Denis' grimaced at his cigarette, threw it on the floor and stubbed it out with his foot. Then he bent over Susana again, and put his hand on her shoulder.

'Let's forget him, shall we?' he said. 'I'm sure you can. He's nothing but a poor storyteller . . .'

He saw me on the far side of the bed and jerked his head for me to leave. I pretended not to have noticed, so he said:

'And you, kid, you can go. It's late.'

Susana's unfinished drawing, the one she had wanted to send her father so that he could see her lying on the bed in her green silk *chipao* with a stream of bright-coloured light flowing in through the window, was still on the table with my box of pencils, rubber and sharpener. I stuffed everything into my folder, managed to stutter 'Good night, Susana', and went home.

2

Nandu Forcat left the villa the next morning. The Chacón brothers saw him leave carrying his battered cardboard suitcase and with his coat slung over his shoulder. They said hello and asked where he was going, but he did no more than stare at them. He crossed the road, walked through the market under a grey, lowering sky and disappeared round the corner of Calle Cerdeña.

I learnt all this that same afternoon. I was expecting to see Juan and Finito outside the garden wall as usual, but they had moved their stall to the opposite pavement.

'It was that loudmouth who came yesterday,' said Juan. 'He's in Susana's house.'

'He moved us on. He claims we're spying on Susana,' Finito added. 'And he wanted to know if we had a permit from the Council to set up our stall in the street, the bastard . . . Who does he think he is? What's he doing here, Danny?'

'He's a friend of her father's. Did he come back before or after Forcat left?'

'After.'

'I reckon he's worried we're going to spy on him, the creep,' his brother said.

The verandah blinds were drawn. At that time of day Señora Anita must be stuck behind the box office window at the Mundial cinema. I knocked on the door and 'Denis' opened it. He was in shirt sleeves, a cigarette dangling from his lips and his tie hanging loose round his neck like a dead snake. His raven black hair was so straight and well-combed it looked like a wig. He told me Susana was not feeling well and did not want to see anyone for at least two or three weeks, perhaps longer, so thanks for your concern, goodbye and good luck, kid. With that, he slammed the door in my face.

I tried another couple of times, but the answer was always the same: Susana needed rest. Later on I learnt that 'Denis' was not living in the villa, but went there every day, and that on the way he usually stopped off at the market to buy fruit and occasionally fish for Señora Anita and her daughter. One boiling hot afternoon in early September he came out of the house in his vest, walked across the street fanning himself with a newspaper, and sent Finito off to buy him a jar of haircream and a bottle of Floid massage oil. He gave him a good tip. Another day he appeared holding a pair of two-tone shoes and asked the boys to take them to have a new set of soles put on; the tip was equally generous this time too.

It was around then, early one gloomy Monday morning, that with a great deal of embarrassment I first put on the long grey dust-coat my mother had bought me and set off to become an apprentice in the Calle San Salvador jeweller's workshop. From that day on I spent most of my time travelling round Barcelona hanging from trams as I delivered pieces to shops or private customers, or took others to be engraved or mounted in workshops smelling of heated lacquer, always it seemed inhabited by a little man wearing a green eye-shade. Contrary my mother's expectations when she chose this profession for me, I never managed to design a brooch or ring, and my supposed talent for drawing was never called upon. On the other hand I can say that at fifteen I knew all the streets and squares of the city like the back of my hand, all the tram and metro routes from the Barrio Chino to the Parque Güell, from Sants to Poblenou. When there were no deliveries, I waited for instructions from the thirty craftsmen sitting at three long benches in the workshop, or stood with my hands behind my back next to the quickest and most expert of the jewellers, watching how he handled the tiny saw, the files or the blowtorch. My apprenticeship lasted two years and I earned fifteen pesetas a week, and although in the end I came to like the trade, at first I thought I was not going to last a fortnight.

Yet two months sped by without my noticing, and it was not until one evening at the end of October when my mother had again invited the chiropodist to dinner that I shut myself in my room and finished Susana's drawing from memory. I suppose it was my way of being back with her on the verandah, of seeing her again: stretched out on her pillows, I made her look like a china doll in a glass box, threatened by the black chimney smoke and the insidious gas that had so obsessed Captain Blay. I was pleased with the result and decided to take it to her. I was not sure she would accept it – I was even running the risk she might tell me to go to hell with my stupid drawing – but at least it was an excuse to visit her. I called at the villa one Sunday morning, expecting Susana or her mother to answer the door. The Chacón brothers' stall had long since disappeared from the pavement opposite. I noticed that the white rocking-chair was out in the garden, next to a wicker table that had magazines and an ashtray on it.

Señora Anita opened the door. She looked extremely nervous, and was holding a wine glass with lipstick stains round the rim. She seemed very pleased to see me. She scolded me in a friendly way for having abandoned her poor sick daughter, then clung to my arm and whispered with a laugh: 'Daniel in the lions' den!' We walked together along the dark corridor with its high, grimy ceiling, that long corridor which on sunny days ended in such an explosion of light. Halfway down it she suddenly stopped; her head sank on her chest and she reached out to steady herself against the wall, spilling some wine as she did so. She ran her fingers over the surface of the wall, as if trying to locate something, while silent tears welled up in her eyes. I thought that perhaps Susana had had a relapse . . . She turned to me, a smile in her glistening eyes, put her hand on my chest, and said: 'You must come whenever you like, sweetie.' As she spoke, the stink of sour wine on her breath hit me. I felt paralysed by her desolate gesture, as her fingers clawed at my shirt, and was unable to react. Eventually she made an effort to recover and said:

'I need some parsley. I'll go and ask the neighbour for some.' And with that, she floated unsteadily down the corridor like a vanishing wraith, raising the glass to her lips as she shut herself in her room.

3

If she had suffered a relapse, by now Susana had recovered splendidly: she did not look the same – she was not the same. She wore her shiny black hair swept back in two plaits, with a perfect parting. A fringe of curls hung down over her moist forehead, but despite the plaits and curls she looked older: her eyes were more sunken, her face was thinner and more tanned, her lips seemed plumper. She was sitting up in bed wearing a baggy man's jersey over her nightdress, her knees pulled up and legs apart under the thin sheet. Her hands were clutching a small flat box, a game where balls the size of buckshot had to be trapped in tiny holes. All the time I was there, she never once took her eyes from the box; when I came in, she glanced at me out of the corner of her eye and greeted me in a parody of comic-book language:

'Why, hello . . . who have we here?'

'I was told you didn't want to see anyone . . .'

'Probably. I don't remember.'

'Are you feeling better? Has the fever gone?'

'They say I'm right as rain. Ha!'

'Have you still got a temperature?'

'Less and less,' she interrupted impatiently. 'And I go out into the garden.'

I noticed that Kim's photo, hat tilted over his brow as he smiled at the future, was no longer on the bedside table. The stove was lit, but there was no pot of eucalyptus simmering on it.

'Did you know I'm working now?' I told her. 'I've only got Sundays free these days.'

'Well, Sundays and Saturday afternoons isn't it?'

'No, I have to sweep the workshop floor then.'

'My, so you're a jeweller now!' she said, rolling the balls round the box. 'Do you like it?'

'Everyone tells me it's a good profession.'

'They do, do they? And what do you think?'

'Me? Nothing.'

She had not looked at me once since I came in. The game she was holding between her legs was a little bigger than a metal box of Craven A cigarettes, but it was made of plastic with a transparent top. The balls rolled over a wavy emerald sea full of sharks with wide-open mouths in which they were meant to lodge. I asked her who had given it her, but she did not reply.

'I've never seen anything like that before,' I said. 'Is it a new game?'

'Of course it is. You're as slow and dumb as ever, Danny.'

I sat on the edge of the bed next to her and leaned over to get a better look.

'I finished your drawing,' I said, letting the folder slide down from under my arm. 'Do you want to see it?'

'Oh shit shit shit,' she said, as if to herself. 'I've only got one ball left, but it won't go in ... You and your drawings, kid. You're so soft.'

'I thought you'd like ...'

'Ha!' she cut in. 'A real artist. Can't you see you should have drawn me very differently, booby. Yes, completely different ...' she said nervously, because she still could not get the ball into the hole. 'You make me laugh. Why didn't you draw me having a shit? Yes, that's it, a nice big turd at the foot of a tall chimney, and with a blackamoor fanning my arse, no, a Chink would be better! What d'you think? Don't you think that would be better?'

She finally looked up from her game to glance at me, and added in a sadder, gentler voice: 'Tear it up, silly. What do we want it for?'

'Well, I like it.'

'Oh, the artist likes it!' She concentrated again on her game, and muttered: 'Just fancy that!'

'Yes, I know, I know ... But you look good in it. Why don't you want to see it?'

'You can keep it. And now be off with you. You're a poor, ridiculous kid.'

She turned towards me and made as if to hit me with the game, but I seized her wrist and she went limp, dropping her head on my shoulder. As so often when she had been close to me during those long summer evenings when Forcat was telling us his stories, it seemed to me the salty tang of the sea that he was describing had somehow got caught in her hair, and that when she narrowed her eyes there was a sudden gleam of distant light, the glint of a far-off dream in them. I was encouraged to think she might accept my drawing and my candour. But then she knelt up in bed, grabbing my wrists, and I let myself fall backwards as she climbed on top of me, still clutching my hands.

'See?' she said. 'I'm stronger than you now.'

I lay still as she squeezed me between her thighs and jigged up and down as though riding a horse. Her hair spilled down round my face and in among the black tresses I caught a brief flash of cruelty in her dreamy, mocking eyes. She continued energetically rubbing herself against me, her warm inner thighs taking over not only my docile body, but also my helpless imagination, my betrayed, vanquished sense of complicity, my secret longing to share her fever and her microbes, my surrender to the vagaries of a will that no longer seemed entirely her own, a perfume of sex which I somehow sensed was no longer all hers either, and which she could not share with me. 'Wise up, kid,' she said, and for a second time through the flailing hair I glimpsed the cold glint in her eyes. Then all at once she pulled herself off and pushed me out of the bed. My folder fell to the floor. 'Go on, get out,' she repeated. It was when I bent down to pick up the folder that I noticed him standing in the doorway.

'Denis' was doing up the watchstrap on his left wrist. He was wearing a white shirt with the sleeves rolled up, and his lank black hair was thick with haircream. I will never know if he was hiding in the villa from any real danger, if there was still a police warrant for his arrest, or if he was just pretending and was there sponging like Forcat before him. Whatever the truth, his sometimes extravagant gestures and attitudes, even his walk – always looking carefully where he was putting his feet, and casting rapid sideways glances all around him – betrayed an intimate knowledge of clandestine life.

This feeling of living a clandestine existence, which years later I was to become acquainted with myself, is like an extension of your dreams. It becomes a way of being, a kind of introspection, even a sort of coquetry. That was how I had always imagined Kim: sparing in his movements, forever on the alert, cat-like, on the prowl, hopelessly romantic. But even though this lent 'Denis' a certain esteem in my eyes, because of the ideals and the bleak destiny he had shared with Kim, and because he had brought the plain truth to the villa, unmasking Forcat and revealing him as a fraud, I could not help reflecting that the truth he had brought from France that rainy afternoon had pitched Forcat out onto the street, and as a result I never liked him.

'You heard, boy,' 'Denis' said, pushing past me as he made for the bed. He looked at Susana and added: 'It's a nice day and it's time for your hour in the sun, so up you get!' He swept the sheet off her with one hand, picked up the crumpled cover from the foot of the bed, and wrapped it round her shoulders. Then he carried her in his arms out into the garden. She lay back, eyes closed and her arms round his neck.

I stood there for a moment watching them go out, staring at Susana's scarlet finger-nails on her hands cupped behind him, the way her head and half-open mouth nestled against his neck, her lips brushing his prominent Adam's apple. Then I also went out into the garden, but I did not follow them to the sunny corner beyond the willow-tree, where he laid her gently down in the white rocking-chair, covered her legs with the bedcover, and whispered something in her ear. Seeing them like that, something fell to pieces inside me. I walked to the garden gate without a word, and it was not until I had opened it, clutching my folder and cursing under my breath, that I turned back to look at them. Susana was enjoying the sun as she rocked back and forth, wrapped in the bedcover. 'Denis' was sitting on the ground beneath the tree, staring up at its drooping branches. Beyond him, the wall that Forcat had whitewashed, the corner filled with irises, the dusty ivy and the hyacinths, all lay exposed to the menace of the black chimney smoke. 'Denis' shut his eyes.

That is how I shall always remember him, his back up against the willow trunk, hands behind his head, eyelids slowly closing. I associate my impression with the twisted, implacable hatred that must already have taken hold of him, the cold obsession that guided his every move. If the hurt he was about to inflict was premeditated, I could swear he decided on his course of action one sunny noon-day similar to this one, in this corner of the villa garden while he watched the consumptive girl dozing peacefully, and breathed in the sweet scent of flowers.

As I walked down Calle Camelias I saw Señora Anita coming home up the same side of the street. She was holding a small bunch of parsley in her trembling hand like a bunch of roses. She was shaking her short blonde curls as she returned from next door, and passed by without even noticing me.

4

A long time went by, and at a point when I thought that nothing concerning the villa could matter to me any more, I heard that Susana was completely cured, that her mother was a poor drunkard but still managed to keep her job in the box office at the Mundial, and that 'Denis' was running a bar in Calle Ríos Rosas, spending lots of money and dressing like a film star. In those days nobody, least of all me, suspected his wealth came from blackmailing former Republican militants and holding up shops.

In February 1951, three years after my last visit to the villa, I ran into Finito Chacón, who was delivering beer crates from a Damm lorry. He was proud of his wispy moustache and the fact that he knew all the brothels in the Barrio Chino as well as all the city's best pick-up bars. He told me he had seen Susana cleaning glasses behind the bar that 'Denis' ran in Ríos Rosas; he said she had been very friendly and was a proper bombshell nowadays, a real temptation, her skin even softer than her mother's, and with an arse to die for, I swear, although he wasn't certain whether she just worked there as a barmaid or was 'on the game' like the other girls, in any case he was going to call in there one Saturday night in his new suit and find out, because apparently Susana was not living in the villa any more . . .

'Why are you telling me all this?' I butted in, irritated. 'Who says I'm interested? Why should I care what she gets up to?'

When she moved out of her home to live with her lover, Susana had just turned eighteen – she was a year older than me. Her mother could be seen coming and going between her house and the cinema or the local bar: she looked increasingly frail and slovenly, was often drunk and talked to herself. It seemed incredible she still had that delicate skin of hers and her beautiful blonde hair. She told anyone willing to listen that Susana had gone off to look for her father, and that the two of them would soon be coming home together. That summer she fell ill and Doña Conxa, Captain Blay's widow, went to the villa every day to look after her. Then one day nobody could exactly place, not even Doña Conxa, Forcat reappeared in Señora Anita's life, to save her from craziness and drink. By that time, Susana had been gone from the house for more than six months.

From this point on I have had to rely on snippets of news and gossip from our neighbours, but that does not make their version any less trustworthy than my own account. A fortnight after his return, Forcat was seen getting out of a taxi outside the garden gate. Then he helped Susana down: she seemed to be very weak and was carrying a small suitcase, with a cheap fur coat over her arm. Forcat took the case and linked arms with her as they went into the villa. This was one Saturday morning in July, and the market was very busy.

No one could be sure at first whether Susana had come back for good, or simply for a few days to take care of her mother. Most people thought it had been Forcat who had sought her out and persuaded her to come home, although some said it was the girl who had decided to return because she couldn't stand the dissolute life and the way her pimp was treating her. You had only to look at her when she arrived, they said, so skinny and ashamed of herself, although in all honesty it had to be admitted that, however harshly you judged her and not forgetting whose daughter she was, she didn't really look like a whore, she wasn't all painted and didn't even dress like one; there was nothing in her appearance to suggest what she had become. In fact it seemed more as though she had suffered another relapse and had just got out of hospital, with that haggard expression, the dark lines round her eyes, and the bruises on her face . . . Whatever the truth, on the evening of Monday 7 July, the second day after her return home, 'Denis' turned up at the villa.

A long time afterwards, when drink and an uneasy conscience had ruined her memory, Señora Anita insisted repeatedly about certain details of his visit. She had not been the one who had opened the door to him, because she had never been happy to have him in her home. She had known from the start he was a trouble-maker, a gangster, even though it upset her to see him always so bitter and obsessed, unable to forgive and forget his wife. And she said she could never have imagined her daughter going off with a man like that, or that he could be so wicked, so determined to bring about her perdition. The bastard could have taken it out on me, she would say, people have played so many lousy tricks on me in this life of mine that one more here or there would not have mattered, I've got a tough hide, but no, that son of a bitch knew the poor sick girl was what Kim loved most of all in the world . . . She said that night she, Señora Anita, had gone to bed very early because she had a temperature and was sweating like a pig, so it was Forcat who had opened the door, no doubt thinking it must be Doña Conxa who had come back from the bar with some ice; Susana had just had a shower and was in her bath-robe. She was drying her hair and went up to Forcat's room to get some aspirin, and that was when it happened. Señora Anita said she had not actually seen it, but had felt it deep in the heart: 'Denis' bursting into the house and shouting like a madman for the girl as he ran along the corridor into the verandah; Forcat trying to calm him down, first trying to reason with him and then arguing violently, why was he so bitter, so full of groundless hate, such a coward, then 'Denis' drowning him out, calling him a clown and a parasite, threatening to throw Forcat out into the street again or kill him if he tried to come between him and Susana. I'm going to take her with me, he roared, and not even God can stop me. She said she was horrified to hear her daughter rush downstairs, so she decided to get up, but by the time she had put her dressing-gown on and rushed down to the corridor it was too late, she heard the two shots echoing through the house. When she reached the verandah, she found Susana standing with her back to the wall, the towel wrapped round her hair, staring paralysed at the revolver Forcat was wielding, probably for the first time in his life. She saw 'Denis' stagger to the door, open it, take three steps out into the garden, then pitch headlong to the ground. Forcat ran out after him and right there, with one foot on the lowest step, cocked his head to one side, slowly and steadily took aim with his cross-eyed stare, then emptied the gun into the motionless body stretched out on the gravel.

It was Forcat himself who rang the police, handed over the revolver, and allowed himself to be handcuffed. As he was being led away he looked at the girl but did not say a word, it's not true he said now you've got nothing to be scared of, or take care of your mother for me and behave yourself, other people made that up, or perhaps I did, who knows I may have dreamt it, Señora Anita would tell everyone, I was so confused I didn't know what was going on, the sound of those dreadful shots still wakes me up at night, I'll hear them until the day I die. And it's not true either that he kissed me goodbye and said we'll meet again or anything like that – he knew perfectly well what he was in for, and anyway what use would it have been, even if he had wanted to, the poor fellow had no hope of getting round me with his fine words the way he had done so often in the past . . . Forcat never took his wall-eyed stare from the dead man's bullet-riddled back, she insisted, and never once opened his mouth again, not even to answer the police's questions or to complain about the way they were manhandling him . . .

That was how she told it, from the muddy depths of her stagnant memory, struggling to free herself from conjectures other people and she herself made about the killing, as if she too were prey to emotions and prejudices that might cloud the truth, feelings which did not belong to that fateful evening and had little to do with what really happened. Cruel fate, she would complain, had toyed with her daughter like a ragdoll, like one of the buds on the sick rose bush in my garden which wither and die before they even bloom. It was our evil star, the cursed bad luck of the poor, that damned tuberculosis and the nonsense that good-for-nothing Forcat put into her head, as fake as a Seville *duro* he was; and worst of all the revenge that wretched pimp wreaked on her. Lord, lord, why did you lead her on with the fantasy about her father only to snatch that happiness from her? Why this endless rosary of longing and suffering? she would ask herself, why does God create all these hopes in men's hearts only to dash them or to let them rot?

On one occasion, while she was at the counter of the Viadé bar telling everyone about her daughter's final cure and how she had recently left the convent where the nuns had looked after her for more than a year, she fainted. When she had recovered, thanks to the help of the bar owner and a couple of customers, she went on to explain in a thoughtful but bewildered voice, as if she were continuing another conversation perhaps already begun in her dreams, that no sir, it was not true what was said of her daughter, that she had already been cured of tuberculosis when she succumbed to 'Denis's' vengeful, furious love. Then apparently without rhyme or reason, she added that it was not true either that Susana had defended herself against the degenerate with a kitchen knife, but had used a revolver although she had never even touched one in her life before. She herself, she said, had been so close when it had happened that the shots had deafened her . . . This tale gave rise to lots of wild speculation. One version had it that the first two shots, which Señora Anita always maintained she had heard from the corridor, were fired by her daughter, and that these were the ones that had killed 'Denis'. Immediately afterwards, Forcat had grabbed the still-smoking gun from her, and emptied the remaining four bullets into the back of an already dead man.

I personally like this version: I liked it the very first time I heard it, and I have kept it secretly in my heart ever since. On reflection, who else but Susana could have got hold of Forcat's revolver? After all, she was in his room when her lover barged in shouting and threatening them. It did not make sense that Forcat had it with him when he answered the door . . .

But this was a feeling more than a hypothesis. It felt right that by finishing off the body lying on the garden path in order to protect the girl, the wall-eyed impostor should have lived out his lie.

5

My mother married the chiropodist Braulio. He took us to live in his home, a large, sunny apartment in Plaza Lesseps that he shared with an unmarried sister. It had four rooms, a bathroom, kitchen and inside balcony on the top floor of a newly-built block. It was quite a long way from Cerdeña-Camelias, but was close to the workshop, so I could ride there on my new bike, a present from Braulio. The chiropodist was a hearty, optimistic sort of fellow with a big nose. He was affectionate with my mother, and could be funny: he had a parrot called Clark Gable and liked cooking and singing in the shower. All this brought a bit of joy to my mother's life; but he felt he had to try to be a father to me, and I would not let him. I could not take this big oaf with his Popeye arms and good-natured smile at all seriously; he was a bore talking about himself, and I never had anything but trivial conversations with him. He had a gift for making everything seem meaningless and silly, and me above all: we would start chatting, and at the end of five minutes I could not bear to listen to the nonsense I was coming out with. As time went by, his unruffled sincerity and calm influence ceased to provoke my adolescent rage, and I learned to love him, but at that moment the memory of my father had returned to haunt me, although the idea of his lonely death did not cause me as much anguish as it had in my childhood. By now I knew he would never come back, and that we would probably never know what had happened to him, but in the most sacred and protected corner of my mind I kept the image of his body slumped in a trench as snow fell on it. Then one day something happened that stripped the memory of all its emotion, and showed I had in fact invented it. That day my mother, staring at me with affectionate disbelief, asked me where on earth I had got the idea of a trench and a snowstorm, something I had believed since I was small and which she had never dared contradict, because for a child with no memories of his father, that was better than nothing. She said she had never told me any such thing: when it happened I never even managed to find out if your father died at the front, and far less exactly how he died, or whether it was raining, snowing or the sun was shining, so you see, all that is pure invention on your part . . . It's just as well that time erases everything, son, she added with a smile which I was not sure was relieved or sad.

After we had moved, my mother kept on visiting Doña Conxa regularly and helping her however she could. This was how I learned that Susana had worked for a while as an assistant in a florist's in Plaza Trilla, and then in a toyshop in Calle Verdi, and now filled in for her mother at the Mundial cinema. On several occasions I wanted to go and see her, but it took months for me to screw up the courage. I had thought that because I was a widow's son I would escape national service, but a year after my mother married again I was called up and posted to Xauen, in the north of Morocco. I was delighted at the idea: the further away, the better; I would cross the Straits of Gibraltar and perhaps even the Sahara Desert, would get to know Sidi Ifni and the Rif mountains . . . Africa, another continent . . . I felt as if I was about to embark on a journey to the far side of the world, just at the moment when I needed to say good riddance to a lot of things.

Two days before I left for Algeciras I went to say goodbye to Finito Chacón. He was no longer delivering Damm beer because they had caught him stealing crates; now I heard he was helping out in a car repair workshop in Calle Ros de Olano, not far from the Mundial cinema. When I went to the garage they told me he did not work there any more either: he had been sacked for stealing some tyres and a motorcycle headlight.

I knew it, I thought as I left the garage, it was bound to happen, Finito; and then I said to myself, so what, forget him. I tried to convince myself that nothing which happened to the Chacón brothers had anything to do with me any more, or could affect me in any way. I told myself I was glad I no longer felt part of the neighbourhood and its sad little dramas. I repeated this over and over as I headed for the Mundial, strangely determined to prove that the past and its illusions meant nothing to me now. How good it is to feel so distant and apart from all that, what a relief I couldn't give a damn about all my adolescent expectations, my gifts as an artist which finally came to nothing, all of Captain Blay's crazy efforts to drum up solidarity for a poor consumptive girl who would end up as a prostitute, his anger and despair at not being able to collect even twenty signatures, how lucky I was to find that the memory of those two men stuck like fence posts on the street corner was fading fast, to feel I was detached from my father's frozen, mournful death, from the boring chiropodist married to my mother, as well as from the future as outcasts and delinquents that awaited the Chacón brothers. What a lucky break, I thought . . .

It was so much wasted effort: I could not believe a word of the nonsense I was telling myself, because I did not feel a thing. Wasn't it the very emotions I was trying to deny that were pushing me towards this small neighbourhood cinema? I had no idea then that however much we grow and look towards the future, in fact we are reaching back towards our past, in search perhaps of our first moment of awareness. I felt a certain morbid curiosity when I thought of Susana and imagined her having to erase from her mind and her blood all traces of the trade and the behaviour she had learnt in her pimp's arms. I wondered whether if, after a year shut up with the nuns, she could have rid herself completely of all that, as she had of her tuberculosis, or if there would still be something in her gaze or the way she treated men that gave her away. Above all, I wondered if I would be capable of asking her if she really had been the one who took the revolver and fired the first, fatal shots? All this and a vague sense of loss overwhelmed me as I approached the Mundial, and in no time at all left my arbitrary attempts to select and direct my memories in tatters.

As I went into the foyer and saw her crocheting in that dark port-hole where her mother had sat so often, the grimy window in a stuccoed wall full of pockmarks and the torn remains of posters, an instant before I forced myself to recognise her and started to wish I was no longer there, almost in spite of myself I could see her sitting on her bed again, clutching her raised knees and her beloved felt cat, listening, eyes lovingly closed, to the muffled sounds of the inviting city outside, or curled up in her dreams of distant worlds and illusions, happy in her glass box, her tiny, fortunate bubble. The image quickly faded: the person before me was a young woman with rather chubby rosy cheeks, who wore glasses and looked healthy and sensible, with her hair in a pony tail and no make-up. Aged a little over twenty-three, she still looked beautiful and had wonderfully smooth skin, but there was no trace any more of the pink, sensual effusion of her mouth, that pouting fullness of her top lip, her disturbing restlessness. As she patiently gazed down at her crochet work, neither she nor the circular hole in the wall of the deserted foyer where she sat seemed to bear any relation to anything surrounding them – the traffic in the street or the scurrying passers-by – she was so cut off from it all, so absorbed in the difficult task of renouncing everything that should have happened and now never would, that she did not seem to be aware of where exactly she was. How often I've considered her wretched, empty memories as the exact reflection of my own!

Just as Kim did that fateful night when he stared down at himself in the sluggish, dark waters of the River Huang-p'u, I felt the city all around me like a chaos of waste and scrap metal. I did not know what to do, so I looked at the photos in the panels. After some moments pretending I was interested in faces and shapes that appeared to have been pinned there forever, and which in fact I hardly even saw, I turned towards the box office. Something that was not even my shadow – perhaps it was the faint sounds of my approach, the air my body displaced as I advanced, or simply the habit of being aware of someone standing in front of the window – alerted her to my presence without her having to look up. She laid down the crochet work, picked up the roll of tickets and asked: 'How many?' still without raising her eyes. I said: 'One,' paid, and before I knew it was almost inside the auditorium, promising myself I would speak to her on the way out as I struggled clumsily with the unending mouldy red curtain, eventually managing to push myself through and take refuge in the darkness of the stalls. I slumped into a seat in the back row, feeling more sorry for myself than for her.

It took me a long while to realise what was happening on the screen. What I saw passing time and again before my eyes was a single frozen image flickering silently, as though stuck in the projector: the reflection of a light even more illusory than the cinema's, one etched more deeply on my heart than on any retina, one which was to stay with me forever:

White as snow, a steamship sails, all flags flying, across the China seas under a starlit sky, while on deck a young girl strolls in the moonlight, wearing a green silk *chipao* with deep slits up the sides; the wind ruffles her hair, and her whole body yearns for distant shores, as she stares fascinated at the vast phosphorescent ocean and the silver crests of the waves that stretch to the horizon: Susana is carried along on her dreams and in my memory, now as always, despite all the disenchantment, the betrayed ideals, the remorseless passage of time, heading for Shanghai.